10/13

MAGIC
ZERO

GHOSTFIRE

Also by Thomas E. Sniegoski
and Christopher Golden

Magic Zero

Dragon Secrets

Coming soon

Battle for Arcanum

MAGIC ZERO

GHOSTFIRE

Thomas E. Sniegoski

and

Christopher Golden

Aladdin

New York London Toronto Sydney New Delhi

ALADDIN

An imprint of Simon & Schuster Children's Publishing Division

1230 Avenue of the Americas, New York, NY 10020

This Aladdin paperback edition June 2013

Copyright © 2005 by Christopher Golden and Thomas E. Sniegoski

Originally published as the series title Outcast.

All rights reserved, including the right of reproduction in whole or in part in any form.

ALADDIN is a trademark of Simon & Schuster, Inc., and related logo is a registered trademark of Simon & Schuster, Inc.

Also available in an Aladdin hardcover edition.

For information about special discounts for bulk purchases, please contact Simon & Schuster Special Sales at 1-866-506-1949 or business@simonandschuster.com.

The Simon & Schuster Speakers Bureau can bring authors to your live event. For more information or to book an event contact the Simon & Schuster Speakers Bureau at 1-866-248-3049 or visit our website at www.simonspeakers.com.

Designed by Karina Granda

The text of this book was set in Bembo Std.

Manufactured in the United States of America 0513 OFF

2 4 6 8 10 9 7 5 3 1

Library of Congress Control Number 2004105708

ISBN 978-1-4424-7313-3 (pbk)

ISBN 978-1-4424-7314-0 (hc)

ISBN 978-1-4391-1341-7 (eBook)

For LeeAnne Elizabeth Fogg Sniegoski,
our silent partner (Don't we wish.)

Thanks and love to Connie and our brood, Nicholas, Daniel, and Lily. Thanks to Tom, as ever, and to the ever-patient Samantha Schutz for all her hard work. Thanks are also due to my whole clan, with love, as well as to Jose Nieto, Rick Hautala, Amber Benson, Bob Tomko, Pete Donaldson, Lisa Clancy, Allie Costa, Liesa Abrams, and Ashleigh Bergh.

—C. G.

Special thanks to LeeAnne for putting up with me, and to Mulder for being Mulder. Thanks to Mom and Dad Sniegoski, Dave Kraus, Liesa Abrams, David Carroll, Kenneth Curtis, John and Jana, Harry and Hugo, Lisa Clancy, Bob and Pat, Jon and Flo, and the cast of crazies down at Cole's Comics in Lynn, Lynn the city of sin.

—T. S.

CHAPTER ONE

Anticipation crackled in the air. His expectations were so high that it tingled upon his skin like magic. Or, at least, the way Timothy Cade imagined that magic would feel. Yet in this world where everything and everyone was connected by magic, Timothy was a blank space. Magic could not touch him, and he could not wield it. He was uniquely alone, cut off in a way that no one else could ever understand, and so he had to create his own kind of magic.

That was the source of his excitement today. He felt jittery, and his stomach fluttered, and he felt a prickling all over his face and hands and the back of his neck, and wondered if this was what it felt like to be in tune with the magical current that ran through the world. In his heart he suspected that even this wonderful feeling could not compare with the sensation of magic that would always be denied him.

But even so, he could not erase the grin on his face. If this was all the magic he would ever have in his life, Timothy would still consider himself lucky. It would do. It would most certainly do.

On that crisp, cool morning, Timothy and several of his friends had gathered in an open, grassy knoll behind the servants' entrance to SkyHaven's kitchen. SkyHaven was a magnificent estate, an island fortress that floated hundreds of feet above the ocean, just a short distance from the shores of Arcanum. High above the water, the wind could blow quite cold, and so the boy raised the collar of his tunic and renewed his focus upon the task at hand. His friends had come to see him test his latest invention.

Timothy called it the Burrower, and he had built it to drill into the earth. The original design had occurred to him in a dream, back in the time when he had lived on the Island of Patience. He had woken and quickly sketched out a rough design, thinking that if he could only get the parts together, it would allow him to build an underground workshop that would be a safer refuge when the tropical storms swept across the island in the spring.

Now, that dream had gone from rough sketch to reality. Or, almost. The vehicle he stood before now was the prototype for a much larger digging machine that he would build if this version proved successful. It was a boxy-looking thing, about the size of a sky carriage, with a studded, conical nose that would twist to tear into the ground and funnel the disturbed soil toward the back of the Burrower. It had one seat behind a thick shield of metal to protect the driver from flying debris as the cone spun, digging into the earth. There was a small window at the center of the metal shield so that the driver could monitor the progress of the dig. The window was made of a transparent and quite durable material called vitreous that he concocted by mixing together the gummy saps of two of the land's most prevalent plants. The vitreous would not shatter. The Burrower's power source was located behind the seat, a steam engine also of Timothy's design, and powered by the burning of the heatstone Vulcanite. The entire craft rested on a six-wheeled chassis.

Timothy walked around the Burrower and made yet another final inspection, feeling the expectant eyes of his audience upon him. He had been readying the craft for its trial run for nearly an hour.

"Are we going to do this today, or should we come back later this week?" a grating voice squawked, and Timothy turned to glare at Edgar. The black-feathered bird was his familiar—his animal companion—as well as his friend.

"Caw! Caw!" Edgar squawked, waiting for Timothy to speak. Taunting him in the way the rook always did. Timothy smiled. The bird could always get a smile out of him.

Three of Timothy's other friends were also there for the test run of the Burrower. Edgar flew in a circle and came to a fluttering stop on the shoulder of Sheridan, a steam-powered mechanical man Timothy had built while growing up on the island. His other companion during those years had been his mentor and teacher, Ivar, the last surviving warrior of the Asura tribe. Last but not least, there was Verlis, a new arrival to Timothy's company of odd comrades. Verlis was a Wurm, a race descended from the Dragons of Old, and his presence in the world of Terra was the subject of much debate. But for the moment, not one of his friends was focused on anything other than the success or failure of his latest endeavor. Their attention was making him nervous. Timothy could tell by their expressions that they shared Edgar's impatience.

"You *know* how I am about testing my inventions," he said. "I have to be absolutely certain that everything will function properly before I give it a try."

"Oh, we know. We're just getting bored waiting for you to start her up," Edgar squawked, feathers ruffling.

A blast of steam erupted from a valve at the side of Sheridan's head, and the mechanical man reached up to take a swipe at Edgar. The bird's talons clicked and clacked upon the metal as he evaded Sheridan's attempts to silence him.

"Keep quiet, you!" Sheridan scolded. "Timothy can take as long as he likes. 'Better safe than sorry,' that's what I always say."

Over the years Sheridan had become so much more than one of Timothy's inventions. As far as the boy was concerned, he was as much flesh and blood as any of his other companions, even though made of metal and powered by steam.

"Thanks, Sheridan," Timothy called. "It's nice to know that *somebody* understands."

Edgar flapped his wings, taking to the air, flying in a circle around the gathering. "You've been over the thing ten times already," the bird complained. "It's time to give it a go."

Timothy looked back to the Burrower and thought of all the things he'd like to check one more time, just to be safe.

"My friend," came a rough, deep voice. The boy turned to see Verlis unfurling his large, leathery wings. "The bird is correct. There is still much to be done to prepare for the expedition to Tora'nah," the Wurm reminded him. "I mean no disrespect, but time is of the essence."

Timothy nodded. It was true enough, but he was still reluctant to go ahead until he was absolutely certain he had done everything possible to ensure a safe trial of the Burrower. He did not want to waste his friends' time, but he had to be sure. Too much depended on the success of this latest invention. For the first time since he had come to live in this world, the Parliament of Mages—the ruling body of Terra—had asked for his help. Many of them were still suspicious of him because he had no magic. They called him the Un-Magician . . . and many other things, far less kind. Abomination. Freak. And worse. But now the Parliament had asked him to help them prepare to defend all of Terra against the threat of an impending invasion. The Wurm had been banished years ago to an alternate dimension, and now, led by a cruel, vengeful commander called Raptus, they intended to return to Terra and make war.

With the safety of every man, woman, and child hanging in the balance, Timothy could not say no, regardless of how he felt about Parliament. He needed the Burrower to work properly. He didn't want to fail the Parliament. He didn't want to fail this world.

Frustrated by Edgar's attitude, he turned his back on his friends and continued his examination of the craft. There could be no room for error. Timothy concentrated on the Burrower's engine, flipping open the door to the compartment that contained the craft's power source. The Vulcanite rocks glowed white-hot, heating the large, metal container of water that would create the steam necessary to fuel the Burrower.

"Timothy?" said a soft voice, like the whispering of the wind, very close by his ear. He jumped, startled. He hadn't heard Ivar's approach, but that shouldn't have been a surprise. The last of the Asura was the stealthiest being Timothy had ever encountered. It was natural for him to move about unheard.

"Is there something wrong with the machine?" The Asura leaned closer, looking for signs of trouble.

So far, Timothy had found nothing out of order. "No. But you can never be too careful with these things."

"Then you expect to find something wrong?" Ivar asked, eyeing the Burrower calmly before turning his gaze upon the boy.

Timothy shook his head. "No, but it's just that . . . this has to work right. There is too much at stake for it to fail."

"And if there is nothing wrong," Ivar said, cocking his head and raising an eyebrow, "it will work."

The boy took a deep breath and let it out in a sigh. He stared at the beautiful black patterns that shifted and moved across the surface of Ivar's flesh. They were tribal markings of a people who no longer existed. The Asura could control the pigment of their skin so that they could change their color to blend in with almost any environment, becoming nearly invisible. But at rest, those tribal markings were always there. Something about them had always calmed the boy.

"But what if it *doesn't* work?" Timothy asked quietly.

The Asura shrugged. "Then we will fix it so it does." He bowed his head slightly to indicate that he had spoken his mind and that, for now, the conversation was done. Ivar turned to walk back to join the others who had gathered to watch.

"Thank you," Timothy called after him. Ivar had always tried to instill in him a sense of confidence. *As is our confidence, so is our ability,* he had said on more than one occasion. Timothy marveled at the simplicity of the thought. The Asura had always been able to see things with such clarity.

Ivar stood with the others, crossing his arms over his barrel chest, waiting patiently.

And deep down, Timothy knew. It was time.

"Sorry for the delay," Timothy apologized. "Let's see if this thing does what it's supposed to."

Timothy pulled himself up into the seat of the Burrower.

A pair of protective goggles dangled from one of the machine's operating mechanisms. He grabbed them up and pulled them on over his eyes. He looked toward his gathering of friends and again felt anticipation crackling in the air. He thought of all the things he would have liked to check one final time, but quickly pushed them from his mind. The time was now, and there would be no turning back.

His hands went to the first of the valves, and he turned it as far as it would go. A hiss like that of a gigantic serpent filled the air. The craft shuddered slightly as the steam that had been building up in a storage tank was released into the main body of the Burrower through a series of pipes. Timothy turned the next knob ever so slightly, and a smile blossomed across his face as the conical-shaped drill at the front of the craft slowly began to turn, with each full rotation growing faster and faster still.

Quickly he pressed his foot on a thick pedal and began to pump it. The rear of the Burrower began to gradually rise as the front of the craft angled toward the ground. As he released the brake, the craft slid forward.

Timothy held his breath as the furiously rotating drill touched the grass, cutting through it with ease and then into the dirt and rock beneath. He pumped the pedal further, and the machine's back end continued to lift. The drill spun faster, emitting a high-pitched whine, digging deeper and deeper into the ground, creating the beginnings of a tunnel. The Burrower was working exactly as Timothy had planned.

Cassandra Nicodemus removed the cover on the old chest and stared down at the rolled pieces of parchment stored within. A musty smell wafted up from within the box, and for a moment she thought that she might sneeze. Suppressing the need, she went about her task. She had an important job to do this morning that required her full concentration, but try as she might, she could not stop thinking about Timothy Cade.

A flush of warmth flowed into her cheeks. She didn't know why, but she found everything about him strangely fascinating, most especially that excited twinkle in his eyes when he talked about the fabulous inventions he intended to build.

Cassandra moved her hand over the top layer of scrolls in the old box, muttering the words of a magical incantation. The rolled parchments on the top slowly rose and began to unroll to reveal what was written on them. And again she found herself thinking of Timothy.

He was unable to perform even the simplest acts of magic. *How different everything must be for him,* Cassandra thought as the contents of the scrolls were exposed to her. She could barely focus on the information they revealed, lost in her thoughts about the boy and how much he had changed the world since his arrival.

"Have you found anything yet?"

Startled from her daydreams, Cassandra turned toward the large, bearded mage who sat behind the desk on the other side of the office. Leander Maddox was surrounded by ancient writings, from the oldest parchment scrolls to more recent texts. He was the one who had found Timothy, hidden away in a pocket world by his father, the great magician, Argus Cade, and had brought him into this world upon the mage's death.

There was an unusual edge of impatience in Leander's voice today.

"Not yet," she told him, attempting to clear her mind so that she could focus on the documents floating in the air before her. But there was so much to think about.

Leander was the current Grandmaster of the Order of Alhazred, the guild of mages to which the Cade and Nicodemus families had always belonged. Cassandra could not help but wonder how the burly mage felt about the changes that had come since he had brought Timothy into this world where the boy was an oddity.

An outcast.

It had been Timothy who had revealed the insidious plot of the former Grandmaster—her own grandfather—to try to take control of the entire Parliament of Mages, to rule all of the various Orders. Cassandra felt a pang of sadness as she recalled the death of her grandfather during a battle with Timothy, and the resultant chaos that followed in the Parliament of Mages.

So much had occurred in so little time.

She thought about the coming of the Wurm, Verlis. This was seen by many as yet another threat, but in fact, the descendant of the Dragons of Old had come seeking help against a much larger evil, an evil that now threatened to spill into her life—into her world. Long before she and Timothy had been born, the Wurm had existed peacefully on Terra alongside mages. But in time there had been conflict, and the Wurm had been driven from the world and forcibly relocated in a parallel dimension named Draconae.

Now, on Draconae, their leader, Raptus, was planning to breach the barrier that separated the dimensions. According to Verlis, Raptus sought revenge upon the world of mages and planned to take control of Terra and destroy the Parliament entirely. The mages had been manipulated in those dark days by Alhazred, founder of Cassandra's own Order, and thus Parliament had betrayed the Wurm. Raptus and his followers would not rest until they had their vengeance.

With a sigh, she at last focused upon the documents floating in the air. She and Leander had been charged by Parliament with the task of studying the ancient scrolls, searching for anything that might help in their defense against the impending Wurm attack. Cassandra found nothing of use on four of the scrolls, allowing them to roll closed again and drop to the floor. It was something on the fifth that caught her eye.

"Leander," she said, reaching up to pluck the scroll from the air before her. "I think I may have found something of interest."

The Grandmaster looked up from his own work, his eyes

red and his face haggard with exhaustion. Cassandra knew the job was a taxing one, but had never really stopped to think about the toll that leading an entire guild might exact upon a grandmaster. Though it was something she would have to seriously consider, if she ever planned to assume the mantle of Grandmaster to the Order of Alhazred. For, as granddaughter of Aloysius Nicodemus, the previous leader of the guild, the post was hers as soon as she felt ready to take it upon herself.

"What is it?" he asked, rising from his chair.

She brought the scroll to him. "It's nothing specific, but in this correspondence between two guild craftsmen, there is some talk about what I presume is the original mining operation near the original Wurm settlement at Tora'nah."

Leander snatched the document from her hand. "Give that to me," he hissed, and she was taken aback by his abruptness. She had noticed some subtle changes in the Grandmaster of late, and was worried that the pressures of the position may have had an unpleasant effect on the normally unflappable gentleman.

"Yes," he said, scanning the ancient writing. "Yes, this may indeed prove very useful to us on our journey."

Leander, along with Timothy and Verlis and some specially chosen representatives of Parliament, were planning an expedition to the former home of the Wurm race to check on the stability of the magical barrier between Terra and Draconae. In addition, they were to oversee a new mining operation there and begin formulating plans to defend against invasion if the Wurm were indeed able to breach the barrier.

"The writer of the scroll talks about the creation of a map designating the areas of the Wurm territories richest in natural resources," the Grandmaster said, and looked at her intensely. "We must find this map at once. It could save us weeks of surveying the land, allowing us to begin digging for Malleum almost immediately."

"Do you have any suggestions where I should begin my search for the map?" Cassandra asked, returning to the chest where she had found the scroll. "Perhaps it's still in here?" she suggested, kneeling down to begin her search anew.

She heard the rush of air and glanced toward the Grandmaster to see him in the midst of conjuring. The spell struck the wooden chest and Cassandra jumped back, watching in amazement as the remaining contents of the box flew into the air, unrolling in unison.

Leander moved out from behind his desk, his robes of scarlet and black billowing around him as he studied each of the many floating documents. One by one, as they proved not to be the map he sought, they fluttered to the floor, discarded.

"There is no time," he muttered beneath his breath as he walked among the scrolls. "The fate of all we've known hangs in the balance."

Leander stiffened and reached out for one of the floating pieces of parchment. "This is it," he said, turning to her excitedly, and the remaining scrolls fell to the ground. He held the parchment out before him. "Crude, but useful nonetheless."

And then the Grandmaster started to laugh, an eerie sound the likes of which she had never heard from him before, and hoped never to hear again.

"Master Maddox?" she said.

He looked away from his prize to glare at her, and for a frightening moment she did not recognize him. Then his features relaxed, and the older gentleman she had come to admire and respect had returned.

"Yes, child?" he answered in a voice that seemed much too weak for a man of his usual vigor.

"Are you . . . are you unwell?"

Leander slowly rolled the scroll. "I'm quite all right," he told her, forcing a sad smile upon his wan features. "Just a little bit tired. There's no need for concern, my dear."

Yet as she watched him make his way slowly back to his desk, clutching the map to his chest, she wished that she could believe him. For as long as she had known the mage, Cassandra had found him tireless in his exuberance. In fact, she imagined that when the time came for the position of Grandmaster to be passed to her, Leander would be the example upon which she would model her own authority. But something was amiss.

He slid the last of the scrolls into a leather satchel with other documents they had found over the last three days, a spell of closure keeping the contents sealed tightly away. "I think we're just about ready to go."

She watched him carefully, searching for any clue as to

what might be troubling him, but all she could detect was weariness. Perhaps the Grandmaster really was just exhausted, his nerves frayed by the demands of his post.

Leander glanced at the large timepiece on the wall and then back at her. "Cassandra, please go tell Timothy that it is time." He gathered up his things. "I shall await him with the other members of the expedition at the main entrance."

She bowed her head and left his study. Cassandra thought she had heard Timothy mention something about testing his new invention in one of the open areas at the back of the estate, so she headed in that direction. She bustled along the seemingly endless corridors, hiking up the hem of her emerald green dress so as not to trip as she descended staircase after staircase. To the uninitiated, SkyHaven would be like a maze, but she had made a study of the place upon her arrival following the tragic death of her parents. She doubted that there was any place left in the floating manor that she had yet to see.

Cassandra descended a set of marble stairs that would take her to the back of the estate through the kitchen. When she entered the room she was a bit surprised that the staff was not hard at work preparing the afternoon meal. Instead, she found them all clustered at the back door, watching with rapt attention some display outside. There was a loud clamor from outside the building, accompanied by a high-pitched whine.

She made her way toward the gathering, nobody taking notice of her approach, and stood on tiptoe to see over the heads of the servants and cooks. Cassandra laughed softly to herself. *Timothy Cade, I should have known,* she thought, watching the boy astride a strange contraption that was digging into the earth, tossing dirt here and there.

Cassandra cleared her throat once, and then a second time, louder. The staff of SkyHaven's kitchen gradually reacted, reluctantly returning to their jobs, fearful that they would be scolded. She didn't blame them for their fascination. After all, how often did people see a boy riding a machine that could burrow down into the earth? Not every day. Never, in fact. Not until Timothy Cade had come into their lives. There was really no one like him in the world.

She stepped through the back door and strolled across the grass toward the gathering of Timothy's friends, who now stood around the hole he had dug, marveling at his latest accomplishment. Cassandra hoped Timothy was smart enough to know when to stop the machine. SkyHaven was a floating island, and if he dug too deeply he could find himself breaking through the bottom and falling into the ocean below. *What a sight that would be,* she thought, and had to stifle a giggle.

"Does he know when to stop?" she asked aloud, cupping her hands over her mouth and raising her voice to be heard over the sound of the digging machine.

Verlis glanced at Ivar, and the Asura then looked at Sheridan.

Edgar, who was perched upon the mechanical man's shoulder, flew into the air and landed on her waiting arm.

"Are you serious?" the rook asked, speaking loudly. "After everything he's done, you still have to ask that question?" The bird shook his head in disgust.

"I meant no disrespect. I just want to be sure he's careful."

Edgar ruffled his feathers indignantly. "The kid's a genius. Of course he knows not to go too far."

And as if on cue, the engine of the digging machine cut out and the sound of another, far quieter, device kicked in. Cassandra leaned forward and gazed into the hole to see that the machine was now ascending. The new sound was that of its wheels slowly turning, backing the craft up and bringing it to the surface.

"See," Edgar said to her. "Nothing to worry about. He knew just when to stop."

The digging machine backed out of the hole and up onto the grass. Timothy busied himself turning knobs and switching levers to shut down his invention's power source.

"Good thing I remembered to stop," Timothy said, removing the goggles from his eyes and jumping down from the craft to the ground. "I was so excited that it was working, I almost kept going."

Cassandra arched an eyebrow and smirked, glancing at Edgar, who quickly looked away, flying from his perch on her arm to the top of the boy's head.

"Good job, kid," the rook cawed. "The Burrower worked like a charm, just like I knew it would."

"Thanks, Edgar," the boy said, beaming.

Verlis approached the machine, resting a claw upon its

metal surface. "Fascinating," he growled. And he then looked toward the boy. "As are you, Timothy Cade, as are you." He then walked to the tunnel dug into the ground and peered down into the darkness.

Ivar and Sheridan went to congratulate Timothy next, but Cassandra hung back, not sure that Timothy had even noticed she was there. The breeze whipped her red hair across her face and she pushed it away from her eyes, trying unsuccessfully to tame it.

"Did you see?" he asked, striding toward her with a grin on his face. "It worked just as I'd hoped."

Cassandra smiled in return. "It's incredible." She wanted to say more but was having difficulty finding the right words with Timothy so close and smiling at her like that.

What's happening to me? she pondered, on the verge of panic.

Their eyes locked for a moment, and then Timothy quickly looked away, scratching the back of his head nervously. He turned his focus back to the Burrower. "Can't wait to tell Leander it worked," he said, reminding her why she had come to find him.

"Oh, right," Cassandra said, her hand quickly going to her mouth. "With all the excitement, I almost forgot. They're ready to leave now. The expedition to Tora'nah . . . they're waiting for you."

CHAPTER TWO

Timothy couldn't have picked a better moment to take his leave.

Across the rich green lawn, he saw Leander's personal assistant, Carlyle, appear at the open kitchen door, his face flushed with annoyance. Timothy quickly snatched his satchel up from the ground and looked inside to be sure he had everything he'd need for his journey.

"Timothy Cade!" Carlyle shouted, hurrying toward them.

"I think Verlis and I had better be going," he told his friends, and Cassandra. He caught her eye as he said his farewells, and she quickly looked away, pretending to be studying the clouds in the sky.

Strange, he thought, before concentrating on more important matters.

"Be sure to bring the Burrower back to the workshop," he told Sheridan, Ivar, and Edgar.

"Not to worry, Timothy," Sheridan said, release valve hissing. "I'll be sure to give it a thorough cleaning so that it is in tip-top shape when you return."

Ivar was already working on getting the craft back up onto the wheeled cart they had used to haul it from the workshop.

"What in the name of the blessed mage have you done to the grounds?" Carlyle yelled in a shrill voice. "When Grandmaster Maddox hears of this . . ."

"You think he's talking about the hole?" Edgar asked from his favorite place atop Sheridan's metal head. If the rook could have smiled, Timothy was certain he would have.

"Think so," the boy answered, backing away from the gathering.

"Hrrrrm. He sounds upset," Verlis growled, scratching his leathery chin with a clawed hand. "Perhaps you should explain the—"

Timothy gripped the Wurm at his elbow. The rough, scaled skin was strangely cool to the touch. "Perhaps we should get away from here as quickly as we can."

"Timothy Cade!" Carlyle shouted again, almost upon them.

Edgar flew toward him, circling around the stocky man's head. Carlyle waved his hands in the air, obviously enraged. "I have no desire to speak with you, bird. I want to talk to the boy!"

"Maybe you are right," Verlis replied, and the Wurm

opened his great wings, grabbing Timothy beneath the arms.

As Verlis lifted him up, wings flapping heavily, churning the air, Timothy noticed that Cassandra was looking at him. Once again he experienced that odd sensation in the pit of his stomach.

"Luck be with you," she called over the pounding of the dragon's wings, and he waved good-bye to her just as Verlis soared skyward with him.

Carlyle had reached the hole the Burrower had made and was gesticulating wildly. It appeared that Sheridan and Cassandra were attempting to calm him, but to little avail. Timothy almost felt bad leaving them to deal with the rather unpleasant man.

Almost, he thought with a chuckle.

Verlis winged his way around to the front of the sprawling fortress and remembered the first time he had ever seen SkyHaven. It hadn't been that long ago, but in a way, after all that he had seen and experienced, it felt like a lifetime. Timothy wondered what still lay ahead for him, what wonders and horrors he had yet to experience. These were exciting times for a boy who was raised in near solitude.

"There they are!" Timothy yelled over the sound of the wind in his ears and the beating of wings. He felt Verlis's grip beneath his arms tighten.

Two sky carriages hovered in front of SkyHaven, and members of the expedition traveling to Torah'nah milled about the crafts. The Wurm angled his body earthward, and they began their descent.

The ground came up at them quickly, and Timothy instinctively closed his eyes, fearing that they would not be able to stop in time. Just as it seemed too late, Verlis spread his great wings wide, cutting the speed of his descent and allowing them to glide safely to the ground.

Timothy adjusted the strap of the satchel he wore slung over his shoulder and checked to see that the metal clasp was still fastened. He wanted to be certain that he hadn't lost any of his notes or drawings in flight with Verlis. Everything was fine.

The boy looked up to see Leander Maddox walking toward them, his hands clasped behind his back. Timothy felt a surge of excitement, quickening his pace to meet up with the Grandmaster, eager to share the news of his latest success. It had been Leander who had assigned the boy the difficult task of designing and building a machine that could dig down into earth, but that was not powered by magic.

He hurried to the burly mage, barely able to contain his excitement. "The Burrower, it works," he blurted out. "I tested it in the back of the fortress and it went perfectly. The hole was smooth and deep. It's a good thing I stopped when I did, because I could have kept right on going and dug straight through and Carlyle showed up and—"

Timothy's ramble came to an abrupt stop as he watched Leander bring his wrist up to his face to gaze briefly upon a timepiece fastened there.

"You're late," the Grandmaster said shortly, barely hiding his irritation. He clasped his large hands behind his back again. "Didn't Cassandra inform you that we were ready to leave?"

Timothy could have blamed Cassandra, but he did not want to get her into trouble, so he nodded. "Yes, but we were testing my machine and . . ." He stopped, realizing that he had no real excuse. "I'm sorry to have kept you waiting, Leander. I guess we just lost track of time."

The big man said nothing, and Timothy looked up to see him gazing off into space, one of his hands slowly stroking the coarse hair of his bushy red beard.

"Leander?" Timothy said softly, looking off in the same direction and seeing nothing but blue sky and the churning ocean. "Are . . . are you all right?"

The Grandmaster started as if awakened from a dream and gazed again at his timepiece. "We have no time for this foolishness," he growled, abruptly turning around and walking toward the other members of the expedition and his waiting sky carriage. "We must depart at once if we are to reach Tora'nah by the morrow."

Verlis moved up alongside him. "Is all well between you and Grandmaster Maddox?" he asked the boy.

Timothy did not answer at once, mulling over Verlis's question. He had noticed slight changes in his friend and mentor over the last few days, but nothing to really cause him concern. This, however, was something else entirely.

"I'm not sure," he whispered, watching as the Grandmaster went to his sky carriage and spoke to Caiaphas, his navigation mage.

When Leander had gone on to the second sky carriage to speak to the others who were a part of the expedition, Caiaphas motioned for Timothy and Verlis to approach.

"Master Timothy," the navigator said with a slight bow of his head. The lower portion of the navigation mage's face was covered in a dark blue veil, but his voice was pleasant enough to let the boy know he was smiling. At least someone seemed happy to see him. "Great Verlis," the navigator then said, addressing the dragon.

Verlis responded in kind, ruffling his leathery wings as he lowered his horned head in a bow of greeting.

"Grandmaster Maddox has informed me that we are to leave at once," Caiaphas said, pushing up the long sleeves of his blue robes, readying himself to cast the spells used to lift and propel the carriage. "And that you and Verlis are to ride with him inside."

The driver motioned toward the lower portion of the carriage, and a spark leaped from one of his fingertips. The door into the vehicle swung open slowly to admit them.

The Wurm leaped back from the sky carriage. "I will not ride within this contraption," Verlis growled, shaking his large, horned head. "I will fly to Tora'nah under my own power."

Caiaphas folded his hands upon his lap. "I'm afraid that will not do. Grandmaster Maddox gave precise instruction that you were to ride *inside* the carriage."

Trails of smoke began to rise from Verlis's flaring nostrils. "I will not fly within this . . . this box," he spat, and Timothy could see that the Wurm's anger was on the rise.

The boy placed a calming hand upon Verlis's arm. "Can you tell us why he wants this?" Timothy asked the navigator, keeping his voice soft so as not to arouse the interests of the others around them.

Caiaphas brought one of his hands to his covered mouth, reflecting momentarily before speaking. "In no disrespect to you, great Verlis, the Grandmaster believes that you will appear more . . . civilized if you were to travel in the same manner as the others in the expedition."

"Civilized?" Verlis barked, and hissing streams of burning orange spittle, liquid fire, began to leak from the sides of his mouth.

"Calm yourself," Timothy said quickly, his voice still low. "You already know what they think of you—the other mages of Parliament."

"They think me a monster," Verlis replied. "A savage beast not fit to walk amongst them."

"Exactly," Timothy said. "Look at this as a chance to prove them wrong again."

The Wurm sneered, revealing his razor-sharp teeth. "But to ride inside this . . . thing." He gestured toward the carriage.

"I will attempt to make your journey as pleasant and as comfortable as it is within my power to do so," Caiaphas said, raising his hands. Indigo magic arced from the tips of his fingers.

Verlis said nothing, glaring at the carriage, as if preparing to challenge it to battle.

"Prove them wrong," Timothy whispered again.

As if sensing discord, Leander approached.

"Is there a problem?" the Grandmaster asked, looking from Timothy to Verlis.

Many of the other representatives of Parliament who were a part of the expedition were watching them now. Timothy tensed. This was not the time for Verlis to lose his temper. The Parliament already feared the descendents of the Dragons of Old. One Wurm was bad enough, but now there were dozens of them on Terra, all of Verlis's clan, who had fled Draconae and the brutality of Raptus. Now wasn't the time for trouble.

"No," Verlis stated firmly, moving to squeeze his large frame through the doorway into the sky carriage. "There is no problem at all."

Timothy did not know whether it was the fact that he had stayed up all night putting the finishing touches on the Burrower prototype, or the relief that the digging device worked, but he found himself growing incredibly sleepy as the sky carriage flew above the clouds on its journey south. Though he tried to fight it, he found his eyelids growing heavy, and eventually closing.

I'll just rest for a moment, he told himself, laying his head back against the seat. But it wasn't long before he was asleep, pulled into the realm of dream as if caught in the current of Patience's emerald green ocean.

* * *

He dreamed of his father's embrace.

"I've missed you so much," he told his father, running to him across the beach of his interdimensional hideaway, burying his face in the thickness of his father's robes. Timothy felt his father's arms around him, and could even smell the scent of him—a pleasing aroma, equal parts old books and parchments and the spicy aroma of the Maddis leaves Argus Cade had often smoked in his pipe. The smell immediately put Timothy at ease, making him feel safe and secure. Here in his father's arms, nothing could harm him.

But the air around him grew suddenly cold and damp, and Timothy looked up to see that he was no longer upon the beach on Patience, but somewhere else entirely. The place was poorly lit and made of stone, and all around him he could hear the moans of those who had been jailed for crimes against the Parliament of Mages—for crimes against the world.

Timothy knew this place well.

Abaddon.

Arcanum was the capital city of Sunderland, which was still a country in its own right, though such boundaries no longer meant very much with the worldwide Parliament of Mages having become so powerful. Even so, there was still a certain amount of local government, and that included the imprisonment of criminals. Sunderland's major prison was Abbadon, located deep beneath the Sunnis Ocean. It was where Verlis had been briefly imprisoned by Parliament, not for any crime, but for what he was. Timothy had broken him out of there. Abbadon was one of the most horrible places Timothy had ever visited. He had wished never to see the inside of Abaddon again, but here he was.

"Why are we here?" he asked.

"It's where you belong," said a cruel, cold voice. Not his father's voice at all. Timothy looked up into the face seething with hate.

Constable Grimshaw smiled, his teeth incredibly sharp. The Constable's grip upon Timothy's arm tightened as he struggled to get free.

"What's the matter, boy?" Grimshaw asked. *"Haven't you missed me as well?"* The Constable started to laugh; one of the most horrible of sounds he had ever heard.

Timothy awoke with a gasp to find Leander and Verlis watching him with cautious eyes.

"Dreams?" the Wurm asked, shifting in the seat across from the boy, still not comfortable with the flying arrangements.

"More like a nightmare," Tim replied. He wiped cool drops of sweat from his brow and leaned his head back with a sigh. "I dreamt of my father."

"And that is a nightmare?" Verlis asked, confused.

"He didn't stay my father; he turned into Constable Grimshaw, and we were in Abaddon."

The Wurm nodded his horned head. "I see. *That* is a nightmare."

Timothy rubbed the sleep from his eyes and glanced over to see Leander busily writing in an oversize journal. It was unusual to find the Grandmaster actually using a writing instrument, magic being the typical means by which words were put to parchment. But Timothy was seated right beside the mage, and the strange magic-negating aura that surrounded him could sometimes wreak havoc with writing spells. In close quarters, particularly traveling together, Leander had found it much wiser to use a pen.

Leander looked up from his scribbling. "You needn't worry about Grimshaw. In dream or reality." The Grandmaster closed his book. "It appears that the Constable has joined the ranks of the missing."

Timothy felt a cold finger of dread touch his neck. Mages were still disappearing in the city, and no one could figure out what fate had befallen them. It was one of Parliament's chief concerns, along with the impending Wurm invasion. But Constable Grimshaw was an evil man, and whatever happened to him was deserved as far as he was concerned. If he shared the fate of the other missing mages, Timothy had no sympathy for him.

He gazed out the window of the carriage to see that they were now traveling over a densely wooded area, the forests of Yarrith. He had read that the forest stretched for miles, and had always wanted to see it. It was like a blanket of green, extending for as far as the eye could see. It was considered one of the last truly untamed regions in Sunderland.

"Not long now," Verlis said, also gazing out at the thick green below. "I sense that we are close."

"You *sense* it?" Timothy asked.

The Wurm nodded. "In here," he said, placing a clawed hand against his chest. The scales there were thicker, almost like armored plating. "As the spirits of your dead live on in the blazing energy that is ghostfire, the spirits of the Wurm continue to exist as well, leaving a piece of themselves behind before soaring on to a land beyond."

Timothy was fascinated; there was still so much that he did not know about Verlis and his people, their customs and beliefs, and he hoped that someday he would have the chance to learn all there was.

"Tora'nah is a special place," Verlis said as they flew above the forested land. "A spiritual place. Hopefully there we will find the answers we seek."

Timothy looked away from the window and placed his hand upon his satchel. Inside were his notes and plans for the construction of the larger Burrower machine they would need for mining in Tora'nah. The Parliament believed that under the ground there they might find a solution to their current predicament.

"So all the materials needed to construct the full-size Burrower are already at Tora'nah?" he asked.

"Everything to your specifications," Leander confirmed.

Timothy stared at his sketches and notes again. "Do you really think this will work?"

Leander gestured for the boy to hand over his papers, and he did so willingly. It was the Grandmaster's turn to peruse the intricate drawings and designs.

"If we're careful," Leander said. "And if your machine works as well as we hope."

The ancient Wurm had mined a rare mineral from the

soil at Tora'nah. A Wurm scientist called Malleus had discovered natural deposits of a metal ore that was unusually soft and pliable . . . until it was touched by magic. Once it came into contact with magic, the metal—called Malleum after its discoverer—was the hardest substance on the planet. Unbreakable. Impenetrable. All of which meant that it had to be removed from the ground by physical rather than magical means. If they tried to use magic to unearth it, the metal would harden instantly and be useless. It could not be made into weapons or armor then.

No, the Malleum had to be dug up without the use of magic, forged in fire, and hammered into whatever form it would eventually take. Only then would it be touched by magic . . . which would transform it from soft to unbreakable.

"The Burrower will save a great deal of time," Verlis said. "We do not know when Raptus will break through the barrier, so there is no time to spare. The sooner the Malleum can be forged into weapons and armor, the better for all of us. The time for war has come to Terra again."

Verlis turned away, gazing out the window of the sky carriage.

Timothy took the plans back from Leander and studied them with a new eye, already thinking of revisions to the machine that could smooth the process. "You know," he said, mostly to himself, "I think we could do this better— make it more efficient."

He borrowed the pen that Leander had been using and started to draw.

Hours passed and many miles passed beneath them before Timothy Cade again lifted his head from his work.

They called it Alhazred's Divide, the wall of magical energy that had been erected to seal the breach between the other-dimensional world of Draconae from Terra, keeping the Wurm race away from the world of the mages forever. It extended as far as the eye could see to the north and south, and from the ground to the sky. The barrier distorted the air so that it shimmered. Timothy Cade had been to that world and back with Verlis, and sometimes still had night-mares about the Wurms' volcanic city and about Raptus, the cruel general who commanded them all. He had seen with his own eyes the Wurm sorcerers who worked with fierce determination to tear down that barrier from the other side. The very thought made him shudder.

From the window of the carriage Timothy could see the other sky craft that had been journeying with them as they prepared to set down at the Tora'nah encampment. The land around them was bleak, rocky, and foreboding, not at all like the rich and fertile regions they had traveled over on their way here. He could see the small village that the workers at Tora'nah had set up for their mining operation. One of the buildings was a large rectangular structure with tall chimneys.

"What is that? Not living quarters?" Timothy asked, pointing.

"No. That is the Forge," Leander replied. "Where the Malleum will be fashioned into tools for war. Other than your Burrower, it is the most important part of the operation."

"We are descending," Caiaphas called from his seat, and Timothy felt the craft's downward motion in the hollow of his belly.

He had learned to love the sensation of flying in a sky carriage, but was still always a little nervous when it came to landing. Since he was not able to do it himself, he had never learned to trust the power of magic. Timothy looked over at the powerful form of Verlis. The Wurm was still gazing out the window as the cold gray landscape came up to meet them.

"I was but a young hatchling when last I was here," Verlis said quietly. "But the memories of what it once was—before the conflict with the mages—are still incredibly clear."

The sky carriage gently touched down upon the uneven ground, a testament to Caiaphas's skill.

Leander opened the door. "That was the past, friend Verlis," the Grandmaster said, stepping from the craft. "Let us see what we can do about forging a far better future—for both our races."

Timothy followed Leander, waiting as Verlis carefully extracted himself from the carriage. It was much colder at Tora'nah, thick gray clouds blotting out the sun. Timothy shivered, pulling the collar of his tunic up around his throat, but he wasn't sure if the reaction was entirely from the cold. There was something truly foreboding about this place, something that filled the boy with unease.

"What was it like before?" Timothy asked his friend. "Before the war with the mages?"

Verlis stretched his wings and glanced around, plumes of smoke rising from his snout. "There was life here then—in the sky, in the dirt and rock—but the fighting, the amount of combat magic released . . . it has left the land spiritless."

Leander had gone to speak with the other members of the expedition force, but in the midst of their conversation, the men and women sent by Parliament were all staring at Timothy and Verlis. Grandmaster Maddox noticed that the others of his group were not listening especially closely to him, and Timothy watched as Leander realized how rude they were behaving. Yet in that moment when he ought to have chided his fellow mages, he instead shot an angry glance at Timothy and Verlis.

"Is something wrong?" the mage asked, an edge in his voice.

Timothy glanced at Verlis, who still seemed distracted by this return to the ruins of his once great society. The boy was about to reply for both of them when Verlis spoke up.

"Much is wrong here," said the Wurm, turning toward the Grandmaster and the other representatives of Parliament. "Much has . . . changed, since I last walked this ground."

A sudden, cool gust of wind arose, and the way it whipped across the desolate landscape seemed to cry out in a mournful voice. The entire gathering seemed affected by the sorrowful wind of Tora'nah. The mages ended their conversation, and the tension evaporated. With the sad song of the wind in his ears, Timothy remembered what Verlis had said earlier about the spirits of his people, and wondered if this might be the voice of their loss.

Movement off to his right caught Timothy's attention, and he moved away from the sky carriage to get a better look. Atop a small hill, Timothy saw a village of huts, an encampment set up by the first of Parliament's workers to arrive. The workers were coming out from their shelters to welcome them.

"Greetings!" called a tall gentleman with a thick head of graying hair. "You must be Timothy Cade," he said, bowing at the waist in greeting. "I am Walter Telford, the project manager, and I am very pleased to make your acquaintance. I've heard some amazing things about your skill as an inventor."

Timothy liked the man almost immediately due to his friendly demeanor as well as the fact that Walter Telford didn't seem at all put off by the knowledge of his . . . handicap. He bowed back. "Pleased to meet you as well."

"Walter," Leander called, striding ahead of the other members of the expedition. "It's good to see you again."

The two men embraced warmly.

"Are you well?" Telford asked. "You look so pale, my friend. Don't tell me that the comfortable life of a grandmaster is too much work for you."

Telford laughed and hugged the burly mage again. It was reassuring for Timothy to hear that others were concerned for Leander's health.

"A by-product of the job, I'm afraid to say," Leander replied quickly, waving away Walter's concerns. He quickly changed the subject. "Imagine my surprise and elation when I heard you would be supervising this operation. I'd thought they would have put you out to pasture years ago."

Telford laughed aloud again. It was a cheerful sound and one that seemed a bit out of place in the grim landscape of Tora'nah.

Timothy looked around for Verlis and saw the Wurm standing alone in front of Alhazred's Divide. He approached, but did not get too close, so that his aura of negation would not affect the ancient spell.

"Verlis?"

"Raptus is on the other side," the Wurm said. He reached out a clawed hand and placed it upon the shimmering wall of magic. "I can feel his anger—his rage. He will do every-thing in his power to tear this barrier asunder."

Timothy started to move closer, but thought better of it, remaining where he was. "Don't worry. We'll stop him."

The Wurm lowered his horned head and sighed, small jets of fire shooting from his nostrils. "I wish that I felt your confidence. But I sense impending disaster."

They were interrupted by the sound of someone walk-ing toward them across the rock-covered ground. The boy turned to find Walter Telford approaching.

"Timothy?" Telford called. "We're about to show everyone to their quarters. Would you and your friend like to come?"

The boy smiled, liking the man even more. Telford treated

both him and Verlis as true members of the expedition team, not as freaks. He glanced back at Verlis, still standing before Alhazred's Divide, and guessed that the Wurm might like some time alone.

"I'll show him later, if that would be all right," he said. "But I'd like to go."

Walter responded with a smile, gesturing for him to follow, and Timothy did just that, accompanying the man back to the encampment. Each hut was small but cozy, consisting of a cot and a small desk to work on. Verlis's quarters were located right next door to Timothy's.

The project manager left Timothy to settle in, recommending that he take a short nap to refresh himself after his long journey. Walter had laughed heartily, saying that the boy was going to need his rest, for they planned on working him quite hard. The cot did look thin and lumpy but turned out to be surprisingly comfortable, and he soon found himself drifting off.

Timothy wasn't sure what it was that awakened him, but as his eyes opened, he sensed that something was wrong. It was dark now, and as he got up from his bed he wondered how long he had been asleep. He removed from his satchel a small lantern capable of containing hungry fire. Using a match from his tool kit, he lit the lantern. Hoping to dispel his uneasiness, he shone the light about his quarters, throwing flickering firelight into the inky pools of shadow.

Something moved in a gloomy corner, swiftly scurrying

from one patch of darkness to the next in an attempt to remain unseen. Timothy gasped, nearly dropping the lantern. It was an animal of some kind, large for something that could move with such speed and stealth. From the quick glimpses he got, it seemed almost furless, its skin a sickly pale hue.

The unknown animal darted beneath his cot, and Timothy stumbled back away from it. He was tempted to cry out for help, but he knew that the representatives from Parliament and many other members of the expedition were probably watching him, waiting for him to do something foolish. If this was just some local wildlife, he didn't want to cause an unnecessary ruckus. No, unless he was sure he was in danger, he would deal with the matter on his own.

He quickly hauled the rumpled blanket from the bed and then leaped up onto it. Standing in the center of the cot, he crouched tensely, ready to use the heavy cover as a net to trap his unwanted visitor the moment it attempted to escape. When it did not immediately race out from its hiding place, Timothy began to jump up and down on the cot, trying to drive it out. For a moment he thought he would have to find something to poke it with, but then the pale-skinned creature shot out from beneath the bed.

Timothy sprang from his perch, a scream equal parts excitement and fear escaping his lips. He landed on the floor in a crouch, throwing the woven blanket over the scurrying intruder, then leaped atop it in an attempt to restrain the beast.

The animal was far stronger than Timothy expected, and it thrashed, growled, and hissed, trying to escape the blanket. Timothy was thrown aside and before he could regain control, the creature escaped, moving with incredible speed toward the door. Timothy was up in an instant and tried to pursue it, but such was its speed that it was already gone. He stared dumbfounded as the door to his hut swung back and forth in the evening breeze.

How did it get in here? he wondered, positive that Walter had closed the door firmly when he had left. He ran to the door in hopes of seeing where it had run off to, and collided with Leander.

"Arrrgh!" Timothy screamed, startled by the large man's sudden appearance.

"What in the name of the seven mystics is wrong?" Leander demanded.

Timothy looked past him. "Did you see it? Did you see the . . . the animal that came from here? It was in my room and I chased it out. I don't know what it was."

Leander looked behind him and then back to the boy. "I saw no such thing," he said, placing his hands on Timothy's shoulders. "And I've been standing out here enjoying the night air for quite some time now."

"But—"

"I heard you screaming and came at once to find out what was the matter."

Timothy looked up into Leander's eyes. "But I saw it. I tried to catch it in this blanket." He held up his bedclothes to show the archmage.

Leander shook his head. "It was a nightmare, boy," he explained. "Likely brought on by your change of surroundings and the dire importance of our mission here. Nothing more."

For the briefest of instants, Timothy almost believed his friend, thinking that perhaps he had imagined it all, still in the grip of sleep. But then he saw the jagged rips in the blanket, obviously made by very sharp claws.

CHAPTER THREE

It wasn't the most restful of nights.

After the business with the animal intruder in his hut, and Leander's insistence that it had all been part of an elaborate dream—Timothy had even brushed off the rips in the blanket as something he might have done himself in the throes of a nightmare—Timothy attended a team meeting to address the following day's goals. That was followed by a hearty meal served in honor of the new arrivals. Later that evening, when he had at last gone to bed, he had slept restlessly, fearing the return of the mysterious animal.

In the morning Timothy arose groggily from his bed. Outside his hut there was a metal trough of water where he splashed his face and attempted to clear away the cobwebs from his mind. The water was cold, and exactly what he needed to wake himself up. He grabbed the towel hanging on a peg outside his door and headed to the next hut over, drying his face and hands on the coarse material.

There was no response to his knocks on Verlis's door, so Timothy opened it a crack to peer inside. No one was there. A flicker of concern went through him. From the look of the room, it did not appear that the Wurm had ever entered it. So where had Verlis passed the night?

"Ah, you're finally up!"

Timothy was startled by the voice and turned quickly, only to relax the moment he saw Walter Telford approaching, a steaming cup of brew in one hand and a piece of fruit in the other.

"Good morning to you," Timothy said. "Are we the first to rise?"

Walter's laugher boomed. "Are you serious, lad?" he asked. "The entire camp's been up since the first rays of dawn." He threw his arm around Timothy's shoulder and steered him away from Verlis's hovel. "We let you sleep in today, but come tomorrow, you'll be expected to rise with the rest of us." He gave the boy a friendly squeeze. "Can I interest you in a bit of breakfast before you begin your workday?"

Timothy grabbed his satchel from his quarters and headed to the dining area with Walter. There, he had something to drink and some dried fruit—not the elaborate breakfast he had come to expect at SkyHaven, but surprisingly quite satisfying.

When he'd finished eating, Timothy and Walter walked over to a larger structure that served as the camp's command center. Timothy entered the building and was shocked to find the workers and all the Parliament members waiting inside. Leander was seated in a chair up front, and nodded in greeting as the boy entered.

Walter placed a hand upon his shoulder. "So, now that you've had a good night's sleep and a bit of breakfast, how do you feel about sharing your plans for the digging machine?"

Timothy looked up at the man. "Do you mean they're all here to listen to me?" he asked incredulously. Sure, Parliament had asked him to come up with designs for the Burrower, but he never imagined his involvement would be much more than that.

"Who else?" Walter asked. "You're the creator, the one who knows the craft. We're just the builders."

Timothy glanced around the room. "I'd like to help build it as well."

Walter smiled. "And we welcome your assistance." He directed Timothy toward a small table that had been set up at the front of the room. "Now why don't you tell us about this fabulous machine of yours?"

And Timothy did just that, opening his satchel and revealing the many drawings and diagrams he had made since first being asked to create the Burrower. He was a bit nervous at first, but he went through each of his drawings and blue-prints, often leaving the table to walk among those in attendance. Some had questions about the construction of the craft, and he was more than happy to answer them. He told them about the prototype he had built back at SkyHaven and how it had worked exactly as hoped, and he told them he would apply what he had learned in building the first craft to the creation of the much larger Burrower.

When he was finished, Walter conjured a floating map to show the audience where they intended to begin mining the Malleum. "Thanks to some documents Grandmaster Maddox uncovered and a study of the rock formations in the region, our geologists have determined that this area here is where we'll find the most success." The project manager circled an area upon the magical map with his index finger and the spot immediately turned a brightly glowing red, highlighting the zone for all to see.

"With Timothy's fabulous machine to help us, we can extract the Malleum, and hopefully strengthen our defenses against the impending invasion."

Walter stepped back, allowing everyone in the room a clear view of the mystical map. He had another cup of brew in hand and was sipping it gingerly as he eyed the audience seated before him.

"Are there any questions for me or for our great inventor here?" Walter gestured toward the boy, and Timothy could not help but smile. He liked this feeling of importance.

A Parliament member raised his hand and stood.

"This gathering recognizes Grandmaster Lokus of the Chakraz Order," Walter said, directing him to speak.

Lokus smoothed the wrinkles from his golden robes before speaking in a high, singsong voice. "The Malleum is crucial to our defense. It can withstand both the fires and the weapons of the Wurm and will give us an edge in battle. But we cannot begin the process of its extraction without the benefit of this digging device. When can we expect the building of this . . . Burrower to begin?"

Walter looked toward Timothy. "I think our designer and inventor would be the best person to answer that question," he said. "What do you think, lad? When can we begin construction on the Burrower?"

All eyes were on him again, and momentarily, Timothy's mind went blank. This was too much; from outcast to resident expert in a matter of days was more than he could handle. He saw Caiaphas in the gathering and felt a little better. Then he spotted Leander in the front row, and the great man smiled ever so slightly, urging him on with a look that said, *Go ahead boy, show them what you know.*

Timothy glanced down at his designs and, before he was even aware, he was speaking. "Well, since we have all the materials we need to put the Burrower together, I guess it all depends on the area where we'll be digging." He looked up from his notes and stared at the floating map. "I'd like to take a look at the dig site first so I can make some last-minute adjustments to the basic design before we begin its construction." Timothy shrugged. "After that, I guess it's only a matter of how fast we can work. With all the parts available, a matter of days."

Walter downed the remainder of his brew and waved his hand through the floating map, causing it to dissipate in a crackle of mystical energy. "Then I think we should give Timothy a tour, and we can begin in earnest."

Timothy agreed, and within moments the entire encampment was following Walter and his assistants to the excavation site. Timothy walked with Leander at the back of the line and noted with concern that the Grandmaster was moving much more slowly these days.

Leander stopped suddenly, swaying on his feet.

"Are you all right, Leander?" Timothy asked, his brow knitting with concern. "We can stop and rest if you need to."

Leander chuckled. "I'll rest when I'm dead," he said.

"Don't even suggest such a thing," Timothy cried, horrified.

"It's just an expression," the Grandmaster explained. "No need to get upset. And do you know who taught it to me?"

Timothy shook his head, but had a vague suspicion as to who it was.

"Your father." As Leander spoke, he let Timothy lead him to a large rock and leaned against it to catch his breath. The boy sat down beside him.

"It's an awful saying," Timothy said.

Leander chuckled again and threw his arm around the boy. "Come now, Tim, no need to be upset. All it means is that there are far too many things to accomplish in life— that we must try to do each and every one of them, to live life to its fullest."

They fell silent then, the two of them sitting on the large stone in the cold, barren wasteland that was Tora'nah. The landscape had never seemed as bleak and depressing as it did at that very moment, and Timothy wanted nothing more than to change the subject and lighten the mood.

"Did you see how the guild members listened to me this morning?" he asked. "Looking at my drawings—asking me questions. Can you believe it? They were asking *me* questions."

Leander slowly stood. "Times are changing, Timothy," the Grandmaster said. "And you are a very important part of that change." He stretched his large frame with a contented grunt, looking healthier than he had in days. "Whether they care to admit it or not."

Timothy stood as well, ready to rejoin the others. "That must really infuriate them," he said, smiling.

"That, my boy, is an understatement."

They both started to laugh, continuing on the path that would take them to the Malleum excavation site, their mood much lighter. They were nearing the top of the hill that would take them down into the valley when they heard the first of the screams.

Screams, followed by the roar of an enraged Wurm.

Timothy quickened his pace, sprinting to the top of the hill. What he saw in the valley below took his breath away and made his heartbeat quicken. Verlis was attacking the Parliament expeditionary force, flying above their heads, liquid fire spewing from his screaming mouth. The members of Parliament were in a panic, running to hide among pillars of gray stone that protruded from the rocky earth, as the enraged Wurm soared above them.

"Verlis, what are you doing!" Timothy cried, running down the slope. He reached the bottom, running among the great stones that provided hiding places for the various guild members.

"I knew this would happen!" Timothy heard one of them snarl as he passed.

"The Wurm can't be trusted," said another. "This one and his tribe are just as dangerous as the ones trying to break through Alhazred's Divide!"

Timothy did his best to ignore their hurtful words, concentrating on reaching his troubled friend and figuring out what could have caused this horrible turn of events. A blast of fire erupted nearby and Timothy leaped back, falling onto his backside. He gazed up at the fearsome visage of a Wurm caught in the grip of madness.

"Verlis, what's wrong?" Timothy screamed, but doubted that the Wurm could hear him as he flew overhead.

"Get to cover, Tim!" somebody called from close by, and he turned to see Walter emerging from behind one of the towering stones. "He's gone mad!"

Walter darted to him, keeping his eyes on the sky, and tried desperately to take Timothy to safety. "Come with me." They could still hear the flapping of the Wurm's wings from somewhere close by.

"What happened?" Timothy demanded, pulling his arm from Walter's grip, refusing to be taken anywhere.

"I haven't a clue," the project manager explained breathlessly, afraid for his safety. "The Wurm was here when we arrived and when he asked what we were doing and I explained that this was where we would begin our digging for the Malleum, he became incensed, screaming that we are heartless monsters, and then he attacked us."

"'Heartless monsters,'" Timothy repeated, mulling the words over, trying to understand. He gazed at their surroundings, at the odd stone structures sticking up from the ground, and then at the cliff face that rose up toward the south, dotted with strange rock formations. "It has to be something about this place."

Walter was trying to get him to leave again, to seek better cover, but Timothy wanted no part of it. "Let me talk to him. Verlis is my friend. He'll listen to me."

He darted out into the open, gazing up into the sky. "Verlis, it's Timothy!" he cried, hands cupped to his mouth. "Please, tell me what's wrong!"

Fearing for the boy's safety, Walter chased after him. "You're going to be killed," the man cried, reaching out to take hold of the boy's arm.

A sizzling torrent of fire rained down from the sky, driving Walter back. Timothy flinched away from the scorching hot air and looked through the billowing smoke to see the fearsome shape of Verlis as he touched down upon the ground before him.

"Run, Tim!" Walter cried, struggling to stand, his clothes singed and smoldering.

The Wurm then turned its attentions to the man. "Defiler of the dead!" Verlis growled, and stalked toward him, menace in his gaze.

"Verlis, no!" Timothy cried, but the Wurm was not listening.

Walter's hands began to glow feebly with a spell of defense, but Timothy could sense that it would have little effect upon the enraged Wurm. This was not the sort of magic for which Walter had been trained. Timothy snatched up a rock and was preparing to throw it at Verlis's head—to prevent him from doing something that he would most certainly regret later—when the air around the Wurm began to crackle with the release of vast amounts of magical energy.

The great stone fell from his grasp as he watched as Verlis was suddenly frozen in his tracks, his body encased in a bubble of shimmering, supernatural force. Verlis struggled against the confines of his magical entrapment, but to little avail.

Leander emerged from the garden of tall stones, representatives of Parliament trailing nervously behind him.

"Kill it before it has the chance to escape!" one of them cried out, her voice raised in panic.

"I'll do no such thing," Leander replied in a commanding voice. "There has been some kind of misunderstanding here, and I intend to find out what has caused it."

Verlis dropped to his knees within the translucent sphere as Timothy approached.

"Verlis?" Timothy called, kneeling upon the stony earth, just far enough away from the bubble of magic so as to not disrupt it. "What happened here? What's made you so angry?"

Leander strode closer as well, his hands still crackling

with the residue from the spell he had just cast. "Explain yourself."

The Wurm kneeled within the sphere, his great horned head hanging low to his chest. It appeared that his rage had substantially subsided.

"They were going to dig *here*," he said, his voice tinged with indignation. "Here, of all places. . . ." Verlis lifted his head to look at them, and Timothy saw that his friend's eyes swam with raw emotion.

"I could not stand the thought of it being desecrated in such a way. It cannot be allowed. I apologize for my outburst, but this place must be protected."

And then Timothy understood. He gazed at the forest of tall stones and realized their powerful significance.

"Your ancestors—the Dragons of Old—they're buried here, aren't they?"

Verlis nodded. "As are many who fell in the war with the mages," he explained. "Before our banishment to Draconae. These cairns mark many graves. And there are far more tombs in the mountainside."

With one claw he pointed to the south, to the steep hill Timothy had noticed before. It rose up into a craggy cliff face that was covered with intricate rock formations.

"The idea of their remains being disturbed was too much for me to bear." Verlis shook his head from side to side, pulling his wings tighter about him. "I lost control, and for that I am sorry. I beg your forgiveness."

The magical sphere surrounding the Wurm dissipated as

quickly as it had appeared, and the members of Parliament immediately began to grumble their disapproval.

"Do you think that wise, Maddox?" one of them asked in a tone laced with caution.

"Verlis was caught up in the emotion of the situation," Leander explained. "He was protecting the graves of his ancestors, just as any of us would have done. I don't believe we have reason to fear him."

The regal beast nodded slowly as he rose to his feet. "I mean none of you any harm."

A large woman with a round, ruddy face, clad from head to toe in robes the color of mud, pushed her way to the front of the crowd. "Then we can still assume that we'll be digging for the Malleum here?" she asked. Other members of the expedition came to stand with her, as if challenging Verlis to react.

"But . . . ," the great Wurm sadly began. He held his tongue and balled his clawed hands into fists at his sides. He said no more, seething in silence.

Timothy could stand it no more. "No!" he said loudly.

They all looked at him quizzically.

"No, Master Cade?" the ruddy woman asked condescendingly. She looked to the others for support.

"You heard me," he said again. "No. We will not be digging for Malleum here."

A gasp went up from the gathering, and he felt Verlis's eyes upon him. "Timothy, please," he begged. "Do not become involved."

The boy did not listen. "Walter," he called, walking around Verlis to address the project manager. The man's clothing was a bit singed here and there, and covered with dirt and dust, but he seemed otherwise fine; for that, Tim was glad. "From your geologists' reports and research, are there any other areas you think might be ripe for Malleum mining?"

Walter stroked his chin in thought. Timothy hoped that the man understood the importance of what was being asked of him.

"A few, yes," he replied. "A short way south and nearer the Divide is another area we had considered."

"One of those might be better. This area *is* awfully rocky." He kicked at the loose, stone-covered ground with the toe of his boot.

"Now see here," the ruddy-faced member of Parliament began. "We were told that this area . . ."

Walter placed his hands on his hips and stared off into space, ignoring the woman's bluster. "In fact, I believe the area closer to the Divide might be even richer in Malleum than any other area we've considered."

"This is an outrage," the angry female mage spat, her round features even redder than before. "I know what you are doing. Are we going to let this . . . this *Wurm* dictate to us where we will conduct our business?"

There was some grumbling among those gathered as they all turned their attentions to Walter Telford.

"Well, Telford?" the woman asked. "What do you have to say for yourself?"

Walter remained quiet for a moment, brushing some more dust and dirt from his clothing. Timothy stared at him hopefully. If the Parliament ever wished to regain the trust of Verlis and his tribe, they couldn't defile the burial ground of his people. Timothy just hoped the man understood the gravity of this situation.

Walter squatted down to the ground and picked up a handful of the dry dirt, letting it run through his fingers.

"The boy's right," he said. "The ground here *is* too rocky. We don't want the Burrower to break before we get the first ounce of Malleum. We'd be wise to dig someplace else." He challenged the representatives of Parliament with a gaze, but none of them rose to the challenge. They would acquiesce to his expertise. Walter looked at Timothy, nodding his head ever so slightly.

"I'd very much like to see this new area," Timothy said, barely able to contain relief.

"Then let's go," the man replied, rising to his feet and gesturing for all to follow. "It's right this way."

"It's impossible!" Cassandra Nicodemus cried, throwing down upon Leander's desktop what could very well have been the thousandth scroll she had read since that morning. "I can never be a Grandmaster. There's just too much to remember!"

Edgar flapped from the stone windowsill to land on the desk. "Spoken like a true grandmaster in training," the bird squawked, pacing. "If I had a gold coin for every time I've heard that very statement, I'd have more coins than I'd care to count."

Cassandra leaned back in the ornate desk chair and sighed. "I can't recall even half of what I've read. It's hopeless."

Sheridan was there too, as was Ivar. The mechanical man was in the process of tidying the office, dusting the furniture with a cloth as he busily moved about the room and straightened anything that seemed out of order. Cassandra wasn't positive, but she was under the suspicion that Leander, or maybe even Timothy, had asked these three to keep an eye on her while they were away.

She smiled at the thought that it was Timothy—the first real smile that she'd had all morning.

"Now don't be too hard on yourself, Miss," Sheridan said, followed by a short burst of steam from the valve on the side of his head. "A true grandmaster is not forged in a day. It takes time and great commitment."

Cassandra reached for another scroll but didn't have the strength to read anymore, her thoughts traveling to Timothy and the fabulous adventures he was probably having in Tora'nah.

"I wish Leander had allowed me to accompany him," she said with a pout. "I'm sure I could have been of help to him."

"And you would have been able to spend more time with Timothy," Ivar said quietly, causing her to jump. His unique skin coloring made him nearly invisible, allowing him to blend with the office wall. She had almost forgotten he was there.

Cassandra blushed slightly at his implication.

"I guess he would have been there as well," she replied, turning her attentions again to the desktop, not wanting to talk about her fascination with Timothy, especially with his friends.

A small sphere of light suddenly blinked into existence in the air above her desk and she gasped, startled.

"Caw!" Edgar cried out, surprised as well.

Ivar dashed across the room, his hand resting on the hilt of the knife he wore in a sheath at his side.

The glowing ball gradually drifted down to the desktop and began to change form. At first Cassandra was curious, but that curiosity soon turned to distaste as the ball took the miniature shape of Carlyle, Grandmaster Maddox's fussy assistant.

"Good morning, Mistress Nicodemus," the tiny image of the man addressed her. "This is just a spell to remind you that a meeting has been set between yourself and the grounds staff to discuss the rather large and unsightly hole that has been dug—"

Cassandra swatted the flat of her hand down upon the magical construct, squashing the image in a flash of mystical light.

"I despise that man," she growled. She felt the others' eyes upon her and smiled sheepishly, a bit embarrassed that she had allowed her temper to get the better of her. "I'm not sure I've ever met anyone quite as annoying."

"Caw! Caw!" Edgar crowed, ruffling his inky black feathers as he stood upon the desktop. "Truer words were never spoken," the familiar said, turning his head to look at Sheridan and Ivar.

"He is quite a pest," the mechanical man said, returning to his efforts to tidy the room.

"A very unpleasant being," Ivar stated flatly, the black patterns upon his flesh changing, flowing across the surface of his skin and becoming thicker, darker, as if to reflect his distaste for the man.

"If I were Grandmaster, there would be no way that I could have him for an assistant." Cassandra frowned, picking up the scroll she had most recently been perusing. "Not that there's a chance of it ever happening."

Ivar remained before the desk, studying her with a slight tilt of his head. His eyes were piercing, and she became self-conscious in his gaze.

"Is there something wrong?"

"You hope to be Grandmaster someday?"

Cassandra shrugged. "Of course I do, but the question is *should* I be Grandmaster. Am I capable? Consider all the knowledge and experience that Leander has. I can't even begin to compare myself with him."

"But you are not him," the Asura stated flatly. "You are you."

"Of course I'm me," she said. "I don't understand what that has to do with—"

"Now is the time in your life when you begin to acquire

your own knowledge and experience," he explained. "You will shape the title to fit your own self, growing into the role of Grandmaster as *you* define it, not as others have."

"But how do you acquire the kind of strength and wisdom that seems such a natural part of Leander? If I am one day to replace him, I would not be worthy of the job if I could not do at least as well."

"If that is your goal and you are willing to struggle to reach it—so shall it be. It is all in your hands, Mistress."

As Cassandra considered those words, the Asura tilted his head as if hearing something off in the distance. Ivar turned away from the desk and padded across the room to gaze out through the magical spell-glass at the grounds below.

"The groundskeepers have gathered and are waiting for you," the Asura said, turning away from the view to fix her again in his dark, soulful stare.

Cassandra stood up, feeling a sense of confidence that had not been there just moments ago. "Then I must be on my way," she said, filled with a sense of purpose as well as a new respect for a man she once believed to be a savage. "A grandmaster in training must never keep an appointment waiting."

CHAPTER FOUR

Timothy couldn't sleep.

The encampment at Tora'nah was much like a small village, and growing more each day as more workers arrived. The full-size Burrower was under construction, and excitement was building. He and Verlis had been moved to a larger hut, a two-story structure, and his bedroom had a small balcony. He was grateful for this, because inside that tiny room he felt claustrophobic, so far away from everything and everyone that mattered to him. The balcony was a place to retreat to, especially at night.

Tonight he had been more melancholy than ever, and when it had become obvious that sleep was going to be elusive, he had pulled on linen trousers and padded onto the balcony quietly. There were guards out in the encampment and torches burned atop posts at the edges of the village, and he did not want to draw attention. He just wanted a little time to be by himself in the cool night air, to gaze up at the heavens, at the stars and the moons above Terra. The smallest moon, Hito, always seemed to catch his eye, and he felt a real appreciation for it. Distant from the others, as though it were too small for the other moons to even notice it.

He felt torn between progress, the adventure of the days to come, and the past, the people and places he had left behind. During the day it was easy to get carried away, to let the excitement and danger that surrounded their mission at Tora'nah and the creation of the Burrower get his heart working. Easy to laugh and to cheer and to lose himself in the intensity of the job at hand.

But at night his mind would drift back to the Island of Patience. He missed the serenity of the peaceful isle where he had spent his childhood, and he missed his father's house, the sprawling Cade Estate, which he had adapted to his handicap, his lack of magic. And, gods, how he missed his father. Thoughts of Argus Cade, of his kindly eyes and gentle hugs, never failed to bring a hitch to his breath and wishes about what might have been.

Tonight, though, it was not only Patience and his father that he missed. Leander had been distant of late, and Verlis was so troubled by the mining at Tora'nah and preoccupied with thoughts of Raptus and his army chipping away at the barrier between Terra and Draconae that he had little time to spend in conversation. Timothy felt alone. How strange it was to wish he was back at SkyHaven, yet he wanted to hear the whistle of steam from Sheridan's head and Edgar's cawing voice, and to see the wisdom and warmth in Ivar's eyes.

And Cassandra . . .

There on the balcony, beneath the stars and with the wind ruffling his hair, Timothy closed his eyes and an image of her swam into his mind. Her rich, red hair flowing about her shoulders and those green eyes that shone like gemstones, the way her nose crinkled when she smiled . . . he wished she was right there beside him, under the stars. He had found himself thinking of Cassandra more and more since leaving SkyHaven. The truth was that it worried him. He still was not certain he could trust her entirely. After all, what did he know about her aside from that she was Nicodemus's granddaughter? And yet in her eyes he felt he saw all the truth he needed.

He wondered if she was on a SkyHaven balcony at that very moment, staring up at the moons. Wondered if she felt the same kinship to Hito that he did.

Stop, he told himself. *She's just a girl.*

But that was it, wasn't it? Timothy had very little experience talking to girls. Though he had seen many women in Arcanum and even at SkyHaven during the time since he had left the island, he had only seen a handful of girls, and had spoken to none of them. Only Cassandra. She was perhaps two years older than he was, if that, and yet possessed so much confidence that he envied her.

He was enchanted. Yet it wasn't magic . . . or if it was, it was a simpler sort than the magic of spells and curses.

With a deep sigh and a twist to his lips that was not quite a smile, Timothy opened his eyes. The cool night wind made him shiver and he hugged himself. It was dark, but there was starlight, moonlight, and torchlight in the village, and so the darkness was far from complete.

He began to turn, to retreat back into his room, when motion down below caught his eye. In the deepest shadows between two huts, where the torchlight did not reach and the moonlight could not penetrate, something darted through the night. An animal, perhaps the very thing that had been in his room several nights ago. It moved swiftly and low to the ground, and was out of sight in a moment. He'd only glimpsed it, but now he locked his gaze upon that spot, hoping it would show itself again.

And a dark, cloaked figure moved across the space separating the huts, moving stealthily, clearly sneaking about in hopes no one would notice.

It took Timothy a moment before he realized that the hut they seemed to be emerging from was the one in which Leander had been quartered.

His pulse quickened and the boy shook his head. There was something very wrong here, something sinister. Cloaked figures and strange, murderous animals lurking about at night, sneaking away from Leander's hut. He recalled the attack he had suffered, and now his skin prickled with fear for his friend.

"Leander," he whispered, barely aware that he had spoken aloud.

Timothy stared at the shadows for a moment longer, then he raced out the door and down the rickety steps. When he found himself standing on the cool earth in his bare feet in the moonlight, he hesitated. If there was trouble, or some danger, he ought to have woken Verlis.

But his concern for Leander drove him on. He was already outside, and he did not want to waste another second by going back in. His heart was heavy with the certainty that something terrible had happened.

Timothy ran across the rough earth to Leander's hut. He raised his fist to bang on the door, but his hand froze when he saw that it hung open several inches. His chest was tight and it hurt to swallow. He could barely breathe as he pushed the door open.

In the darkness within, lit only by the dim illumination coming from the open door, he saw the massive figure of Leander Maddox sprawled across the floor, twisted up in his bedsheets. He was twitching, and his eyes were wide as he stared blankly up at the ceiling.

A tiny trickle of blood ran from the corner of his right eye and down his cheek.

The sky was lightening above Tora'nah, the morning coming on. The stars faded and the moons were like ghosts in the pale blue sky. Timothy had not slept at all, had not even returned to his quarters. Still barefoot, he sat in the dirt with his back to the outer wall of Leander's hut. Verlis stood perhaps twenty feet away, wings folded against his back, eyes slitted with concern and plumes of smoke swirling up from his nostrils. Between them, the navigation mage Caiaphas paced up and down, at a loss as to what to do with his hands. He wrung them, clasped them first in front of him and then behind his back, adjusted the veil that covered his face below the eyes, and at last dropped them to his sides, clenched with worry. When he finished he would begin the sequence all over again.

Doctor Gryffud and Walter Telford were inside with Leander, and had been for hours. After Timothy had woken Walter, the project manager had roused the doctor and then some of his crew, who had searched the encampment for the mysterious figure Timothy had seen leaving Leander's hut. The entire night had passed with no word about Leander's condition. Just before dawn the search party had given up, having found no evidence of intruders in camp. Construction of the Burrower had been completed the day before, and with sunrise these men and women would have to begin their mining operation on very little sleep.

Now it was morning and Timothy was exhausted and shivering. The sun was rising, but the last chill of the long night still lingered.

Verlis snorted, twin jets of flame sputtering from his snout. "You ought to sleep. I will wake you when there is word."

The boy shook his head. "I couldn't sleep," he said. "Not without knowing."

Caiaphas paused in his pacing to gaze first at the Wurm

and then at the boy. He gave a soft sigh of frustration, blue eyes gleaming above his veil, and then continued wearing a path back and forth in front of his master's door. Timothy was sure that the navigation mage understood why he could not leave until there was news.

The sky continued to lighten. The night had gone from deep, dark blue to a rich color the hue of Caiaphas's robes and then to the pale sky of early morning. In time, all traces of the night were gone and it could no longer even be considered dawn. The sky was clear and bright blue with only wisps of clouds. A light wind blew through Tora'nah, and from time to time Timothy felt sure he caught a scent that might have been sulfur, a smell that reminded him of Draconae, and the volcano there where he had once been held prisoner. He told himself it was only memory, that there was no way the odor could pass through Alhazred's Divide, that magical barrier between Tora'nah and Draconae.

The barrier would have had to be very thin for such a thing to happen. Too thin.

The morning whistle had blown shortly after dawn, and even now he could hear and perhaps even feel a rumble in the earth. Not far away the crew had begun to dig again.

And all the while, fear trembled in Timothy's chest like the heart of a captured animal.

In his mind he could picture the day that the magic door had appeared on the sand of the Island of Patience. Leander had seemed so massive to him then, stepping through the door and throwing back his hood to reveal that shaggy mane and beard and those kind eyes.

Kind, sad eyes. For he had been there to tell Timothy that his father was dead. And now the man who had taken Timothy in, Leander, lay unmoving, obviously ailing, and perhaps even . . . dying?

No.

As he sat outside Leander's hut now, Timothy's lip quivered. His eyes burned, but he refused to cry. To him, crying would mean he did not have enough hope, enough faith that Leander would be all right. And he would not give up.

Caiaphas stopped pacing. Verlis's eyes widened with expectation. Timothy frowned as he looked at them, tired enough that it took him a moment to realize what they were reacting to. He turned to see Walter leading Doctor Gryffud out the door of Leander's hut. Timothy scrambled to his feet.

"Well?" he said, trying to keep his voice down. He looked from the project manager to the doctor. "How is he?"

Verlis and Caiaphas joined him, and the five of them came together there in the narrow space between huts.

"Grandmaster Maddox is stable," Doctor Gryffud grumbled. The medical mage was short and round and he ambled when he walked. At the moment he rested his hands across his voluminous belly. "He's had a small heart attack—"

"No," Timothy whispered.

Verlis laid a heavy talon across his back to comfort him.

"He's going to be all right, Tim," Walter Telford said, nodding in assurance. "Leander's weak. Very weak, actually. And no matter what the doc says, truth is, he's only guessing about the heart attack."

"What?" Caiaphas snapped. Usually so calm and collected, at the moment he was most impatient. "You're a healer. How can you not know—"

"I stand by my diagnosis," the doctor said, glaring at Walter grumpily. "Nevertheless, Walter is correct. The Grandmaster is very weak; he still has chest pain. I've done what healing spells I can, but . . . well, frankly, I'm somewhat mystified. Grandmaster Maddox needs to be examined by Parliamentary physicians with access to greater magic than I have at my disposal here."

Timothy let the words sink in. He nodded slowly, glancing around the small circle of men he trusted.

"All right," he said, looking from Walter to Caiaphas and then back again. "We'll take him back. Today. Back to Arcanum."

Verlis had to fly.

It had been difficult enough for him to be around the mages when Timothy and Leander were there, but now that they had gone—his only friends in the ruins of Tora'nah—he felt surrounded by suspicion and animosity. Walter Telford was a kind, open-minded man, but the crew who worked for him had already proven themselves angry and unpleasant.

It was not only the feeling of being alone among enemies that made Verlis take to the skies. There was something else lurking at the back of his mind, something he could not quite explain. It was not knowledge or memory, but a general feeling of unease. The Wurm believed that some were gifted with prophecy, allowing certain of their kind to have glimpses of the future, sometimes in dreams and sometimes in visions. Verlis had never known anyone who claimed to have *the sight* to be accurate. Most of them were just overly dramatic, desiring of attention, or charlatans.

But still, he had this feeling. Nothing specific, really, save for the certainty that events were coming together that would propel the world into disaster.

Disaster, perhaps that's too strong a word, he thought, spreading his wings and soaring above Tora'nah, the blue sky soothing him, the view of the forest unfolding below, filling his heart with its beauty. The air buffeted him, and Verlis slipped among the winds, beating his wings powerfully as he soared higher and then began to swoop down toward the tops of the trees, enjoying the rush of it, the feeling of flight. He had needed this. The freedom of flying was glorious.

Yet he could not be entirely free. Not here. Not when he could see the miners using the much larger version of Timothy's Burrower to bore enormous holes in the hillside, then carting enormous loads of metal ore from the ground. Not when the barrier that separated Tora'nah from Draconae shimmered and from time to time he thought he caught the sound of ancient chanting drifting through from the other side. DragonSong. The hymns of his ancestors. He could not relax completely with his wife and all of his clan back in Arcanum, always under suspicion even as they attempted to fit into the mages' world. He could not relax when Leander was ill and Timothy had departed an hour earlier to escort him back to the city.

But it helped to fly.

Verlis opened his jaws and let loose a stream of liquid fire that burned the air. When he closed his snout, dark smoke billowed from his nostrils. The edges of his mouth turned up in what passed for a smile among his kind.

Fire always made him feel better.

He beat his wings several times and then banked to the right, riding air currents in a long arc that brought him back above the mining operation. Several of the mages paused to point up at him but he ignored their rudeness. There was a task he had set for himself today and despite the trouble with Leander and the departure of Timothy, the Wurm intended to fulfill it.

His heart soared as he came into view of the highest ridge of the hills at Tora'nah. There were stone ruins spread all across the hills, tumbled down structures that had been constructed by the Wurm in the years before the mages banished them to Draconae. But on that highest ridge were far more ancient ruins, even more sacred than the graves he had driven the miners away from. There were caves in the steep, rocky hillside here, many of them covered over by what appeared to be landslides or blocked by enormous stone slabs that seemed to have broken off of the ridge. But none of those caves had been blocked by nature or by accident.

They were the earliest tombs of the Dragons of Old. Kings and Queens and heroes. Sacred ground. The cairns that had been created as stone markers for the graves of Dragons had seemed only rock and earth to the miners, who cremated their dead rather than buried them. But here . . . this cliffside and the caves within were monuments to history, the resting place of the greatest of his ancestors, and Verlis could not imagine how the miners could not see the grim dignity of the place.

He alighted beside the first cave on a rocky outcropping. This tomb had a huge slab of stone in front of it, but time had long since eroded the marking that had been engraved in the slab in the language of the Dragons of Old. There were only traces of those symbols now.

Verlis surveyed the entire ridge. There must have been dozens of such markers. He meant to restore each one. No matter how long it took him, he would carve those symbols anew, marking those ancient tombs, so that when his clan finally made their way to Tora'nah—when the treat of Raptus was over—they would find the sacred land properly cared for.

First, however, there was one other chore.

Beside the slab that covered the tomb was a spire of stone, and atop the spire, a bowl made from Malleum. The metal bowl was empty, but long ago a flame had burned in front of each tomb to mark the graves of the Dragons of Old.

These memorials would blaze anew.

Verlis curled his wings around his body and lowered his head. He spoke long strings of words in the ancient tongue of his people. He bowed to the spire and bowl, scraped his talons across the air itself, and then he opened his jaws. A narrow stream of golden fire rose from his belly and churned in his chest, at last erupting from his maw to ignite a fire in the bowl atop that spire.

A torch of remembrance.

No one would ever forget this place again.

Caiaphas was capable of navigating the sky carriage at great speed. Several times Timothy had been made breathless by the swiftness of the vehicle and the skill with which its driver guided it. Leander Maddox might have been the owner of the carriage, but Caiaphas was its master.

This was why Timothy remained mostly silent as they journeyed back toward Arcanum from Tora'nah. It would take well into the afternoon hours to make the trip, but if there was a way to shorten the duration, Caiaphas would find it. The navigation mage was kind-hearted and very loyal to his employer, and though they had not discussed it, Timothy knew he would do everything he could to get Leander to the healing mages in Arcanum as quickly as possible.

All Timothy could do to help him was to not become a

distraction. So the boy sat on the plush seat inside the carriage and watched with concern as Leander slept fitfully, spread out upon the bench seat across from him. His eyes moved rapidly beneath his eyelids. Whatever dreams Leander was having, they were not pleasant.

The man did not look well at all. The blood that had run like tears from his eyes had been cleaned off of his face, and there had been no further sign of injury. But Leander was pale, and though it was cool enough outside—and in the sky carriage—beads of sweat glistened on his forehead. There was a yellowed cast to his skin that disturbed Timothy deeply. It was as though he had been tainted, even poisoned. If he sought deep within his heart, Timothy would have had to admit that other than the sweat upon him and the way he shivered, Leander looked almost like a corpse.

"No," he whispered, there in the sky carriage, alone save for the unconscious mage. From atop his high seat Caiaphas could not hear him speaking so low.

He's not going to die. He can't.

Timothy swallowed hard and his throat hurt. He hugged himself and slid further down in his seat, staring at Leander. He gnawed on his lower lip and when his eyes burned, threatening to shed tears, he bit down harder, the pain clearing his head.

Yet he could not rid himself of the emotion, of the specter of his father's death that now haunted him. Over and over again he had asked himself what he would do in this strange and unfriendly world without Leander.

He had yet to come up with an answer.

With a deep sigh he forced himself to sit up straight and he gazed out the window. Yarrith Forest spread out ahead of them, but it took him a moment to realize he saw something other than trees. They were quite high above the green forest now, and far ahead something flashed in the sunshine. Far off in the distance there was a building . . . and then he realized there were several. Perhaps even more. He had only a glimpse of the distant structures before the sky carriage dropped much closer to the trees below and his view was eclipsed, but he thought the tops of those buildings were terraced, like pyramids but built in steps.

"Caiaphas?" Timothy called.

The sky carriage slowed just slightly. "Yes, lad?" the navigation mage replied.

Timothy was about to ask about the terraced buildings he had seen, but a shiver ran through him and he felt sure something moved at the edges of his vision. He frowned, glancing down at Leander.

The ailing mage had opened his eyes. He was still sweating and the yellow hue of his skin had deepened, so he looked even worse, but Leander was staring right at Timothy. His eyes were alert.

The boy smiled hopefully. "Leander?"

He'd barely gotten the word out when the mage shot from the seat, silent and swift. His size and weight, shifting so suddenly, tilted the sky carriage a bit. Caiaphas called in to them, wondering what had upset the vehicle. But

Timothy barely heard the words and certainly could not respond.

Hate was etched upon Leander Maddox's face.

The burly mage reached out and grabbed Timothy by the throat with one enormous hand, and twisted his fist up in the fabric of the boy's tunic with the other.

"What is it?" Timothy cried. "What's wrong with you?"

But his frightened queries were ignored. Leander hauled him across the carriage with powerful hands. A cruel grin spread across the mage's face, and in that moment Timothy saw that he had stopped sweating. Then the mage thrust Timothy's head at the window of the sky carriage and Timothy flinched . . . though he knew there would be no impact. Instead of striking the spell-glass, his head passed right through. The glass winked out of existence and the wind whipped into the sky carriage, screaming past his ears.

"Leander!" Timothy screamed. "Stop!"

Twisting around, he tried to beat at the mage's hands as Leander forced him out the window. Timothy had one glimpse of Caiaphas as the navigation mage turned around on his high seat at the front of the sky carriage, eyes wide with horror.

And then Timothy was falling.

Screaming.

He plummeted toward the trees, arms flailing, terror hammering in his chest. As he dropped, spinning in the air, he saw the sky carriage one last time. The door had been thrown open and Leander was climbing out, dragging himself up onto the roof, reaching for Caiaphas with hands ablaze with crackling, darklight magic.

Timothy's free fall ended when he struck the uppermost branches of a tree. Several small branches snapped beneath him, knocking the breath out of him. When he collided with a much thicker limb, Timothy grunted in pain as something cracked in his chest.

He tumbled only a few more feet before he at last struck the ground. Pain shot through his body and he could barely breathe. Black spots swam before his eyes, and Timothy Cade slipped down into darkness.

CHAPTER FIVE

Timothy was aware of the birds before anything else. His mind was cloaked in darkness, his awareness simply shut down. It was only the singing of the birds that he noticed, somewhere beyond him. One bird in particular had a bleating, insistent call that he found aggravating. It made him frown, though the other birdsong soothed him.

A cool breeze washed over him and he heard it rustling the branches above him.

It was sort of nice.

His eyes opened to slits. He saw the trees above and the deepening blue sky beyond. The sunlight was rich and golden, and long afternoon shadows surrounded him.

Trees. Broken branches. And the sky.

Only then did he remember what had happened. An image of Leander, eyes lit with madness and cruelty, swam into his mind and Timothy felt grief and fear welling in his chest. What had happened? What had become of Leander?

Then he moved, just a small shifting of his weight, and pain shot up from his right side so sharply that it pricked tears from his eyes. Timothy groaned, taking in a deep, shuddering breath that burned in his chest. He lay still, one hand pressed against his side where the pain throbbed in his ribs. After a few moments, though, it subsided to a dull ache and he felt that he could breathe more easily. Even so it took another minute before he could muster the courage to try to move again.

Careful to use his left arm to prop himself up, trying not to strain his right side, he got onto his knees and rose to his feet. Fresh pain spiked into his side and he gritted his teeth, but it passed more quickly this time. Afraid his ribs might be broken and worried what damage a broken rib might do to his insides, he raised his shirt and carefully pressed his fingers over each rib bone. There was a massive, purple-black bruise larger than his hand with all fingers splayed. He winced despite how softly he prodded those bones, but after checking his chest, Timothy believed that though he might have cracked a rib or two, none of them were broken. There was no danger of him puncturing a lung or damaging other organs.

Growing up on the Island of Patience, climbing trees and hills and scrambling over rocks, he had once broken his left arm and twice had cracked ribs. Fingers and toes were simple enough if broken; a basic splint and the bones would heal fine. He had sprained muscles and worse. Ivar had taught him a great deal about injuries and how to treat them. There were poultices, for instance, made from simple plants and berries, that would diminish swelling and cause bruises to disappear more quickly. But the bones would have to knit on their own.

"All right," he whispered. "I'm all right."

Timothy drew in a long breath. The pain in his side was sharp, but bearable. He could breathe. Though it would hurt, he could also travel. And that was vital, for he had to make his way out of these woods and somehow return to Arcanum.

He glanced up again and it was as though he saw it all playing out before his eyes once more. The sky carriage, dipping lower toward the forest—thank the gods that Caiaphas had chosen that moment to descend or he would have died—then Leander shoving him out of the window to tumble end over end, striking the branches as he fell.

Timothy frowned. *Caiaphas.* The last thing he had seen was Leander climbing on top of the sky carriage to grapple with the navigation mage. He wondered what had happened next.

With a deep, painful breath, he surveyed the woods around him. The sun had moved through the sky, and the shadows continued to deepen. It was a simple thing to gauge direction this late in the day from the position of the sun. The sky carriage had been heading north. If Leander had done the same thing to Caiaphas as he had to Timothy, the navigation mage ought to have fallen a short distance farther north.

His heart filled with the fear of what he might find, Timothy started north, moving in among the trees. He walked as swiftly as he could without adding to his pain. The bruises would fade, the cracks would heal. At the moment, even the madness that had befallen Leander was not his first priority. No, foremost in his mind was Caiaphas.

The forest thinned and he found the going much easier. A handful of minutes after he had begun walking, however, Timothy paused. He shook his head sadly as he stared at what lay ahead . . . a clearing in the trees.

In the clearing was a sprawled figure cloaked in deep blue robes. In that great forest, Caiaphas had had the ill luck to plummet from the sky into a clearing devoid of any branches that might have broken his fall. He lay unmoving.

"Caiaphas," Timothy said, staring into the clearing. His heart hammered in his chest and he felt a terrible grief welling up inside of him. "Caiaphas!"

One hand clamped upon his bruised side, he hurried over. Strands of long grass stuck to Caiaphas's robes. Though he knew he would see only birds, Timothy could not help glancing up into the afternoon sky as though the sky carriage might still be there, as though he could imagine the fall of the navigation mage who had been his friend and Leander's loyal servant. He bit his lip as he stopped beside the fallen mage. Timothy knelt gently beside the body, wincing at the pain in his side.

Caiaphas lay on his chest, legs outstretched, left arm tucked at his side. The mage's right arm had been trapped beneath him in the fall. His head was turned to one side and his veil had been pulled away to reveal rugged, dark features. He was very still.

But not completely.

Timothy's heart leaped as he saw that the mage was breathing. Caiaphas uttered a soft groan of discomfort.

"Hello?" the boy ventured. He reached out to touch the navigation mage's shoulder. "Caiaphas?"

With a grunt, the mage opened his blue eyes, which glowed with the deep blue of his robes. The man's features contorted in pain, but there was a kind of tenderness in his eyes as he gazed at Timothy.

"Well, well, my young friend," Caiaphas rasped. He uttered a single, short, pained laugh. Then he used his left arm to prop himself up, cringing in pain as his right hung there, useless.

Timothy flinched as he saw that arm, so obviously broken. Caiaphas used his good arm to cradle the broken one against his belly, letting it rest on his lap as he sat cross-legged in front of Timothy, in no hurry to even attempt to stand up.

"I know how I survived that fall," Caiaphas said, grimacing in pain before studying the boy more closely. "But how did you? With no magic, how did you survive?"

"I . . . well, you were flying low, just above the trees, and I hit the branches and they sort of broke my fall. And maybe my ribs. But I don't understand. You . . . how did you . . ."

Caiaphas gestured to his useless arm with a resigned expression. "My studies were always magical navigation. That includes levitation, certainly. Unfortunately, levitating an object or even flying a sky carriage is not at all the same as levitating yourself. Particularly when one is falling from a great height. I was able to slow my fall. A mage with more general skill rather than a special vocation such as mine might have been able to suspend it entirely, to bend gravity to his desires. I did my best."

"You broke your arm."

With his good hand, Caiaphas slipped his veil back up over his mouth and nose, leaving again only his icy blue eyes peering over the top. "I had my fingers extended, casting and recasting the spell to prevent me from striking at full speed. It would have killed me, likely as not. I managed it, but I still had my hand out, trying to cast that spell, when the ground at last rushed up at me."

He twitched with obvious pain as he gestured to the broken arm. "Now this. But better my arm than the rest of my bones."

Timothy smiled and let out a long breath as he relaxed. He sat down in the long grass, though his cracked ribs made any position uncomfortable.

"That's wonderful. Well, not that you've broken your arm, but . . ." He laughed.

"That we're alive!" Caiaphas said.

The boy nodded and the two of them just reveled for a

moment in their good fortune. Then, almost as though some signal bell had sounded, their smiles disappeared. They gazed at each other for several long moments. Timothy swallowed, and his sadness and worry returned.

"What happened to him?" the boy asked.

Caiaphas shook his head. "I don't know. But that was not Leander Maddox as I have known him."

"You think . . . you think he's being controlled? Some dark sorcerer has got him spellbound?"

The blue eyes over that veil seemed brighter than ever. "Don't you?"

Timothy considered it a moment, then nodded. "Of course. I can't see any other explanation." He looked around the clearing. There was nothing in sight but trees and the sky above. Birds still sang, but the annoying bleating of whatever winged creature had woken him before was now silent.

"We must get back to Arcanum," Caiaphas said, his voice grave, his brows knitted intently.

"Yeah." Timothy thought a moment, staring at the branches of the nearest trees, and then at the tall grass. He gazed intently at Caiaphas. "Yeah. First, though, let me take care of your arm."

"I know a bit of healing magic—"

"Enough to fix this?"

"No," Caiaphas admitted. "As a navigation mage, it was hardly my specialty. I can help it mend faster, but not instantly."

"Then you speed the healing process as best you can, but

let me put a splint on it, and we'll fashion a sling. It will help the bone set properly and it will be less painful while we travel. We're going to have to go quite a ways on foot."

"Perhaps only to the nearest village," Caiaphas suggested, beginning to rise, gritting his teeth in pain.

"Wait," Timothy said, one hand on his shoulder. "Let's see to that arm first. Afterward . . . the last thing I saw before Leander . . . before we fell, was some kind of town. At least I think it was a town. Terraced buildings, spread far apart from one another. Two or three hours' walk to the north. Right in our path."

"Yes, I saw it as well," Caiaphas said, settling again upon the grass.

As the boy rose and started toward the trees to find straight, thick branches for a splint, the navigation mage called after him. Timothy turned to face him.

"If I must endure this trial," Caiaphas said, "I'm glad to be in your company."

Timothy smiled. "Thank you," he said. And for the first time since he had awoken in pain and confusion, he felt hopeful.

The sky over Arcanum was gray with clouds, only a few patches of blue sky showing through. A light rain fell. In the Grandmaster's study on the floating fortress of SkyHaven, Cassandra Nicodemus was curled into a comfortable chair, legs drawn up beneath her, writing in her personal journal. The patter of raindrops on the honey-colored spell-glass in the octagonal window behind her chair was a comfort to her. It went perfectly with the cup of tea that rested on the small table beside her.

Cassandra rested her pen in the cradle of her open journal and reached out to take a sip of tea. The rain had put a chill in the air and the tea was pleasantly warm as it went down her throat. She set the cup down and looked at the journal again.

. . . I must put aside thoughts of Timothy, along with all other distractions, she wrote. *If I am to be Grandmaster one day, I must immerse myself in Parliamentary procedure and the business of the Order of Alhazred. Professor Maddox is a good man, a powerful mage, and wise, but this was not a role he had ever desired. One day, when he sees I am ready, he will likely cede the position to me, and rightfully so. If I can make up for the evils that my grandfather perpetrated upon the Order and the Parliament, that is what I must do.*

And yet . . . can't I do all of these things and still have room in my thoughts for Timothy? I'd never speak of such things to him, but the boy fascinates me.

I miss him.

Once again she picked up her teacup. As she brought it to her lips, her eyes still on those words in her journal, the air was filled with a loud cawing, a cry of alarm. The noise startled her, and Cassandra fumbled the cup. It dropped from her fingers.

"Stop," she said, pointing at it.

The teacup froze in midair, as did the spray of liquid that spilled from it. Gently, the cup settled onto the floor and the spilled tea poured back into it. Even as this bit of magic concluded, Cassandra rose from her chair and started for the study door.

She threw it open.

"Caw! Caw!!" cried Edgar. The rook fluttered his black wings as he slowed, then circled above her head in the high-ceilinged corridor. "The courtyard! Come to the courtyard, and hurry! Leander's back. Something awful has happened."

The bird cawed loudly again and started back along the corridor.

"Wait! Edgar, stop! What is—"

But the panicked rook did not slow down. In an eyeblink, he had turned a corner, perhaps on his way to alert Ivar or Sheridan. Cassandra glanced down at herself. She was dressed casually in a magenta tunic and loose pants, hardly appropriate for a grandmaster. But Edgar was not the sort to panic unnecessarily.

Brow furrowed in worry, she hurried along the corridor, up a narrow back stairwell to the main hallway of that level of SkyHaven, and then down the massive central staircase that led to the receiving hall and the doors out to the courtyard.

The windows showed the gray skies. The patter of raindrops had quickened and grown louder, the storm no longer gentle. When she pulled the doors open, several acolytes in service to the Grandmaster were rushing across the foyer toward her, accompanied by Dorian, a Healer new to SkyHaven's staff. The Healer was pale, nervous.

"What is . . . ," she began.

But she had pulled the doors open and Cassandra saw motion now, out in the rain. Though the sun was still out, somewhere above, the storm had cloaked the land with gray darkness. In the gloom she saw figures moving around a sky carriage that had landed in the courtyard, a crash landing if the dirt and grass that had been pushed ahead of it was any indication. One of the figures, ramrod straight and barking orders that were mostly lost in the wind that now whipped the rain into her face, was almost assuredly Carlyle. Tall and thin and authoritative, it could be no other.

Another, standing nearby the carriage with arms crossed as though on guard, she was certain was Ivar.

"Oh, dear! Oh, no, Professor Maddox," came a familiar voice from behind her. The words were followed by a toot of steam.

Cassandra held her breath as she turned and saw Sheridan striding across the foyer with Edgar perched on his shoulder. Another gasp of steam escaped the valve at the side of his metal head. Then the acolytes and the Healer were there and she was blocking their way, blocking the door. She spun and gazed out into the storm again.

"Leander?" she whispered.

Barely aware of her feet moving beneath her, she rushed out into the storm. The wind first fluttered her hair around her head, but quickly the rain slicked it across her forehead and down the back of her neck. She ignored the rain, the wind, the storm.

Her bare feet slid on the grass, sinking into the sodden earth. The girl rushed to the carriage, pushing past Carlyle. He shouted something at her, but Cassandra could not hear him. It was not the wind that deafened her to his words, but the thumping of her heart in her ears. If SkyHaven was in chaos like this, if Edgar was panicked and a Healer had been summoned . . .

The carriage was canted over to one side. Cassandra grabbed the door, which hung open, and peered inside. The rain pelted her now and had begun to puddle on the floor of the carriage. Her breath caught in her throat.

Grandmaster Maddox lay sprawled across one of the seats in the carriage. There was a long cut on his left cheek and blood wept from it, staining his robe. The flesh around his right eye was bruised and swollen. But it was not merely the signs of violence that were so disturbing. The mage was sickly.

He was also alone.

"Leander!" Cassandra said, raising a hand to cover her mouth, hiding the "o" of shock formed by her lips. "What . . . oh, gods, what's happened? Are you all right? And what . . . where's Timothy?"

The question sounded almost like an admission to her, but she pushed away any embarrassment she might have felt. Cassandra was acutely aware that she was not acting like a grandmaster. Not at all. She was acting like precisely what she was: a teenage girl with no experience dealing with a real crisis.

That was going to have to change.

Taking a deep breath, she ducked and stepped halfway into the carriage. She took Leander's hand, trying to soothe him. His gaze drifted, as though he was not entirely aware of his surroundings.

"Leander," she said, more calmly. "Tell me what happened."

The massive mage focused on her. "Attacked," he said, licking his lips to moisten them. "I fell ill. Caiaphas was conveying us home. Timothy and me . . ." He took a deep breath, steadying himself, and let it out. "They came . . . out of nowhere. Couldn't see much. The carriage was rocking, under attack. I . . . I fought."

Leander Maddox seemed to shrink, then. He shook his shaggy mane and would not meet her eyes. "I fought them. When I . . . I suppose I drove them off. But then I was alone, and still ill. Injured. I almost did not make it back."

Cassandra stared at him. She saw his eyes glaze again, and his head bobbed as though he might pass out. Then Carlyle was pulling her away from the carriage, moving her to make room for the Healer and the Alhazred mages. They would take care of him, certainly. The Grandmaster would be well again in no time. They would carry him inside, bathe him in magic that would heal his cuts and bruises and likely his illness as well, whatever strange ailment it might be.

The Grandmaster would be fine.

"But . . . what of Timothy? And Caiaphas?" she called through the whistling winds and the pelting rain.

A gentle but firm hand grasped her arm and she turned to find herself face-to-face with Ivar. The Asura's stony features were grimmer than ever. His eyes were warm, though, and filled with a gravity that made her bite her lip and shake her head in denial.

"The Grandmaster returned alone."

The afternoon shadows had grown even longer as Timothy and Caiaphas trekked northward through the great forest. The land was fairly flat in this region and the trees tall enough that it was easy to walk beneath them without being obstructed by branches. In truth, if it had not been for their circumstances the journey would have been peaceful, even pleasant. Certainly the landscape was beautiful. But Timothy had to constantly grit his teeth against the pain in his side where his ribs were cracked. Several times an hour he had to stop to simply clutch his side and try to steady his breathing, letting the pain wash over him.

Despite his broken arm, Caiaphas had an easier time. Or would have, if he had been used to exercise. The navigation mage was reliant upon his sky carriage. He was not in poor physical condition, but during the third hour of walking, he had needed to sit for a time to recover. When they began their trek again, the going was slower.

Timothy had made him a splint out of branches and twined grass, and a sling from a portion of the mage's robe that the boy had torn off and tied round Caiaphas's neck. It was crude, but it would do the job. The break must have hurt, but Timothy figured at least it wasn't going to stop him from traveling.

The eastern horizon had begun to darken to a deeper, evening blue, when they at last emerged from the trees.

"Amazing," Timothy said, forgetting for a moment the pain of his cracked ribs.

Caiaphas came to stand beside him. "Indeed," he said, voice hushed.

The land sloped away gently down into a valley whose grass was as green as nature had ever created. A narrow, winding river flowed through the valley, turning lazily in among seven massive structures, those same terraced buildings Timothy had seen from the air many miles away. They were all the same color, a rich, earthen clay hue, with four sides, each of which was terraced, as though it was a staircase built for giants.

Timothy gazed with fascination upon this village— though "village" seemed a poor word for the river valley. There were no outbuildings. None at all. No huts or houses, no towers or shops. Only those seven terraced pyramids that shot up from the ground as though they had grown there, bursting from the earth. They were strange, but somehow beautiful in the ethereal light of dusk.

Atop each of those pyramids was that glittering light Timothy had seen before, even more obvious now that the daylight was fading into night. The western sky was still light, but fading, and yet sunlight gleamed from the peak of each building.

"How do we do this?" Timothy asked. "We don't know anything about them. Can we just knock on the door and ask for help? I mean, if there even is a door."

Caiaphas gazed at him, eyes gleaming magically above his veil. "The days of barbaric tribes of mages are long over. But not all guilds are friendly to Parliament. If we avoid politics, we should be received with courtesy, if nothing else. And, frankly, we have little choice. Despite what magic I know, I've few skills that would help us survive alone in the wilderness."

Timothy smiled. "I've had plenty of experience. I could get by."

The navigation mage was thoughtful. "Come to that, I imagine you could. But just the same, let's see if they've got a sky carriage we can borrow."

The boy grinned and they started down that gentle slope together, walking into the valley. To the east, where the river ran its curving course toward the forest, there were fields of various crops. Timothy had seen farms from the air and pictures in books, but he had never seen crops growing up close save for those in the small solarium at SkyHaven, where certain herbs and fruits were grown. To the west they caught sight of the first people in this strange community, a group of children swimming in the river. Timothy shivered at the sight of them. The water must have been chilly today, but there were perhaps two dozen boys and girls of varying ages splashing in the water, the golden light of sunset glinting on the river. Laughter echoed along the valley.

An unfamiliar sadness touched Timothy. He longed to join them. But other duties beckoned and he wondered if there would ever be a time when he might be as carefree as he had once been.

"There. Amongst the buildings," Caiaphas said.

Timothy looked and saw that there were adults strolling along a serpentine path that followed the twists of the river. They wore long, rather plain robes that reached nearly to the ground, most in muted colors, the same earthen shade of the buildings. Those terraced pyramids seemed to have been arranged carefully, one at each bend of the river, with four on the north bank and three on the south. Timothy saw that there were at least four places where small bridges spanned the water. And around the base of each building were gardens full of flowers whose colors seemed vibrant even as the daylight waned.

"It's so peaceful," Caiaphas said. "Nothing like Arcanum."

"You would have liked the island where I grew up," Timothy replied.

By then they had crossed half the distance between the forest's edge and the nearest pyramid, the grass rustling in the evening breeze, and they had been noticed. Many of the people wandering the paths and gardens of the village stopped to stare at them. Even the laughter of the children abruptly stopped, and when Timothy looked over he saw that they had stopped swimming, some climbing out of the water for a better view. There were several boys taller than he was, led by a girl with dark hair and even darker skin, who started away from the river, crossing the valley floor toward them.

At this, a mage left the path and intercepted the children. His head was cleanly shaved, though he had a beard and mustache that were neatly trimmed. His long robe was gray as stone, drab and featureless, and he seemed almost unwilling to look at Timothy and Caiaphas as they approached. The sound of the river was like music, but the mage's voice disrupted it. With an outstretched arm, he commanded the children to go back to the river's edge and they obeyed with obvious reluctance.

"Guess they're not used to strangers," Timothy said.

Caiaphas grunted in agreement. "We may have to alter our expectations of hospitality."

But by then they had nearly reached the mage who had left the path. Timothy took a moment to glance up at the terraced pyramid as they approached. It seemed somehow smaller than he imagined now that he was nearly upon it, but the one impression that did not go away was the idea that it had sprung from the earth not unlike the crops in the eastern fields. He turned to glance at the nearest pyramid, across the river, and a spike of pain shot through his side. Wincing, he put his hand over it again. Pressure on the cracked ribs hurt the bruised area, but that was superficial. On the inside, the pressure relieved some of the pain.

"Good evening," Caiaphas said as they neared the mage,

whose eyes seemed in the dusky light to be the same stone gray as his robe. "Kind thoughts on this day."

The mage regarded them carefully. Timothy paused, perhaps twenty feet from the man, and Caiaphas glanced at him a moment before he halted as well. They were a ragged pair, no question. Timothy's tunic was torn from catching on branches during his fall. He knew he was bruised, and though his injury was not visible, his constant wincing and the way he held his ribs would have made it obvious. Caiaphas still wore the veil of his vocation but his robes were also torn, including an entire swath that had been torn away to fashion his sling.

Still, after a moment, the stony-eyed mage smiled at them. "On this and all days," he said, offering the traditional response. "What brings you here, travelers? We see sky carriages often enough, but rarely received visitors."

"Our Grandmaster—" Timothy began.

"Has summoned us back to Arcanum," Caiaphas interrupted, shooting a meaningful glance at Timothy. "Unfortunately I am not always as cautious navigating as I ought to be. I'm afraid our sky carriage was ruined. We were fortunate enough to emerge with so few injuries."

Timothy saw the way the man's gray eyes narrowed as he listened, trying to find the truth in Caiaphas's tale. The mage was suspicious of them, unsure whether to believe them. Caiaphas was being cautious, but Timothy suspected the man would have treated any outsider the same way.

He glanced past the gray mage. Others had clustered

on the path, watching them parley. Within the terraced pyramid, windows had begun to glimmer with illumination. He had seen little light beyond that spell-glass before, but now the structures began to come alive with warmth.

"Do you admire the ziggurats?" the gray mage asked.

"Is that what they're called?" Timothy replied. "Yes. They're amazing. And lit up like that . . . they're beautiful."

Those stony eyes regarded him for a moment, then he looked at Caiaphas again. He had not responded to the navigation mage's story and he deliberated for several moments longer.

"We haven't a sky carriage, I fear," the mage said at last. "We do not believe in the artifice of such travel."

Timothy's shoulders sank in disappointment and he winced with fresh pain from his side.

"However," the gray mage went on, "evening is upon us, and the Children of Karthagia would not turn away those in need. You are injured and, I wager, hungry as well." He smiled. "Come. We will try to heal and refresh you so that in the morning we may set you on your path with good wishes."

Caiaphas bowed.

Timothy attempted to follow suit, but hissed in pain and could only manage a sort of nod of his head. For the first time Timothy saw sympathy in the mage's eyes, and much of his anxiety about this place dispersed. They would be safe here, he felt. For the night, at least.

CHAPTER SIX

I am called Finn," said the bald, gray-cloaked mage. He walked a step or two ahead of them, guiding Timothy and Caiaphas toward the entrance of the ziggurat. When he spoke he glanced back. "Might I ask your names?"

"Of course. Forgive our rudeness," said Timothy's companion. "I am Caiaphas, navigator by trade."

Finn inclined his head in a casual nod even as he continued walking, his robe dragging on the ground. "Well met, Caiaphas."

"Indeed," Caiaphas replied.

"My name is Timothy Cade," the boy added.

The gray mage paused and turned slowly toward them in the failing light of dusk. One eyebrow was arched and he surveyed Timothy more carefully now. There was no hostility in his attentions, but the boy frowned regardless, uncomfortable with the scrutiny.

"Cade. Son of the great Argus Cade." Finn smiled. "We have heard of you here in Karthagia. The un-magician, yes?"

Nervous, Timothy glanced at Caiaphas before replying. "Yeah. That's me."

The kindness in Finn's expression then surprised him.

"I see you are anxious, Timothy. Worry not. You are welcome here."

He said nothing more, but Timothy felt himself relaxing as he and Caiaphas followed Finn up to the massive doors of the ziggurat. He was exhausted and hungry and the pain in his ribs was agonizing, but the relief that swept over him, knowing that they had a place to rest, even only for the night, was enormous. He and Caiaphas had to get back to Arcanum to find out what was wrong with Leander, to help him and to warn everyone else. But a meal and a night's sleep in a comfortable bed would be like a kind of magic all their own.

Timothy glanced around the village of Karthagia a final time before entering the ziggurat. The last of the day's light was draining out of the western sky. The river burbled quietly as it meandered among the buildings. The ziggurats were lit up, beautiful and elegant crystal towers that shone from within. He felt at peace here.

If things were different, he would have wanted to stay for a time, to learn more about these people. But that would have to wait for another day.

Finn led them inside the ziggurat. At first there was only a high-ceilinged, narrow corridor made entirely of stone, save for the doors, which were fashioned from a gleaming golden material that was neither glass nor stone. Timothy at first thought it was metal, but after passing several of these passages—the doors had neither hinge nor knob nor lock—he determined it must be pure magic, not unlike the spell-glass in the windows.

At the end of the corridor they emerged into what was obviously the core of the ziggurat, and Timothy staggered to a halt, eyes wide. A smile touched his lips and he uttered a soft laugh of amazement.

The entire center of the building, the heart of the ziggurat, was open, the interior a series of staggered balconies that mirrored the terraced design of the exterior, lined with doors Timothy imagined led into the private quarters of the residents of the building. There were gardens and fountains everywhere, and on each level there were people strolling, children laughing. It was as though an entire city existed within that one structure, gleaming with warm, golden light that was like sunshine.

In the midst of it all, an axis upon which the life in the ziggurat turned, was a quartet of elevator shafts. Catwalks stretched from that central core out to each balcony level like spokes upon a wheel. But the lifts did not only go up. Feeling a rush of excitement, Timothy hurried past Finn and Caiaphas to the edge of the balcony. He leaned out over open space and stared down. There must have been twenty-five or thirty levels above the ground. Below, there were easily twice that number.

"Oh," Timothy whispered, and he pulled back a little from the edge. The building continued to widen as it went deep underground, with each balcony farther from the elevators than the last, and looking down into that vast open space made him feel as though he would fall.

He had fallen enough, recently.

"Remarkable," Caiaphas said as he and Finn joined Timothy at the edge of the balcony. "It is beautiful. We saw children, and some of your guild members, outside, but it seems as though your society is all contained within this building."

Finn smiled and smoothed his beard thoughtfully. "Within each building, actually. Though at the lowest level there are passages that connect the ziggurats, one to another."

"Under the river?" Timothy asked.

"We cultivate the land and enjoy it, but we are largely a private culture. Much of our world is subterranean. And we do not hold with all of the traditional beliefs of most guilds in the Parliament. In truth, we are not members of Parliament at all."

Caiaphas blinked several times. Timothy thought he was in shock.

"How can that be?" the boy asked. "I thought every guild—"

"No. Not all. What sort of government would they be if they forced everyone to do things their way?" Finn asked.

Timothy nodded. He had lived on Terra a short time, but

he thought he might be able to tell Finn stories about the Parliament of Mages that would horrify him.

"This is why we cannot be of very much help to you, I'm sorry to say," Finn went on. "We keep to ourselves, and though we will offer courtesy to accidental visitors such as yourselves, we do not invite interaction with other villages or guilds. Our ways are not your ways. We have no sky carriages at all, for instance, for none of the Children of Karthagia ever leaves."

Caiaphas had his brows knitted in thought. Timothy knew they ought to be discussing their plight and what they would do tomorrow, when the hospitality of Karthagia would be politely withdrawn and they would be set on their way. But at the moment he was distracted by his hunger and the pain in his side, and also by the ziggurat itself.

"We are grateful for your help," the navigation mage said at last.

Finn nodded, clasping his hands together in what Timothy imagined was a traditional gesture of thanks or respect. "Come, then," the mage said. "I shall need to speak briefly with a clan chief so that the guild masters are aware of your presence, and then I can show you to rooms where you may wash and be refreshed. I shall send healers to your quarters, and food and drink as well."

"Masters?" Caiaphas asked. "You have more than one leader of your guild? No Grandmaster?"

"Seven. One for each ziggurat," the gray-eyed mage replied.

Timothy barely listened as he took in his surroundings. He followed the two mages across one of the catwalks that led to the elevator core, careful to be sure that the surfaces he was stepping on were metal or wood and not glass or the golden magic that those spell-doors had been made of. Even with that as his focus, his attention was drawn away by what was the most amazing sight to greet them yet.

As they crossed the catwalk, Timothy saw the source of the warm light that suffused the entire central chamber of the ziggurat. On either side of the elevator core there sat a mage, cross-legged upon the floor with hands outstretched and palms upward. From those upturned palms the light streamed, as though they held mini-suns in each hand.

Timothy craned his neck. On every level above—and when he looked he saw that they were on every level below as well—there were two more. Perhaps 150 mages in all, just to light this building.

"Finn?"

"Yes?"

He gestured to the illuminated mages as they walked to the elevators. "Is this your only source of light?"

"At night, certainly," the mage replied.

Caiaphas stared at him, even as Finn passed his hand over a sigil on the elevator door, summoning it.

"These mages are here all night?" the navigator asked, incredulous.

Finn smiled, but there was a flicker of displeasure in it. "Only until the clans take to their beds for the evening. By then they have generated enough power to provide light in the individual quarters if it is needed."

"The lights I saw at the top of each ziggurat—"Timothy began.

The elevator arrived and the doors slid open. The three stepped on and it began to descend, sliding deep into the ground.

"They are mages as well," Finn confirmed. "One mage at the top of each ziggurat. While we all must take our turn illuminating the interior, the mage at the peak is always the same. One chosen from each clan, mastering that magic, and remaining atop the ziggurat for all the long years of his life. It is great sacrifice, but it is the core of what we believe. It would be hard for you to understand."

"It is," Timothy confirmed.

Both Finn and Caiaphas shot him looks of disapproval. Timothy didn't care. He was troubled at the idea.

"The mage at the peak siphons sunlight all through the day. At dusk, her sorcery—for our current illuminator is female—passes that light down to each of those who provide the light within for the evening."

"But . . ." The boy shook his head even as the elevator continued to drop below ground. "What about ghostfire? Wouldn't ghostfire lanterns be so much simpler?"

Finn's smile disappeared. His nostrils flared, and the look he gave Timothy then was full of dismay, even disgust.

"That is the primary difference between our guild and others, young Master Cade. It is the fundamental reason we are not members of Parliament. Ghostfire, lad, is comprised of the souls of dead mages. It is cruel, but worse, it is blasphemous. The spirits of our dead deserve their rest, Timothy, and we would not disrespect them so profoundly as to capture their souls upon this world, to keep them here, twisted to our service. It is a horrid, barbaric practice."

Timothy stared at him, mouth agape. The way he spoke, ghostfire sounded no different from the souls that Nicodemus had tainted and made into his slave-wraiths. He'd always been made to believe that ghostfire was harmless, that the mages' real spirits were not contained, but only a portion of their essence. If what Finn said was true . . .

The boy looked at Caiaphas. The navigator shook his head doubtfully and made as if to argue, but then the doors swept open and Finn walked quickly from the elevator, forcing them to follow.

The conversation was over.

But it would echo in Timothy's mind all through that long night.

Cassandra made her way quickly along a gently curving stone hallway. She glanced over her shoulder from time to time. She could not have said, if asked, why precisely she did not want the residents of SkyHaven to know of the meeting she was about to have. It was simply that she knew something was out of place, and it was more than the attack on Leander's sky carriage, more than the Grandmaster's illness or Timothy and Caiaphas being left behind. These things had started a panic in her heart, but beneath that was something else, a strange, creeping dread that she did not really understand.

But it made her secretive.

She had instructed Carlyle to wait by Leander's quarters until the healers had emerged with word of his condition, not because the man would be needed there but because he was far too inquisitive and she wanted to go unnoticed. Now she paused a moment, took one final glance over her shoulder, and then hurried around the corner to the tall door of Timothy Cade's workshop.

Cassandra rapped softly on the door. She heard a metal rasp from within the room and it took her a moment to realize it must be the mechanical lock that Timothy had installed. It was strange to her. Spell-locks were security enough. With the right spell, the door could have been sealed tight against any visitor who did not have authorization to enter. But even for his own benefit, Timothy did not trust magic. Instead, he had put in a heavy bolt that slid into the frame of the door so it could be locked from within.

Now it opened with a whisper. The workshop flickered with the light of a single lantern. This was not ghostfire, of course, but hungry fire, the dangerous, consuming flame that burned wood and flesh and almost anything else it touched. Yet Timothy had used flax-oil, cloth, metal, and glass to make a lantern in which hungry fire burned safely. The flame danced inside the glass like a darting lightning bug, somehow throwing shadows and light in equal portion.

From the shadows came a ruffle of feathers. Off to her

right, among some of Timothy's inventions, Sheridan was so still that he might have been inactivated. It sent a shudder through her, seeing him like that. Cassandra had never thought of the mechanical man as precisely alive, but now she realized she must have begun to think of him as a person, for in that moment he looked dead, and it frightened her. Then his red eyes flared to life in the darkness and a soft sigh of steam escaped the valve at the side of his head, and she smiled in relief.

"Ivar," the mechanical man whispered, a new assurance in his voice. "Close the door."

Cassandra frowned deeply, glancing around, peering into the shifting light and darkness of the room. She almost shouted in alarm when the shadows behind the open door took sudden form. Ivar had been there all along, the unique camouflage of his skin's changeable coloring keeping him hidden. Now the Asura warrior nodded to her and she stepped out of the way to allow him to close the door. Cassandra watched the way the black tribal markings that decorated his skin shifted as he moved. He slid the bolt back into place, locking the door, and then turned to face her.

"Grandmaster," the Asura said respectfully.

She blinked in surprise, shaking her head. "No, I—"

But Cassandra did not bother to continue the protest. For the moment, at least, she was Grandmaster. In the past few months she had gone through an incredible sequence of emotions on that subject. It was what she had wanted, so desperately: to succeed her grandfather as Grandmaster of the Order of Alhazred. But when the time came, all too soon, she had been forced to realize she was not ready. Leander Maddox had begun to teach her, to help her prepare for her eventual inheritance. And now that it appeared that it might be thrust upon her, even temporarily, while Leander was ill, she did not feel ready.

Fate, however, did not seem willing to give her a choice in the matter.

"I am not Grandmaster yet," she said at last, glancing from Ivar to Sheridan, and then to the gleaming black spot in the shadows of the room that she knew must be Edgar, the rook. "For the moment, I am in charge, yes. While Leander is not well. But only temporarily."

"Perhaps," Ivar said, and his normally emotionless features narrowed with a dark concern. The Asura was deeply troubled, but did not seem inclined to explain why.

Feathers ruffled in the shadows again and with a heavy flapping, Edgar emerged into the lamplight. The bird flew up to roost on the edge of a worktable not far from Sheridan.

"You're in charge, Cassandra," the bird said, no trace of a caw. Cawing might draw attention, and it was obvious that none of them wanted that right now. "But you still wanted to talk to us in secret. So what's going on?"

And then the bird *did* utter a single caw, but very quietly, almost as an afterthought.

She took a long breath, trying to find careful words to express her concerns. Sheridan stepped toward her, another soft sigh of steam hissing from his head. His red eyes grew brighter still.

"We're all afraid for Timothy," the mechanical man said. "But we have talked about it, and have decided we do not believe Professor Maddox's tale of what happened on the return from Tora'nah."

Cassandra flinched. Relief washed over her. "I was afraid you would think I was trying to cause trouble, to cast Leander in a poor light."

"Nonsense," Sheridan said, again with more assertiveness than she'd ever heard in the metal man before. It seemed that fear for Timothy had given him courage. "You've earned our trust. Please speak."

"All right." Cassandra nodded, looking around gratefully. Edgar cawed softly again, so softly, and cocked his head to study her. Ivar seemed distant, distracted, but she knew how troubled he must be, not knowing Timothy's fate. They all felt the same way.

"You've all known him longer," she went on, "but I cannot imagine Leander Maddox—no matter how sick or injured he might be—leaving Timothy behind. He made a vow to his own mentor, to Argus Cade, that he would watch over Tim. The mage I thought I knew would have died before breaking that vow."

Sheridan sniffed, a little whistling noise, and crossed his arms. "My thoughts precisely."

"More than that," Cassandra said, "when I heard Leander's story, I was so upset, so shocked and afraid for

Timothy, that it didn't fully register on me at the time. I was sort of . . . well, numb." She hesitated a moment, wondering if her growing feelings for Timothy were obvious now, if she was giving herself away. But if he was in danger, lost in the great forest, perhaps even now injured or dying . . . Cassandra bit her lip at the thought. Hiding her fondness for him was hardly important anymore.

"The point is, I realized that I didn't believe him. I don't believe it, and I guess none of you do either. I can't explain it. I don't know why Leander would mislead us. I have the greatest respect for him and believe that he is good and decent. Perhaps there is something else he does not want to tell us, something he's hiding from us for our own sake."

Ivar grunted and his brow furrowed more deeply.

Sheridan, though, took another step forward. "Yes!" he said hopefully. "You could be right."

Edgar ruffled his feathers. "Maybe. Maybe not. I've known him longer than any of you, but the healers won't let me in. They say he doesn't want to see anyone right now, not until he's up and around. So I don't know what's going on in his head. It makes sense, though."

Sheridan nodded again, a small squeaking noise coming from the joint of his neck. "All right. We all agree. But that means we have to find out for ourselves what happened."

"Right," Cassandra said. She moved into the middle of the room and spun, glancing at them each in turn, her robes swishing around her feet. "As acting Grandmaster, I plan to send a small detachment of Alhazred mages back along the route they flew, searching for Timothy and Caiaphas. But that's only what I will do officially, and since every mage in service at SkyHaven is loyal to Leander, I have no way of knowing if they will keep his secrets. If there are, indeed, any secrets to be kept."

She narrowed her eyes and stared at the rook. "Which is why I believe Edgar must go as well. To search from the sky, to find the trail, and find Timothy . . ." Cassandra swallowed heavily, a terrible dread in her heart. "No matter what has happened to him."

Ivar seemed deep in thought. The flickering shadows of the lantern moved across his face. Or it might have been the hue of his skin, those tribal markings, shifting again.

The rook cocked his head the other direction, black eyes gleaming. "Ivar should come with me. He could track a fish across the sea."

Cassandra did not want Ivar to go for several reasons, but she only gave one. "You can move faster, and will draw less attention, Edgar. If we want to go unnoticed, putting Ivar in charge of a sky carriage headed south would defeat that purpose."

She did not mention that she would feel better with the Asura there at SkyHaven. Cassandra felt a foreboding, a sense that something terrible was going to happen, and though she knew Sheridan would be a staunch ally, she wanted Ivar with her. Had it made sense to send him with Edgar, she would have put her worries aside, but in truth she was relieved to have reason to keep him there.

Ivar only nodded at her reasoning.

Something was disturbing him, and she wished he would say what it was. But Cassandra knew that the Asura would speak his mind in time, when he thought it was important to do so.

"You've got it, boss," Edgar said, flapping his wings again.

"Go now," Cassandra told him. She glanced at Sheridan. "Stay in the workshop. Edgar will leave through the window here and come back the same way. Wait for his return. Or for my summons, if I should receive word from him in some other fashion first."

Sheridan agreed.

"And what will you do now?" Ivar asked.

Cassandra took a deep breath. "I'm going to look in on Leander and see if I can figure out what he's not telling us."

Timothy slept very little that night in Karthagia. The healers had been incapable of fixing his cracked ribs with magic, which he could have told them if they had been willing to listen to him. In the end they had followed his suggestions to simply wrap his torso in bandages that would put pressure on the bones, keeping them together, and, he hoped, help them to knit faster. The discomfort disturbed him each time he tried to turn over in the bed, forcing him awake regularly.

Each time he found himself in the small bedroom they had provided for him, eyes staring at the ceiling, his mind would drift back to the plight of the Illuminators. The fate of those mages haunted him, stuck at the peaks of the ziggurats of

Karthagia. Their sacrifice was extraordinary, and he knew there must be a kind of honor in what they did, at least by their own judgment, but it still seemed horrible to him.

Some time in the early morning, troubled more and more by this, the spark of an idea ignited in Timothy's mind. It brought a smile to his face. Afterward, when he drifted off again, he was at last able to sleep soundly, even in spite of his injuries.

Hours later there came a rapping on the door. He struggled to open his eyes. What little sleep he'd managed had refreshed him somewhat, but his body protested as he sat up and pulled on his trousers. As he yawned and stretched, the knock came again.

"Come in," he called as he pulled his tunic over his head. His eyes felt itchy, lids still heavy, but he imagined some fresh air and sunshine would wake him fully. And some breakfast if the Karthagians were kind enough to offer it.

The door swung inward and Caiaphas entered, the splint gone from his arm. He still wore the sling and there were bruises visible on his arm, but it was obvious that the break was healing rapidly. At this rate the navigator would be entirely recovered by the following day, or perhaps even by nightfall.

Caiaphas was followed into the room by gray-eyed Finn, who was cloaked this morning in robes of a rich hue not unlike clay, or the coinage of the Parliament. The bald mage smiled warmly at Timothy. It appeared he and Caiaphas had been awake for quite some time.

"Good morning," the navigator said.

"'Morning," Timothy replied. He glanced at Finn. "And to you, sir. Thank you for your help. I don't know what I would've done without a bed last night. And food."

"You were pleased with dinner?"

Timothy grinned in response, some of the sleep lifting from him like a fog. "It was wonderful. After what happened to us yesterday . . . after that . . . well, I never thought we'd be fortunate enough to end the day so comfortably."

Finn crossed his arms and regarded them contentedly. "I am pleased. I only wish that we could make the rest of your journey as comfortable. You are, however, welcome to a breakfast at least as marvelous as last night's dinner before you go."

Timothy's stomach rumbled at the thought of it.

The two mages left him to wash up. Timothy had to use a small tub of water that had been brought to him, because of course the shower was magical and would not function in his presence. It was not the way he preferred to bathe, but it was better than wandering in the woods and hoping for a heavy rain.

At breakfast he asked for a pot of ink and a quill pen. The mages looked at him oddly but they complied. Though Finn was friendly enough, some of them seemed willing to be as hospitable as necessary simply to speed their visitors' departure. When he had the quill, he dipped it into the inkpot and began to pen designs onto a cloth napkin he spread out on the table before him. Though he was sure this was not at all good manners, the Karthagians were obviously hesitant to stop him. Timothy drew first on one side and then the other, after which he folded the napkin carefully and slid it into his pocket.

A short time later, Finn escorted them out of the ziggurat. As they made their way up the elevator, Timothy could not help gazing about him in fascination again. The gardens and the glass, the interior terraces of each floor, descending row by row into the earth, were simply incredible. The sight of that crystal and iron tower was one he would remember for the rest of his days.

The stone-eyed mage walked outside with them. They followed him along the path to the river and over a narrow footbridge that spanned the rushing water. It was early, but already there were many Karthagians about, some striding hurriedly and with great purpose, others strolling arm in arm. Children splashed in the river, laughing, but they stopped their games to watch the outsiders pass overhead.

Finn accompanied them past the other ziggurats and up the slope to the northern end of the river valley. At the edge of the forest, he stopped. It was clear he would go no farther.

"I wish you a safe journey," the mage said, bowing, his bald pate gleaming in the sun.

"We are in your debt," Caiaphas said, bowing in return.

Timothy pulled the cloth napkin from his pocket. "I . . . I have something for you. I don't know if you'll want it, but I thought I should show you, anyway."

Finn's brows knitted in curiosity. Caiaphas raised an eyebrow but said nothing. Timothy held the napkin up so both men could see what he had drawn there. It was a ziggurat, but with certain changes.

"On the top, where the Illuminator sits . . . well, if you set it up correctly, to catch the sun . . . and see here, deep inside the ziggurat . . . if there were mirrored glass on every level, you could catch the sunlight and spread it all through the building all day long. Then, at night," he said, turning the napkin over, showing the basic design of the lanterns he had made for his father's house and for his workshop and quarters at SkyHaven, "you could use oil lamps, with hungry fire—"

Finn flinched at the words.

"No, it's completely safe," Timothy said. "As long as nobody shatters it, of course, and you could use magic to make the glass unbreakable. But this way, you could have light all day with the sun, and have lamps at night, and the Illuminators wouldn't be . . . they would be able to come down. If the ghostfire really is the souls of mages, just kind of . . . well, trapped, then I agree with you. It's terrible. But the Illuminators are sort of trapped too."

He shrugged, embarrassed and feeling awkward under the stare of the two mages. Folding the napkin again, he handed it to Finn. The mage stared at it for long seconds before reverently slipping it into a pocket of his robe.

"I will present it to my clan chief. Thank you for your thoughtfulness, Timothy."

"I just wanted to help," said the unmagician.

Finn smiled. "It is a generous instinct. And now I must return. Be well. May your path be smooth and your journey swift. If you follow our instructions, you should find your way to the settlement of the Lake Dwellers in several hours' time. I hope that they will be able to provide you with assistance."

Caiaphas and Timothy said their final good-byes and then were on their way.

The forest was not so thick here as other areas they had passed through. They walked due north all through the rest of the morning as the sun moved steadily across the sky above. They spoke of small pleasures, of the breakfast they'd had and the hospitality of the Karthagians. Caiaphas told Timothy of Nosgraf, the small village where he was raised, hundreds of leagues north of Arcanum, and the boy told the mage of the Island of Patience, and the peacefulness of the place.

Timothy purposefully avoided discussing the things Finn had said about ghostfire. It lingered in his mind, upsetting him deeply, but it wasn't something he wanted to share with anyone else. Not yet. Most of Terra used ghostfire lamps. To suggest that they should abandon this practice . . . well, given the way they'd treated him previously, he could only imagine how the Parliament would take such a statement from him.

Still, he was haunted by it.

But he did his best to push such thoughts aside while

they were journeying. Other things took precedence now. They had to return to Arcanum and discover what had come over Leander, and what other trouble he might have stirred up once he made it back to SkyHaven.

They rested at midday. Timothy's side had not bothered him much all that morning. The large bandages wrapped around his torso had helped him a great deal, and he began to wonder if perhaps his ribs were only badly bruised and not cracked after all. Or they might simply have begun to heal already. The Karthagians had provided them a satchel filled with dried meats and fresh fruit and a loaf of dark, grainy bread, as well as a jug of water. Caiaphas carried all of these things now that the healers had touched him and his arm was nearly better.

In a clearing they ate and drank and lay flat on their backs for a time. Timothy's legs throbbed from the walking. Still sleepy from the night before, he began to feel drowsy. The sky had begun to cloud over, the sun veiled by a layer of gray gauze. It was not so dark as to promise a storm, but a sprinkle of rain seemed almost inevitable.

"We'd best move on," Caiaphas said eventually.

Reluctantly, Timothy agreed. If Finn had been accurate in his estimation of distance, the village of the Lake Dwellers ought to be only another hour's walk or so. If a sky carriage could be borrowed there, Caiaphas would be able to get them to Arcanum by late afternoon. Otherwise they'd have to continue on. Finn had suggested they might get horses from Romulus and his people, but Timothy was sure that the Grandmaster of the Legion Nocturne would sooner trample them beneath the hooves of his horses than lend them one.

Preoccupied with what the afternoon might bring, he was not as careful rising to his feet as he ought to have been. A sharp pain shot through him from his injured ribs and he hissed air in through his teeth.

"Are you all right?" Caiaphas asked, hefting the now lightened satchel over his good shoulder.

Timothy grimaced. "Not exactly. But there's nothing to be done for it. Let's get going."

They moved out of the clearing and into the woods again. Now that the sky had turned gray, it was dark in the forest. Even so, the trees were still spaced well apart and the going was easy enough, the landscape relatively flat. In time, they emerged onto a path that had been beaten down by the passage of mages and horses. It ran northeast and Caiaphas smiled as he glanced in both directions.

"This ought to take us directly to the lake."

"At least it feels like we're getting closer to someone who can help," Timothy said.

But Caiaphas wasn't paying attention to him anymore. Timothy had been facing the navigator, looking back at the forest from where they had just emerged. The woods were deep on both sides of the path. Caiaphas, though, was staring along their intended route to the northeast, and over the deep blue veil he wore, the navigator's eyes were dark and troubled.

"What is—" Timothy began, turning to find the source of his friend's alarm. Something drew his attention in the woods. A low, swift shape darting from tree to tree.

"Lost and alone," said a rasping, familiar voice.

The woods were forgotten. Timothy turned up the path to see a single figure striding toward them. Moments earlier he had not been there at all, but now they were not alone. Caiaphas only stared uncertainly ahead. But not Timothy. As the new arrival strode through the gloom toward them, his single arm at his side, Timothy balled his hands into fists and prepared to fight.

"There are no Wurm to protect you here, boy," snarled Constable Grimshaw. The cruel-eyed mage raised his remaining hand and smoothed his mustache. The cloak he wore fluttered behind him in the breeze.

"Grimshaw," Timothy said, grinding the name in his teeth. He was stunned to meet the mage here in the wilderness, this horrible man who had called him a freak and a monster, who had imprisoned Verlis and tried to do the same to Timothy. "You know your magic won't hurt me. And you can't beat me hand-to-hand. Get out of our way."

The Constable laughed, an ugly, hollow sound. "I don't have to beat you. I only have to kill the navigator." He sneered on this last word, letting them both know how far beneath him he felt Caiaphas was.

Timothy shook his head, not understanding.

Then something moved again in the woods and he saw

it just out of the corner of his eye. As he turned, he heard Grimshaw speak again.

"Alastor will be the one to spill *your* blood, unmagician."

Timothy spun. At the edge of the path, just emerging from the trees, was a monstrous thing that seemed part man and part cat. It crouched low to the ground, though it walked on two legs. It was much larger than a feline, but smaller than Timothy himself. Its ears pricked up, it raised its clawed forepaws, and it hissed, cat eyes gleaming sickly yellow in the gloom and shadows of the forest path.

Alastor. He knew that name. Nicodemus's familiar. But it had been an ordinary cat. This couldn't be—

Then it no longer mattered.

The cat-creature hissed again, and then it sprang across the path at him, claws descending.

CHAPTER SEVEN

Timothy dove out of the cat-creature's path. Excruciating pain flared in his side, as if someone had jabbed a knife into him. The explosion of agony took his breath away and he stumbled, falling to his knees, colorful stars dancing before his eyes.

The cat-creature—this monster that had once been known as Alastor—landed in a crouch, then spun around to face him, its hairless tail twitching in the air as it crouched, hungrily eyeing its prey.

What happened to you? Timothy's mind raced as he stared at the monstrous feline. When last he had seen Nicodemus's familiar, it had been nothing more than a hairless house cat—a minor annoyance, at best—but now? He had no idea what it had become. It was huge and its body was no longer built like a cat. It was almost as if the cat had become more . . . *manlike.*

The monstrosity sprang at him with a throaty growl and he tried to dodge again, but the beast was too fast. Before he knew it the thing was on top of him. Its needle-sharp claws pricked Timothy through his clothing and he was forced back down to the ground. Pinned beneath its weight, he was forced to look up into its hideous features and, for an instant, he saw something in the large, yellow eyes, something familiar.

It lashed out at him, then, running the claws of one strangely shaped paw quickly down his right cheek.

Timothy cried out in pain, the five scratches burning like hungry fire.

"Get off of him!" Caiaphas screamed from somewhere behind them. And then the navigator's voice was replaced by another.

"You heard the man," Grimshaw growled. "Off the boy—now."

The cat-creature looked down into Timothy's face and hissed, baring its teeth. And then it left him to return obediently to its master.

Timothy crawled to his feet, the throbbing in his side now partnered with a burning pain on his cheek, but both discomforts were quickly forgotten as he caught sight of the latest horror to be played out before him.

"Caiaphas," Timothy whispered. The navi-mage dangled in the air, with what appeared to be a tentacle of pure magic wrapped tightly about his throat. And "tentacle" was the right word, for the appendage grew from the stump of

Constable Grimshaw's missing arm. Caiaphas struggled in its grasp, and Timothy started toward him.

"No tricks, boy," he said with a snarl. "Or your friend's life is forfeit."

"He can't breathe," Timothy said, moving one step closer.

Alastor hissed, crouching at his master's side, ready to pounce yet again.

"I'm warning you, boy, I'll snap his neck with nary a thought. Keep where you are."

Timothy's mind raced with a hundred thoughts and then a hundred more after that, but no plan occurred to him that would guarantee he could save his friend before the Constable did the unthinkable.

"Please," he begged. "He can't breathe."

Grimshaw chuckled before slowly lowering Caiaphas to the ground and loosening the magical tendril from about his throat.

The navigation mage gasped, gulping air.

"Nothing would please me more than to kill the two of you now," the Constable spat. "But that is not my master's wish."

Master, Timothy thought. *All right, so you're holding Alastor's leash, but who is holding yours?*

Leander had hinted of an evil mastermind, someone working in the shadows of the world. Though Nicodemus had been defeated and Grimshaw's own efforts had been thwarted, mages had continued to disappear. The assumption was that they had been abducted or murdered, and

Leander had been assigned the task of helping to investigate those disappearances. So far, however, there had been not a single clue as to what had happened to all of them.

It seemed the only mage who had disappeared and then reappeared was Grimshaw himself, which made Timothy fairly certain that whoever was behind those abductions was the mage that Grimshaw now called master.

Caiaphas was on the ground, still recovering. The Constable's bizarre magical arm writhed in the air above him, ready to attack at the first sign of resistance. Timothy's hands were still tied, and he seethed with anger. There was nothing worse than feeling helpless.

"Do you like it, boy?" Grimshaw asked, glancing at that tendril of shimmering magic that had replaced his missing arm. "Almost as good as flesh and bone—perhaps even better." He uttered a curt, ugly laugh devoid of any humor. "It was a gift. A gift for my services." He drew the limb away from Caiaphas, studying it, as if seeing it for the first time.

Timothy caught the eye of the navigation mage, who had yet to rise from the forest floor. He was on all fours, apparently still trying to catch his breath. But when their eyes touched briefly, Timothy saw something in the man's gaze that warned him to be ready—to be prepared.

"A gift from your *master*?" Timothy asked, mocking Grimshaw.

Rage blossomed upon the Constable's face. The tentacle of magic shot out toward Timothy, away from Caiaphas, only to crackle and dissipate as the negating field around the boy disrupted the magic that had constructed that terrible arm.

"Such a wonderful gift," Timothy continued calmly. "But you still can't touch me."

Grimshaw's face contorted with fury and frustration, and he drew back his tentacle of magic as one would pull back from the searing heat of a ravenous flame. "Right you are, boy," he agreed, a cruel glint appearing in his dark, malevolent eyes as he made sure that his gift had not been damaged. "But I *can* touch your companion."

He might have attacked Caiaphas again, then, but the navigation mage chose that moment to act. He worked his fingers into the dirt of the forest floor and suddenly the woods around them were swept into a frenzy. Dirt, rocks, leaves, and twigs shot up into the air, briefly forming a barrier between them and their foes.

"Toward the lake, Tim," Caiaphas bellowed.

The boy did not hesitate. He bolted into the trees with Caiaphas thundering at his heels, the two of them whipping past low branches and darting between the thick trunks of ancient trees. Timothy chanced a quick glance over his shoulder to be sure that Caiaphas was right behind him. The navigator's diversion would only buy them so much time before Grimshaw and his pet were in pursuit. They had to make this work.

Finn had spoken of Lake Dwellers, and Timothy hoped they could reach that settlement before the Constable caught up to them.

"Faster!" he heard Caiaphas gasp behind him, and he quickened his pace, trying not to stumble in the darkening shadows of the deep forest.

His side and face ached with each rapid-fire beat of his heart, but it did not deter him. In fact, it spurred him to run faster. The river was close. He could smell its rich dampness in the air.

"Almost there, Caiaphas," he gasped.

There came no response.

Timothy faltered and glanced behind him, peering into the darkness. But Caiaphas wasn't there. He did not want to stop, was desperate to reach safety, but he had no choice. What if his friend had fallen, twisted an ankle, perhaps? He had to help.

"Caiaphas," he called out, coming to a full stop. "Caiaphas, where are you?" He looked about the darkened forest for a sign of his friend, wary for any hint of Grimshaw and the monstrous Alastor, but saw nothing. Timothy began to slowly retrace his steps. "Caiaphas," he called again into the infringing darkness. "Where . . . ?"

A whistling sound filled the air, then something struck him in the back of the head, knocking him to the ground. Six figures suddenly emerged from the shadows, converging upon him. He tried to stand, but dropped back to his knees, overcome by a sickening dizziness.

"You'll stay down, freak, if you know what's good for you," said a voice dripping with malice.

One of them rushed at him and launched a savage kick

to his side that sent Timothy sprawling to the damp forest floor yet again. His injured ribs seared with such pain that he nearly passed out, but he struggled to hang on, to stay conscious.

The shapes loomed over him now, their features clouded in the shadows of night. Timothy lay on the ground, aching so badly that it felt as if his entire body were one enormous injury.

"Caiaphas," he said again.

"Don't worry, little one," said another coarse voice. "The navigator is just fine. In fact he's sleeping quite soundly."

They all began to laugh.

And then he heard the voice, unmistakable in its malevolence and cruelty. "Do you have him?"

Grimshaw.

"Of course, Constable," said one of the six. "And we didn't hurt him very much, just as you asked."

"That is best for all of you," Grimshaw snarled as he emerged from the trees to join the assailants. "For it is not I who wishes the boy to remain unharmed, but the master."

"The master," hissed one of the attackers. "Yes. All praise and glory to Alhazred."

Timothy could fight the pain no longer, and the darkness pulled him into oblivion, the name of his enemies' master echoing through his mind . . . the master who was supposed to have been dead for over a century.

Alhazred.

* * *

Shortly after dawn, Edgar flew above the Yarrith Forest, keen avian eyes searching through the breaks in the trees below for a sign that Timothy and Caiaphas were still alive. He had yet to find anything to give him hope, but Yarrith was a very big place, and he would not give up until he had searched every inch.

Feeling a need to rest his wings, Edgar dropped down into the thick woods and perched upon the branch of an ancient and gnarled tree. He fluttered his wings, shaking the aches of his long journey from his muscles. *A short rest will do me good,* the familiar thought as he peered about.

Yarrith was more than a bit creepy, the bird determined, as he heard strange sounds rising from shadows below him. *I need to be careful,* he mused, *winding up in the stomach of some wild beast won't do Timothy and Caiaphas any good.*

Something moved in the brush below, and Edgar cawed loudly to frighten it off. With a crackle of twigs and a swaying of branches, it hurried away. There came another sound, right behind it. At first Edgar mistook it as the soft whispering of the wind through the leaves, but then he realized the sound was coming from nearby. Investigating, he found a large hole in the body of the tree on which he perched. The sound was coming from the darkness of that hole.

Edgar sprang back, prepared to defend himself with beak and talon if necessary, but something told him that wasn't going to be the case. He tilted his head inquisitively.

"Hello?" he asked, and from inside the hole, he heard

the rustle of feathers, and caught the smell of something incredibly ancient wafting out from within.

At first he glimpsed only its large, round eyes, covered in a glistening milky sheen. The orbs floated in the darkness of the hollow in the tree as though there were nothing more to the creature but eyes. Then, after a moment, it emerged, an owl more ancient than any Edgar had ever seen. It was twice his size, faded feathers speckled white and brown.

Edgar searched his memory for the language of the owl. It had been quite some time since he'd had to speak the dialect. "Good morning to you, revered owl," he said, hoping that he remembered all the pronunciations correctly. He didn't want to insult the great old bird.

The owl studied him with his large, cataract-covered eyes. "Why have you awakened me, rook?" he asked in a quavering voice that sounded as old as he looked.

"I meant no disrespect. I did not know that you slept within this tree," Edgar told the owl. "I've stopped only to rest my wings before continuing on with my mission."

The owl considered his words. "Mission?" Owls were an extremely curious race. "What sort of mission?"

"I am a familiar in search of his master," the black bird explained. "The sky carriage he was riding in was attacked two days past, and I believe that he and the carriage's navigator fell from the craft somewhere in these vast woods. Perhaps you know something of this?"

"A sky carriage attacked, you say?" the old bird asked as he gazed off into the great woods around them. "Let me see," he mused aloud. "Sometimes it is difficult to remember. At my age, things have a tendency to slip easily away. I do seem to remember something about two strangers to these woods, but I'm afraid little else."

Edgar cocked his head to one side, feathers ruffling. Strangers did not necessarily mean Timothy and Caiaphas, but it was possible. And if so, it would mean that they were alive.

"Might you know, venerable one, if they had suffered any injuries? Or can you give me a hint as to where they could now be?"

The great owl slowly shook his head. "I am truly sorry, rook, but the years have robbed me of memory."

Edgar felt his body grow slack with disappointment. "That's all right, good owl. At least you have given me some hope that I may yet find them both well."

He knew it was time to be on his way. If these strangers to the forest were indeed his friends, he could at least narrow the area of his search. "Many thanks to you for your time and for this resting place," he said with a bow. "I take leave of you now, for there is still much of the Yarrith Forest left to search."

"I remember that I fed upon fire weasel last night."

Edgar furled his wings, not sure how to respond to the owl's bizarre statement. "Excellent," he replied. "Perhaps this evening you'll feast upon squirrel, but now I must be off and—"

The owl ruffled his ancient feathers in annoyance. "You

misunderstand me, rook. I fed upon the fire weasel as it was startled from its hiding place."

Edgar raised his beak and stared, still unsure of the old bird's purpose. "Go on," he urged.

"There was a commotion in the woods yesterday; the dwellers who live by the lake captured two, I believe. Yes, there were two of them."

Edgar stared at the owl. "These Lake Dwellers, are they hostile? Do you have any idea where the strangers would have been taken? Or how long ago it was when they were taken captive?"

The owl considered the many questions, then turned and headed back to his home in the tree.

"Please, old one," Edgar begged. "Can't you tell me anything more about last night?"

"Yes," the ancient bird said, his head turning almost completely around to gaze at the rook. "Yes I can. The fire weasel, it was truly delicious."

Cassandra rapped lightly on the heavy wooden door to Leander Maddox's living quarters. Each time she visited him she found the poor mage in worse shape than the last. The healers were baffled, treating the man with special herb drinks to help boost his strength, but other than that, they could do nothing.

She was about to knock again, fearing that she had not been heard, when the door suddenly opened a crack and a pale face warily peered out from the darkness within.

"What is it?" Carlyle asked in a perturbed hiss. He saw that the visitor was Cassandra, and his tone dramatically changed. "Ah, Mistress Nicodemus. What may I do for you?"

The Grandmaster's assistant looked tired, large black circles under his eyes from lack of sleep. *He may be an annoying man,* she thought, *but he is loyal to his employer.* Carlyle had not left Leander's side since the Grandmaster's return.

"It is not what you can do for me," she explained, "but what I can do for you."

He eyed her suspiciously, allowing the door to open a little wider. The sitting room and bedroom beyond were in near total darkness, illuminated only by small ghostfire lanterns. A sickly smell mixed with that of poultices and herbs wafted out into the hall, and Cassandra could hear Leander moaning softly in his sleep within.

"What is that supposed to mean?" Carlyle asked doubtfully.

"You have been with Leander for days, never taking any time for yourself. Allow me to sit with the Grandmaster. Go and have a hot meal—perhaps even a bath and a few hours' rest."

"I couldn't," he said, turning from her toward the darkness of the other room where Leander lay. "What if he needs me? What if he calls my name and I am not here?"

"Then I shall send someone to find you," she reassured him. "Do not worry, the Grandmaster will be in good hands while you replenish your strength."

Carlyle looked back to her and she could see that his

resolve was crumbling. Days without proper rest and food had taken their toll.

"You'll come find me if he should speak my name?"

Cassandra nodded. "Immediately. Now go, take care of yourself so that you may better take care of him."

He allowed the door into the Grandmaster's quarters to open wider. "Yes, that's exactly what I'm doing," Carlyle said. "I'm taking care of myself so that I can best see to his needs. Yes, that's it." He smiled tiredly, stepping out into the hall and gesturing for Cassandra to enter the room.

The Grandmaster's assistant suddenly tripped over nothing, catching himself on the doorway. Cassandra's eyes grew large as she watched the man recover. Carlyle looked about the hall, embarrassed.

"I'm so tired that I am tripping over my own feet," he said with a nervous chuckle. "Perhaps it is a good thing that you have come to relieve me."

He smiled at her then and started to leave, only to stop and return. Cassandra had begun to close the door, and he reached out to stop it with his hand.

"Yes, Carlyle?" she said.

"I'll be in the kitchen having a bit of supper, and then I am going to retire to my room to wash up and rest for a few hours."

"Very good," she said, humoring him. "I assure you, he'll be fine. Go."

Cassandra at last closed the door on the man, pressing her back against it with a heavy sigh.

"I was certain he would suspect when he tripped," she said aloud, looking about the sitting room.

"He moved into my path as I was attempting to pass by him," Ivar replied, the colors upon his flesh changing so that he could be seen. "I do not think he suspected anything other than his own clumsiness."

"And we can be thankful for that," Cassandra said, moving away from the door and toward the interior bedroom where Leander was recuperating.

"He is very ill," Ivar said flatly. "The air reeks of sickness."

"The healers are doing the best they can," she explained. "But I fear that there is something far more deadly than illness at work here."

During a visit she had paid the Grandmaster the previous night, Leander had briefly awakened from a fitful sleep, eyes wide in terror. Carlyle had been out of the room following up on some parliamentary business, and she had tried to comfort Leander, but he seemed to be firmly in the grasp of some horrific nightmare, thrashing about in his bed, raving about things hiding in the darkness—about a voracious evil living among them.

She suspected that he was trying to tell her something, and had tried to encourage him to explain, but Carlyle had returned and the Grandmaster had immediately fallen silent, slipping again into a restless sleep. It was then that she decided she must return, accompanied by Ivar. Together she hoped they might make sense of Leander's ravings.

Now they entered the gloomy room together. Dim ghostfire lamps burned in wall sconces and on a dresser across from the archmage's bed. Thick curtains had been pulled across the windows, closing the ailing Grandmaster away in a cocoon of twilight.

Approaching the bed, Cassandra was disturbed at how small the mage appeared beneath the covers, almost as if whatever ailed him were somehow stealing away his size. Leander was sleeping fitfully, his head tossing side to side. Cassandra reached down and took hold of his large hand, giving it a gentle squeeze.

"Shhhh, it's all right," she said softly, leaning close so that he could hear. "You're not alone. Don't worry."

Roused by her voice, Grandmaster Maddox opened his eyes. "Cassandra?" he said, looking about the darkened room. "Ivar?" The sickly mage attempted to sit up, but Cassandra put a hand on his chest and easily pushed him back down.

"Relax, Leander," she told him. "We're here—we're both here."

Ivar had now joined her, standing silently at their friend's bedside.

The Grandmaster looked about the room, eyes wild. "Not sure how much time I have," he said, breathlessly. "It's so hard to fight . . . so hard. Must try . . . try to explain, but haven't . . . the strength."

The Asura reached down and laid a pale hand upon Leander's feverish brow. "Then we will lend you some of ours."

Leander's breathing grew ragged and quick, as if he was fighting something that they could not see. Cassandra held his hand more tightly, willing her strength into him.

"While doing . . . research . . . about Tora'nah . . . I found something . . . something . . . hidden away. . . ."

The Grandmaster began to tremble, his body horribly rigid.

"What did you find?" Ivar encouraged him.

The Grandmaster looked at them, his tired eyes bulging as if he was afraid. Terribly, terribly afraid. "Down in the darkness," he croaked. "Hidden . . . hidden down in the darkness . . ."

The room was suddenly, brilliantly illuminated as the ghostfire within the lantern on the dresser flared, tripled in brightness, and shattered the spell-glass that contained it.

Cassandra gasped as the room darkened once more.

"Down in the shadows," Leander repeated, his voice growing weaker. "Hidden, down in the dark . . . something evil."

A spell of illumination left her lips, and Cassandra's hand began to glow with a soft yellow light.

"He is unconscious again," Ivar said to her, and she noticed that the black patterns upon the Asura's flesh were moving about. Timothy once had explained that this happened when the warrior sensed danger.

"What do you think he meant?" she asked, staring down at the burly mage who had become a friend as well as her mentor. "Hidden down in the darkness. What's hidden—and where?"

Ivar removed his hand from the Grandmaster's brow.

"The *what* still remains to be determined," the Asura said as he studied the broken, jagged pieces of the ghostfire lantern that now littered the bedroom floor. "The *where*, however, I feel is closer than we imagined."

"Then where, Ivar?" Cassandra asked, her hand still burning like a miniature star, dispelling the gloom that tried to engulf them.

"It is here," the Asura said, his dark gaze piercing her. "Somewhere in SkyHaven."

CHAPTER EIGHT

Timothy awoke to the stink of something awful.

Careful not to let anyone know that he had regained consciousness, he examined through slitted eyelids his surroundings. There were dwellings on the shore of the lake and others that were on stilts out in the water. He and Caiaphas were in a makeshift cage above the water. The cage hung by a thick rope from a beam that stretched between two of the structures on stilts. He was lying on his side and, from between the wooden slats of the cage, he could see three figures below him cleaning fish in the shallows near the shore of the lake. They were large, ugly fish with gleaming black scales and large, jagged fins that ran the length of their bodies, all the way to their wide tailfins. The horrible smell was coming from these grotesque fish as they were cut open and their insides tossed into the water.

The Lake Dwellers appeared to be a relatively primitive group, dressed in rough clothing that seemed to be made from the skins of whatever they could catch from the lake, and the woods beyond.

He opened his eyes wider now that he knew he was not being directly observed. Still, he was cautious not to move about too much. If the cage rocked, it would draw attention. Timothy craned his neck to get a better view of his surroundings. The village was a cluster of boxy wooden structures that sat upon thick wooden pillars above the surface of the lake. Platforms connected the dwellings, creating a network of wooden plank pathways high above the water. He was surprised by how unpolished everything seemed, and guessed that the use of magic here was minimal.

A low, throaty moan came from behind him. Timothy could not turn toward his companion without setting the cage in gentle motion and perhaps drawing attention, but he did twist his head a bit, hoping to get even a peripheral glimpse.

"Caiaphas, is that you?" he whispered.

"Yes, Timothy," the navigation mage replied. "Are you well? Did you sustain any injuries in the attack upon us?"

Timothy wiggled a bit to see if anything hurt, and realized that his hands were bound behind his back with rope. His side still ached and the scratches on his face burned, and he had a bit of a headache from where he had been struck on the back of his head, but other than that, he seemed to be fine.

"I'm all right," he answered. "And you?"

Timothy heard a sharp intake of air from the navigator that told him Caiaphas hadn't been so lucky.

"They have injured my hands," he explained. "I think . . . I think that some of my fingers have been broken."

"To stop you casting levitation spells," Timothy said, a sick feeling settling into his stomach. The Lake Dwellers might be primitive, but they were not stupid. He grimaced and stared at the workers below as they cleaned and skinned the ugly lake fish.

"I could cast spells," Caiaphas explained, "but without the use of my fingers there would be no way to guarantee control, and I could injure myself, or cause the cage to fall, endangering us both. I'm sorry, Timothy, but escape does not appear to be in our imminent future."

One of the workers below suddenly yelped in pain, and Timothy looked out to see that he had cut himself badly on the jagged fins that ran along the back of one of those ugly fish. The worker grumbled beneath his breath, plunging his wounded hand into the bloody water to clean out the gash as the others laughed at his clumsiness.

"That's all right, Caiaphas," he said, still watching the workers intently. "We'll just have to come up with another way out."

The worker who had injured his hand paused in examining his wound and glanced upward. He had heard their voices. Timothy cursed silently and tried to pretend he was still unconscious, but it did not fool the man.

"Awake at last," the worker said.

Neither Timothy nor Caiaphas replied, so the man splashed through the water to shore. Reaching land, he climbed a ladder to a wooden platform and disappeared into one of the larger buildings.

It was useless now to pretend he was not awake, so Timothy turned his attention to the sight of multiple boats being paddled upon the vast lake. He watched with interest as those in the boats spread their hands before them and cast spells that wove nets of crackling energy that spread across the water. The Lake Dwellers may not have used magic for all things, Timothy observed, but they did use it to catch their food. He thought it was quite interesting how the importance of magic differed from culture to culture upon Terra. He had little time to pursue such interesting thoughts, however, for in that moment a figure emerged from the building where the injured worker had gone.

Grimshaw.

The Constable stood outside the structure, ebony cloak billowing in the breeze from the lake. Timothy could see the stump where his arm had been bitten off by Verlis, but there was no sign of the tentacle-like magical arm that had replaced it. The cat-creature stood at Grimshaw's side, tipping its nose to the air and sniffing the wind. Two Lake Dwellers, one the injured worker, emerged from the building behind Grimshaw, and the three descended the ladder to the shore.

"Good morning to you, young sir," Grimshaw called out to Timothy pleasantly.

"He is a vile man," Caiaphas sniffed as he shifted his weight and caused the cage to sway.

"You've taken the words right out of my mouth," Timothy agreed. He managed to rise to his knees, hands still bound behind his back.

"What are you up to, Grimshaw?" he asked defiantly. "What use are we as captives? I demand to know what you intend to do with us."

Grimshaw's barking laugh echoed out over the lake. "You demand to know?" he repeated as he regained control of himself. "Your insolence amuses me, freak."

Timothy winced at the word. No matter how many times it was used against him, he could not deny its hurtful power.

"If it were up to me, we would not be having this discussion right now, for you would most certainly be dead," Grimshaw said. Alastor had jumped to the ground and now padded out into the shallows as though it had little interest in their exchange.

"My master wants you alive," the Constable continued with a nasty smile, "as a precautionary measure. He seems to think that you might prove useful . . . can you imagine that? Timothy Cade, freak of nature, useful."

Master, Timothy thought. Then he remembered the words of the Lake Dwellers who had captured him, what he had heard them say as he'd lost consciousness. The name. *Alhazred.* It made no sense to him. Even if Alhazred was alive—which in itself seemed impossible—he had no idea what that ancient mage could want with him. Yet what if Alhazred was also the mysterious master Grimshaw referred to? Certainly a mage as powerful as Alhazred would have many allies, many followers. The Lake Dwellers were belligerent and cruel, just the sort who would associate with Alhazred. And Grimshaw . . . he was truly evil. Timothy shuddered at the thought that the cunning, merciless Alhazred might still be alive.

"Your master, Constable?" he said. "You mean Alhazred?"

He said it casually, as though it meant nothing. He spoke as though it were a fact instead of simply a guess.

The Constable was visibly taken aback by his question. Grimshaw glared at the men beside him. It was obvious they had thought him unconscious when one of them mentioned Alhazred, but Timothy was sure the Constable would make whoever had spoken pay for that mistake. When Grimshaw looked back at Timothy, he had recovered, and his expression was full of ridicule.

"Are you insane, boy?" he scoffed. "Alhazred has been dead for well over a hundred years."

The Lake Dweller beside Grimshaw eyed him with wide, fear-filled eyes as the Constable remained eerily silent. Alastor hissed, charging out into the water toward them and crouching on his haunches as though to leap up at the cage. Grimshaw raised his one hand and snapped his fingers loudly, bringing the animal to an abrupt stop. It turned to look at him.

"Return to me," the Constable commanded, and Alastor hissed ferociously as it eyed the prisoners before obeying its master and slinking back to his side. Timothy wasn't sure if he had ever seen an animal quite as frightening.

"For now, your lives are perceived as having some value," Grimshaw said testily. "But perceptions change." The Constable pulled his ebony cloak about him and turned to leave. "When the time comes, Timothy Cade, I will be the one who ends your worthless life—of that, you can be certain."

Timothy watched the man as he departed, climbing a ladder and then striding across a wooden walkway to the largest of the structures built on those pylons above the lake. When the boy was sure they would not be overheard, he turned to Caiaphas.

"How would you feel about getting away from this place tonight?"

Night had fallen, and a kind of celebration was going on in the village. Torchlight illuminated the entire encampment, and music drifted with the cool evening breeze coming down from the forest hills.

"I'm curious what they're celebrating," Caiaphas said as he shifted his position to get comfortable.

"Perhaps they had a successful day on the lake," Timothy suggested. "Or maybe they're celebrating our capture."

"Do you really believe that Alhazred is alive?" Caiaphas asked.

"I don't want to, but I heard what I heard. One of the

men who captured us said he was their master. And you saw Grimshaw's reaction."

"Yes," the navigation mage replied. "He was not at all pleased. Maybe it is true. For the sake of the world, I hope it is not. Most mages still believe Alhazred was a great man, but if even half of the stories about him are true, he was a monster."

They were quiet for several minutes after that, neither knowing what more to say about this troubling news. Timothy heard a faint grumbling coming from Caiaphas's stomach.

"Pardon me," the navigator said. "But it has been quite some time since last we ate. My belly is telling me that a meal is long past due."

"I've been wondering that myself," Timothy said. "In fact, a meal will play a big part in how we manage to escape."

"A meal?" Caiaphas echoed in disbelief. "How will feeding us—"

"Trust me," Timothy said. "If we're lucky, we may be free soon."

"And if we are not?" Caiaphas asked.

"Let's pray we are."

Timothy was the first to notice the two shapes coming toward them in the distance. The two men were coming from the direction of the celebration, and one was holding two plates. "I hope this is what I think it is," he said in an excited whisper.

"And so do I," Caiaphas agreed. "Even though I haven't the slightest idea what you're up to, I'm still rather hungry."

Timothy watched eagerly as the two men approached the shore and waded out toward them. The one who wasn't holding plates had brought along a ladder that he balanced against the side of their cage.

"Are we famished?" asked the man holding their supper. "If I had my way, you'd not be sharing the wealth of our bounty this night," he growled, starting up the ladder, one plate atop the other. He was an ugly man, covered in filth, and Timothy could not help but wonder when he had last bathed.

When he reached the cage, the filthy man leaned into the ladder and used his free hand to work the knot that held the door in place. "It'd be moss soup for ya if it was up to me," he spat as he pulled the door open. "This meal is too good for the likes of prisoners."

He set the plates down inside the cage and Timothy nearly yelped with joy, but managed to contain his outburst. They had been given fish to eat, the same disgusting fish that he had watched being cleaned in the lake below them.

"Thank you, good sir," Timothy said. "Your kindness overwhelms me."

The man growled, slamming the door closed and retying the rope.

"Wait," Timothy called, struggling to his knees. "Won't you undo our hands so that we can eat properly?" he asked.

"Eat like dogs," the man said, and laughed cruelly. "If you

are hungry enough, you'll find a way without the use of your hands."

He climbed down the ladder, laughing the entire time. They took down the ladder and soon both men were laughing as they splashed their way to shore, and headed back into the village to continue their celebration.

For a moment Timothy wondered about Grimshaw, and if he was participating. He really didn't seem like the celebrating type.

"I guess we should feel lucky that they decided to feed us," Caiaphas said, distracting the boy from his thoughts.

"We are very lucky," Timothy told him, eyeing their meals. "They did exactly as I hoped."

Caiaphas chuckled, shaking his head in mock confusion. "Perhaps now you will explain to me what it is that you were implying earlier."

"Watching the Lake Dwellers today, I gathered that a large portion of their diet would consist of fish, and that if they fed us, we would likely be eating fish as well."

"Continue," the navigator prodded.

"Well, as you can see, I was correct."

They both again looked at their meals. The twin fish were hot, and charred from being cooked over a roaring fire. Steam drifted up from the plates.

"I wasn't sure how they would prepare them," Timothy said. "But as I watched them clean their catch this morning, I noticed that it was their custom not to remove the sharp fins that run down the length of the fish."

Caiaphas looked at him, and Timothy could tell that he still did not understand.

"They leave the fin on, Caiaphas," he said, stressing his every word. *"A fin that is extremely sharp—almost knifelike."*

Timothy moved himself around so that the plate was behind him.

"What are you doing?" Caiaphas asked as the boy leaned backward toward the plate.

He could feel the hot flesh of the fish beneath his fingers and he carefully began to move his bound wrists so that the fish's razor-sharp dorsal fin would be between them. It took some time, but his persistence was rewarded, and Timothy managed to sever the rope tied to his wrists.

With a grin he held the pieces of the rope up for his companion to see. Caiaphas watched in disbelief as Timothy picked through the remains of their meal, retrieving the fin that was still attached to the fish's spine.

"They followed their customs, Caiaphas," the boy said. "They're not used to having prisoners, except in their fishing nets."

"Timothy Cade, you are truly an amazing individual," the navigation mage said as the boy went to work cutting his restraints. "I am honored to be acquainted with you."

Timothy sawed through Caiaphas's ropes in half the time it took him to do his own, now that he could see what he was doing. When he finished, the navigation mage slowly brought his fingers up to look at them.

"Are they broken?" Timothy asked.

Caiaphas nodded. "Some, I'm afraid. I will not be much help to you in this escape."

The music from the village had grown softer, and it seemed to Timothy that the fires burned a little less brightly. They didn't have a moment to spare. If they were going to flee this place, they had to do it at once. Timothy immediately went to work on the door, the fish fin cutting through the rope that held it with ease.

"You go first," he said to Caiaphas as he pushed the door open. "I'll help you down."

The navigator moved toward the door and began to slip over the edge of the cage. Timothy grabbed hold of his wrists, using all his strength to allow the man to gradually lower himself toward the shallow lake water below. When Timothy could hold him no longer, he let go of Caiaphas's wrists and the mage splashed down into the thigh-high water.

They both paused, listening for any sign of alarm from the Lake Dwellers, but there was no response.

"Come on, Timothy," Caiaphas urged, and the boy lowered himself from their hanging prison to land in the cold water beside his friend.

"And now?" Caiaphas asked as they moved up onto the shore.

"We get away from here," Timothy said, sliding into a pocket in his pants the fish fin knife that had given them their freedom.

They ran toward the darkness of the woods. "And once

we are away? Do you have any idea where we should go?"

"I've given that some careful thought," Timothy said as they fled the Lake Dwellers' village.

"We need to find Lord Romulus," he rasped, the very name weighing heavily upon his heart. Finn had told them that the region of Yarrith Forest beyond the Lake Dwellers' encampment was controlled by the Legion Nocturne, but Timothy had hoped they would be flying above it rather than traveling through it on foot.

"The Grandmaster of the Legion Nocturne hates me enough that he may kill me on sight, but I also think he is honest and true to the ideals of Parliament. He may be our only chance of escaping these woods alive."

Timothy was cold and growing colder by the minute.

He and Caiaphas had been walking steadily for hours. He blew warm air into his cupped hands as he followed the navigator, each of them alert to the sounds around them in case they were pursued. They had headed deeper into the Yarrith Forest, walking through the night, moving upward into the colder, mountainous regions in their search for the city that was home to Lord Romulus and the Legion Nocturne.

Caiaphas paused and turned to face him. "Are you well?"

"I'm fine," Timothy said, trying with all his might to keep his teeth from chattering, but not altogether successful. "I'm just cold."

"Here," Caiaphas said, throwing an arm around his

shoulder and pulling him close. "Let me share some of my warmth."

The two started to walk again, more slowly as they continued side by side but still making adequate progress through the dark woods.

"Aren't you the littlest bit cold?" Timothy asked his friend.

Caiaphas pulled him tighter. "Not really," he said. "You must remember, as a navigation mage I must sit out in the cruelty of the elements as I pilot my craft. My body has grown used to the variances in temperature. It is all part of becoming Caiaphas."

"*Becoming* Caiaphas?" Timothy asked. "Isn't Caiaphas your name?"

The navigator stopped walking for a moment, checking their surroundings before continuing. He did this from time to time, verifying that they were indeed moving in the proper direction.

"I gave up my name long ago," he explained to the boy. "To be a true navigation mage—to be Caiaphas—one must renounce one's identity." He pointed to the veil that still covered the lower portion of his face. "It is why we wear the veil. Once the level of Caiaphas is reached within our guild, you are forever and always a navigator, nothing more and nothing less."

Timothy was in awe. There was still so much he didn't know about the world that had become his home. "I had no idea. Did it bother you—to give up your name?"

"To be Caiaphas is a great honor," the navigation mage said, and Timothy could see the hint of a proud smile beneath the blue veil. "I gave away something quite small for something much greater."

The farther they traveled into the higher elevations, the colder it became. Despite Caiaphas's efforts to keep him warm, Timothy found himself growing more and more uncomfortable.

"Do you have any idea how much farther we have to go?" he asked, hugging himself against the bite of the wind whipping through the trees.

"It's hard to say. I'm used to navigating from my perch atop a sky carriage. It's quite different from the ground."

Timothy stamped his feet, attempting to bring some feeling back into his numbed appendages. He wasn't sure how much longer he would be able to go before the cold started to have a genuine effect upon him, but he didn't want to think of such things. They had come too far for him to be brought down by a change in temperature.

"Let's keep going," he told his friend. "I'm warmer when I'm moving."

They talked as they walked, mainly to take their minds off the dropping temperature. They discussed what they would say once they were in the presence of the Nocturne Grandmaster. Lord Romulus despised Timothy. They would need to be extremely convincing if they had any hope of Romulus listening, and not killing them where they stood.

They climbed higher and higher still into the Yarrith mountains, and as if the cold weren't bad enough, a light snow began to fall. He had never experienced winter, but knew that depending on how quickly it fell, snow could prove quite a hindrance.

"Hold on, Timothy," Caiaphas urged. "We must be very close by now."

Timothy wanted to believe him, but fatigue and bitter cold were making it difficult for him to remain confident. The snow began to fall harder and started to collect in the crooks of the tree branches and on the leaves scattered on the ground. He found himself slowing down, his limbs growing heavier with each step they took.

Caiaphas slowed his pace, urging him to continue—to not give up. Gently, he took hold of the boy's arm, with a damaged hand, and helped him along. Timothy was grateful, for he wasn't quite sure if he could have done it without his friend's assistance.

"I've decided that I don't really care for snow," Timothy said over the moan of the wind, and Caiaphas chuckled briefly as they marched on through the accumulating conditions.

Visibility had become nearly nonexistent, and Timothy tried, through squinted eyes, to see where they were going. He prayed silently that they might find a cave or some kind of natural shelter where they might wait out the storm.

Timothy stopped short, attempting to focus through the swirling flakes of frozen rain.

"We must keep moving," Caiaphas yelled over the wailing winds, attempting to pull him along.

The boy pointed to a spot in the distance. "I thought I saw something. Over there, moving through the woods."

Caiaphas looked through the swirling snow in the direction of Timothy's gaze. "I don't see anything. The storm is playing tricks on you. We must keep moving."

And Timothy started to walk again, following Caiaphas—

Right into the path of the creatures advancing on them through the blinding storm.

CHAPTER NINE

They were extremely tall beasts, with four legs and two arms, their bodies covered in heavy fur, horns protruding from the sides of their square heads. The monsters roared as they advanced, and Caiaphas threw himself in front of Timothy to protect him from attack.

"Hold!" bellowed one of the ghastly beasts, and Timothy saw that these were not monsters at all, but armored soldiers on horseback—soldiers of the Legion Nocturne.

"You are trespassing upon the game preserves of Lord Romulus, Grandmaster of the Legion Nocturne," said one of the soldiers from atop his steed, his voice echoing through the metal of the helmet he wore. "A crime that is punishable by death."

The legion drew their weapons; even over the howl of the winds, Timothy could hear the swish of the razor-sharp swords as they were pulled from their scabbards.

"Please," he cried over the winds. "We mean no harm. We've come seeking an audience with your master—with Lord Romulus."

"Audience with the Grandmaster?" one of the soldiers scoffed. "Why would he speak with the likes of you, lad?"

Timothy moved closer so that he could be seen better. "This is Caiaphas, navigator for the Grandmaster of the Order of Alhazred, and I am Timothy Cade—the Un-Magician." He hated to use the insulting title, but it was one that had stuck with him, whether he liked it or not.

"Timothy Cade?" a soldier asked, glancing around at his brethren.

"He says that he is the Un-Magician," said another.

The lead soldier moved his horse closer to the boy, the animal's large head mere inches from Timothy's face.

"If you are lying to us, boy," he growled, "we'll feed you both to our horses."

The great beast snorted, and Timothy felt the warmth of its powerful exhalation on his face, but he did not flinch or move away.

"I'm telling the truth," he said. "I *am* Timothy Cade, and I need to speak with Romulus right away. Lives depend upon it."

"Yes," said one of the soldiers, grinning. "Yours."

With those words, the horsemen reared back upon their powerful steeds and began to turn. All save two of them, who spurred their mounts toward Timothy and Caiaphas. They had no chance to react, never mind object, as powerful arms pulled them up to sit behind the two riders. They were forced to hold on for dear life as they galloped at a break-neck pace through the woods.

The storm seemed to be lightening a bit, and from his place at the back of the steed he saw Lord Romulus's city coming into view in the distance.

Caiaphas was right, he thought. They hadn't been that far away, but the question still remained: Would they have made it to their destination in the snowstorm? Timothy wasn't sure, but he was grateful that Lord Romulus's guards had stumbled across them when they had.

He had heard the name of Romulus's city mentioned once or twice before, and searched his mind for it as the place came more clearly into view. It was awesome to behold, a vast, sprawling empire, seemingly built onto the side of a mountain. From what he could discern, the structures were made entirely from stone, yellow lights burning in many of the windows, and Timothy wondered if they were lanterns of ghostfire that he was seeing. And then he remembered the city's name.

Twilight.

Up a winding path toward an enormous stone bridge that spanned a yawning chasm, they rode, galloping toward the great gates that began to open wide in welcome for the patrol's return.

The horses came to a sudden stop in a courtyard, multiple sentries all adorned in fur and armor converging on them.

"Inform Lord Romulus that we have brought Timothy

Cade, the Un-Magician, and that he requests an audience," the captain of the patrol proclaimed.

Two of the sentries bowed their heads and were gone in a flash with the message. Timothy was helped down from the steed by the captain, and directed toward a large door in the face of an imposing structure of gleaming black stone.

"That way," the captain of the guard said, placing a gauntleted hand against the back of his head and pushing. Timothy turned to scowl at the man.

"Lord Romulus hates to be kept waiting," the soldier said. "And if you are who you claim to be, he will be most anxious to speak with you."

Caiaphas joined him, and the two walked toward the impressive door, which swung open as they approached. There was another armored guard waiting on the other side, and he directed them down a long passage with the point of his sword. The Legion Nocturne was rare among the guilds of Parliament in that they forged their own weapons and hunted without magic. It was their tradition. Somehow Timothy felt he understood them more than he did other guilds, and yet he feared them more as well.

Timothy had started to regain the feeling in his feet and hands, and despite the uncertainty of their situation, was quite pleased to be out of the cold. At the end of the stone passage, another sentry awaited them. The man was huge, clad in heavy armor, and he stood with such unwavering attentiveness that he could have been some sort of intricate sculpture.

"Who seeks passage into the chambers of the lord and master of the Legion Nocturne?" the guard growled, his booming voice reverberating off the walls of the stone passage in which they stood.

"Timothy Cade and Caiaphas," he answered nervously, uncertain if the fearsome sentry would allow them entry.

The armored sentinel turned his awesome bulk to face the metal studded door. He raised a gauntleted fist and pounded three times upon it.

THOOM! THOOM! THOOM!

"Who seeks passage into my chambers?" came an equally fearsome voice from the other side of the door.

"It is Timothy Cade and a Caiaphas," the guard said.

There was silence that seemed to last for an eternity, and then at last the reply came.

"Grant them access," the voice on the other side proclaimed, and the sentry pushed open the great door with a grunt and bid them enter the hall beyond.

"He is waiting," the sentry said as they stepped into the room, and he closed the door behind them.

The room was huge. Its wood-beamed ceiling was at least thirty feet above Timothy's head. On every exposed inch of wall there hung the head of an animal, many of them with large, curved horns. He presumed they were local creatures from the forest of Yarrith.

An enormous fireplace, constructed to form the face of a fearsome, screaming beast, stood across the room, a fire roaring in its maw. Timothy could feel the comforting warmth of the flames and had to fight the urge to lie down on the floor and go to sleep.

"It *is* you," said a voice from the other side of the room, and he and Caiaphas turned to see the grim visage of Lord Romulus. The mage stood up from a large, high-backed chair that could very well have been considered a throne.

Timothy had forgotten how large the Nocturne Grandmaster was. He was even bigger than the sentry that had allowed them access into the room, and Timothy had thought that man gigantic. Lord Romulus was nearly nine feet tall, and three and a half feet broad at the shoulders. He was clad in armor of gleaming black, a cape of gray fur hanging from his broad shoulders to the ground. Upon his head was the ever-present helmet that concealed all the man's features except for his eyes.

The Grandmaster came toward them, crossing the great room in three strides.

"How dare you come here?" Lord Romulus growled. "To my forest—to my home?"

Caiaphas stepped forward as if to shield Timothy from his wrath. "Greetings and many thanks to you, my Lord," he said with a slow bow of his head. "Your hospitality is greatly appreciated this cold and stormy day."

"I should have let the storm take you," Lord Romulus snarled, looking past the navigator to glare at Timothy. "Should have let it take you both."

Timothy guessed that the Grandmaster of the Legion Nocturne was still a bit upset from the last time they had seen each other. The boy had used his unique ability to cancel out the Grandmaster's magic in front of the entire Parliament of Mages. It had been completely necessary, but Timothy could understand why Romulus was still perturbed.

"But you didn't," Timothy said, stepping up to stand beside Caiaphas. "And for that, we thank you—*I* thank you with all my heart." He placed a hand, still trembling from the cold, upon his chest.

Romulus said nothing, choosing to only growl before abruptly turning away from them to pace about the great room.

"I have heard recent reports that you were missing and presumed to be dead," the Grandmaster said. He spun around again to face them, his eyes blazing from within his horned helmet. "How easy it would be—and, might I add, quite pleasurable—to make those reports a reality."

Timothy said nothing, depending on his faith that Romulus was primarily an honorable man and not a murderous monster like Nicodemus and Constable Grimshaw.

"Why do you continue to plague me, boy?" the massive warrior asked, clenching and unclenching his powerful hands, which were covered in studded black gloves. "The world has changed far too much since you have been in it—and there is nothing I'd like more than to forget that you exist."

Timothy swallowed hard before speaking. "We've come to ask for your help."

Romulus laughed, but there was little humor in it. "You're asking *me* to help *you*?"

"Not only for ourselves, but for Parliament, and quite possibly for all of Terra, as well."

The Grandmaster tilted his helmeted head to one side quizzically. "What nonsense are you speaking, Cade?"

"It's not nonsense," Timothy said. "Doubtless you're aware of the expedition to Tora'nah, and the efforts of Parliament to mine Malleum from the ground there to make unbreakable armor and weapons, to prepare for an invasion from Draconae."

"An invasion I am still unconvinced will ever come," Romulus scoffed.

Timothy sighed. "You say that, but I don't believe you mean it. You have seen Verlis and his family, his clan. You have heard the stories of the violence and oppression on Draconae, and the evil of Raptus. The Wurm on Draconae are working tirelessly to tear down Alhazred's Divide, and they mean to slaughter all of Parliament as well as all of their kin who escaped their tyranny. Like it or not, Lord Romulus, you and Verlis share the same enemy.

"Regardless, at the moment, there is another enemy who threatens us all. While in Tora'nah, Grandmaster Maddox fell ill. Days ago Caiaphas and I were transporting him back to Arcanum. He had been behaving . . . strangely. Belligerently. And then he fell ill. But on the journey home, he tried to kill us."

Romulus pulled his fur cloak tighter about his body as he moved closer. "Maddox tried to kill *you*?"

"I believe it was Leander in body only. It was as if he was

no longer in control of himself—almost as if something had taken possession of him." The memory of the horrible event chilled him more than the storm raging outside Twilight.

Romulus grew silent, moving past them to return to his great seat. "Sit by me," he instructed them, gesturing to pillows that had been laid upon the floor in front of the chair.

Timothy and Caiaphas complied instantly. The boy was weak with relief at the realization that Lord Romulus might hate him, but did not consider him a liar.

"Obviously you escaped," Lord Romulus continued as he lowered his massive, armored body into the chair.

"Barely," Timothy said, making himself comfortable upon the cushions. His ribs still ached, but the pain was starting to lessen. The scratches on his cheek had stung him before the cold weather had numbed his face. Now the warmth of the fire reminded him of the claws of Alastor. He realized how extremely tired he was, his body overjoyed by the opportunity to sit. "We were thrown from our sky carriage into the Yarrith Forest, and were lucky not to be killed."

"That was days ago. Where have you been since then?" Romulus asked. There was a bronze goblet and pitcher upon a pedestal by the Grandmaster's chair and he helped himself to some refreshment. This served only to remind Timothy how long it had been since they'd last had any food or drink.

"We spent some time with the Children of Karthagia," he explained.

"Truly?" Romulus asked, taking a sip of his drink. "The Children usually do not concern themselves with matters that occur outside their ziggurats. How did they react to your tale of impending doom?"

Timothy's stomach growled noisily. "Excuse me," he said, embarrassed, before continuing. "We did not yet know the extent of this danger, for we had yet to be attacked by Constable Grimshaw and his monstrous beast."

Romulus paused mid drink. "Constable Grimshaw?" he said. "But he has been reported missing, included amongst the mages no one can seem to locate."

"Exactly," Timothy said. "He and the Lake Dwellers—who we mistakenly believed might help us get back to Arcanum—held us captive by the command of . . ." He paused, reluctant to continue for fear that he would not be believed.

Lord Romulus leaned forward on his seat, setting his goblet down on the side table. The red eyes within his helmet seemed to glow brightly in the ghostfire light. "Under whose command?"

Timothy glanced at Caiaphas, not certain if he should continue. But the navigation mage nodded, urging him on. The boy took a deep breath.

"As impossible as it seems, we heard them speak of Alhazred."

The Grandmaster of the Legion Nocturne rose quickly from his chair. "Alhazred?" he questioned. "Are you certain that you heard correctly?"

"I heard the name spoken as well," Caiaphas announced. "It is indeed Alhazred that Constable Grimshaw and the Lake Dwellers serve."

Romulus began to breathe deeply, as though a fire of rage burned within him. He sounded to Timothy like one of the horses his forest soldiers rode. The mage strode away from them, his fur cape flowing behind him. "How is this possible?" he muttered beneath his breath.

Then he paused and nodded slowly. "And yet, it would explain so much of the recent troubles in Arcanum."

Timothy stood up from the pillow and approached the enormous mage. "You believe us?"

Romulus looked down upon the boy with burning eyes. "Though it pains me to side with the likes of you, in light of recent events I am left with little alternative."

Timothy actually found himself smiling at the fearsome countenance of Lord Romulus. "Then you'll help us?"

"You will stay here tonight in my great hall and know the hospitality of the Legion Nocturne. In the morning you will be given horses to make your way back to Arcanum."

And with those words, the Grandmaster abruptly turned and strode toward the room's exit. "But now, I must think upon what you have told me, and ponder the fate of my people, my guild, and quite possibly my world."

Blending with the surroundings of SkyHaven's vast hallways and corridors, Ivar searched for further evidence of the evil that Leander Maddox had accidentally uncovered. The servants and employees of this vast, floating fortress went about their business, totally unaware that he was among them. He listened to their whispered gossip, and watched as some shirked their responsibilities when they believed themselves to be truly alone.

Ivar imagined the look of absolute terror that would have appeared on their faces if he had allowed himself to be seen. But he would not allow this to occur. Cassandra had entrusted him with this most important mission, and he did not wish to disappoint the young Grandmaster in training.

In the raving of his illness, Leander said that he had been researching Torah'nah, when he had found something—something evil. Now Ivar moved down a darkened corridor toward a storage compartment where older records and documents pertaining to the business of Parliament were stored. He was certain that Leander would have looked here for the sort of information that he had sought.

The Asura stood before the large door, sealed tight by a spell of security. First making sure that he was alone, Ivar willed the hue of his skin back to normal. Cassandra had expected that in investigating Leander's mad ramblings, he would need access to places that normally would be forbidden to him. Individual locks required specific spells to open them, but Cassandra had given Ivar a spell of opening that would act as a key to override whatever magical locks he might encounter.

Ivar looked at his palm, where the young girl had drawn

the symbols that made up the spell. He held his hand out to a magical orb that was built into the frame, and the door slid slowly open to grant him access.

The Asura had found himself growing fond of Cassandra Nicodemus, seeing in her a chance that the future generation of mages could actually learn from the mistakes of the past. He liked the fact that she seemed to have a special fondness for Timothy, and he for her.

Timothy. There was still no word on whether his young friend had survived the attack upon their sky carriage. With the thought of the boy heavy on his mind, Ivar entered the storage room. The door to the large room closed, and lanterns of ghostfire immediately were illuminated. Ivar gazed about the vast chamber at the multiple shelves that adorned every wall. Upon each of the shelves were boxes within which countless scrolls and documents were stored.

Ivar carefully moved through the room, extending his finely attuned senses to seek anything that seemed out of the norm. The room smelled of ancient parchment but, for the briefest of moments, he caught the scent of something else. He prowled toward the back of the chamber, seeking out the odd aroma that now sought to elude him. He was certain that he had smelled it, a scent that did not belong. Ivar shut his eyes. To someone other than an Asura, the scent would have gone completely unnoticed. He imagined his senses as a kind of net, cast upon the still waters of the room. He did not know how long he stood there, eyes closed, but he had almost begun to believe that he might have been mistaken when he found it again.

This time he held on to the scent, following it.

Ivar found himself standing before a particular bookcase in a darkened corner. The bookcase was huge, made from heavy timber, and pressed flat against the far wall. *The smell originated here,* he thought as he eyed the shelving unit. He carefully examined the floor around it and found scrapes there. Something heavy had been moved across the floor. He crouched lower to the ground at the base of the bookshelves and felt the slightest draft from beneath them.

There is something beyond this wall. He ran his hands along the shelves, searching for access.

There came a sudden *click* as his hand passed over a decorative engraving in the wood. At first he was unsure what he had done, but then he remembered the spell that Cassandra had drawn upon the palm of his hand. The unlocking spell had worked upon the enchantments that kept the heavy shelving unit attached to the wall, concealing what was hidden behind it.

He leaped back as the storage unit swung away from the wall, scraping along the floor, to reveal a doorway. Carefully the Asura approached it, peering down through the darkness at a winding staircase that descended deeper into the bowels of SkyHaven. His hand went to the knife that he wore in a sheath attached to his belt, just to be certain it was still there, in case it was needed.

As Ivar began his descent, a faint breeze was kicked up

from somewhere below and he again caught the scent that had aroused his suspicions before.

The scent of death.

Timothy held tightly to the reins of his mount, the powerful animal beneath him trotting along through the freshly fallen snow.

The cold morning air felt good in his lungs, clearing away the last vestiges of the previous night's deathlike slumber. He could not recall a time when he had slept so deeply, certain that it had much to do with what he had been put through since falling from the sky carriage into the forests of Yarrith.

He and Caiaphas had been escorted for a time by a patrol of Lord Romulus's best horsemen, but had been left to go it alone once they were past the Legion Nocturne's borders.

Yarrith Forest was incredibly beautiful covered in snow, and he could appreciate it more now that he was dressed more appropriately for the chilling weather. Romulus had ordered that they both be given more suitable dress for traveling upon horseback.

He had never ridden a horse before, but found it quite pleasant, almost relaxing. It helped him to forget, just for the moment, the problems that would be facing them once they at last returned to Arcanum.

"How are you doing back there?" Caiaphas called to him. His horse was a beautiful animal, the color of night, while Timothy's was pure white, blending with the snow.

The boy reached down and patted the animal. "We're doing just fine."

"It has been quite a journey, hasn't it, Timothy?"

"It certainly has," Timothy said, but deep down he knew that the troubled journey was far from over.

The farther they descended from the mountainous elevations, the warmer it became, and Timothy found himself becoming increasingly uncomfortable in his new heavy clothing. He fumbled with a clasp at his throat to remove the cloak draped over his shoulders.

"Could we stop for a moment, Caiaphas?" he called, pulling back the reins on his mount.

The navigator stopped his horse as well, turning it around to face him. "Do you need some help with that?" he asked good-naturedly, watching as the boy attempted to unfasten the clasp with little success.

"Perhaps you have a special spell for uncooperative clasps," Timothy suggested with a smile. Twilight's healers had been in to visit the navigator after their hearty meal of stew and bread, just before they had retired for the evening in front of the great roaring fireplace. Caiaphas's hands now looked as good as new. It was unfortunate that the magic they could cast would not have any effect on him, or his troublesome cloak clasp.

"Here, perhaps I can help," Caiaphas said, urging his horse closer to the boy's.

A crackling bolt of pure magical force descended from the sky and struck the navigation mage, hurling him from his mount.

"Caiaphas!" Timothy screamed, jumping down from his horse to go to his friend.

The navigator lay upon the damp forest floor, his body twitching uncontrollably as the punishing spell coursed through him like snake venom. Timothy laid his palm where Caiaphas had been struck to disrupt the spell, and immediately felt the navigator begin to calm.

Maniacal laughter filled the air, and Timothy looked skyward through the canopy of trees to see Constable Grimshaw hanging there, shimmering supernatural energies keeping him aloft.

"Why won't you leave us alone?" Timothy shrieked, his fists clenched in rage.

"And here I was thinking that you were a smart boy," the Constable said, drifting to the ground. "Isn't it obvious? We hate you—hate you for what you are, and for what you've done to us."

Timothy heard the rustling of leaves behind him and spun to face the most horrific of sights.

"Isn't that right, Alastor?" Grimshaw asked his monstrous companion.

He didn't believe it was possible, but somehow the cat had changed even further since the last time Timothy had seen it. It had become even more manlike. The cat-creature was even bigger than before, and was now walking erect upon its hind legs. It padded toward him, clawed hands extended.

Timothy stared into the face of the animal and again was

struck with an awful sense of familiarity. What was it about this horrific creature that struck a nerve, making him look upon the beast as something more than animal?

And then it tried to speak, the words coming from its fanged mouth in a growling slur.

"Hate . . . you," it spat, saliva dripping from its open maw.

And Timothy understood why the monster seemed so familiar. He saw it in the cat-creature's eyes, and in the shape of its face. Timothy Cade knew that face, though the one who had worn it was dead. Or so he had thought. Now, staring into the advancing beast's hateful yellow eyes, he knew that he had been wrong.

"Know me . . . Cade?" it asked him, a hideous smile stretching its animalistic features.

And the boy did know him.

"Nicodemus," Timothy said in a whisper of equal parts fear and utter revulsion. "But how?"

CHAPTER TEN

The stairwell wound down into the heart of Sky-Haven, dug out of the earth and stone. The passageway that led to the stairs had been hidden—a secret—and Ivar realized he had discovered something that had been kept from the residents of SkyHaven.

Most of them, at least.

Leander Maddox had discovered that secret passage, these hidden stairs, and whatever lay below, and given his mad ramblings to Cassandra, it seemed that encounter had altered him somehow. Poisoned him. Ivar worried what might have happened to Timothy and Caiaphas because of Leander's discovery, but at the moment he knew he must focus on the secrets of the Order. Perhaps whatever truths he found could be used to help his friends.

The stairwell was dark, but a dim glow shimmered from below and gleamed dully on the stone walls of the spiral stairwell. He slid his fingers along the stone and was surprised to find how dry the walls were. Dry as bone. Ivar had senses far more acute than an ordinary mage. He was upset that he had not felt the presence of these secret passages previously. Now that he was within them, however, it was simple for him to use those enhanced senses to gather information about his location. Perhaps one hundred feet below him was the bottom of the floating island. At the core of SkyHaven was the conference room where Timothy had first encountered the Grandmasters that Nicodemus had gathered to meet him. The aerie, he believed it was called.

This secret segment of the fortress must have been separated only by a few feet of stone and earth from the more familiar depths of SkyHaven and yet had remained unknown. The hidden stairs were on the eastern side of the floating island, farthest from the shores of Arcanum.

No sound came from below. The passages had been built to be truly private. If Ivar was forced to call for help, no one in SkyHaven would be able to hear him. In the darkness he shifted the hue of his skin to match the gray of the stone walls and continued to descend.

The flickering of light upon the walls grew stronger as he wound around and around down those stairs. When the illumination grew so bright that he knew a few more steps would take him into full light, he paused and pressed himself to the dry stone. Ivar was not afraid, but he knew he must be cautious because so much depended upon his remaining hidden and returning to Cassandra with news of this place.

Carefully and silently he descended farther. The fourth step down took him into view of a ghostfire lamp that sat in a sconce jutting from the wall. Ivar narrowed his eyes and peered into the gloom beyond the light, searching for any sign of motion on the stairs, then continued on, his flesh still the hue of the stone. The Asura knew he was invisible to any observer, even in the light.

And yet . . . he felt as he descended that someone had noticed him, that there were eyes upon him even now.

Ivar frowned and paused upon those stone steps, and though he feared nothing, a shudder went through him. He turned and glanced back up the curve of the stairwell, but no one was there. His gaze fell upon the wall sconce and the ghostfire that burned in the lamp there. It trembled. In the flames, for just a moment, he thought he saw a face, eyes watching him.

His every muscle tensed as he dropped into a battle stance. He stared at the ghostfire for a long moment and saw no further sign of that face. The Asura wondered for a moment if he had imagined it, but knew he had not. What it meant, he did not know. But he was even more cautious as he continued down those spiral stairs. His flesh tingled, every nerve ending ready to react to an attack.

Ivar passed beneath two other ghostfire lamps before coming to the bottom of the stairs, where a tall wooden door blocked further progress. There was a sphere of ghostfire on either side of the door. He eyed each globe carefully, wondering what magic had allowed that strange observer to peer out at him before. But he saw nothing out of the ordinary.

He pushed the door open.

As he did, a dozen spheres floating around the room blossomed into light, illuminating a small chamber that reminded him instantly of Timothy's workshop. There were shelves and benches and long worktables. Yet as Ivar blinked his eyes against the brightness of the ghostfire, he saw that the instruments arrayed throughout the chamber were those of magic, not mechanical invention. On the shelves were jars of herbs, the dried skulls and organs of animals, rolled parchments and grimoires, and strange artifacts that Ivar was sure ought to have been in the archive room high in the fortress, where the Grandmaster of the Order was supposed to store such things. The Oracle of Vijaya was there, along with myriad talismans and objects of power.

This was a wizard's laboratory. Yet the Wizards of Old had long since died out, and only the mages that had descended from them remained. Practicing magic in such secrecy was outlawed by the Parliament of Mages. Guilds often kept their magical research, practices, and rituals to themselves, but within each Order, secrecy was not allowed. In this way, the Parliament hoped to prevent the rise of renegades who practiced the darkest magic.

Ivar took a step backward. His discovery of the room was

enough. Someone in SkyHaven was practicing magic in secret—likely black sorcery that would cause the culprit to be turned over to the constabulary and imprisoned in Abaddon.

He paused. With all of the clutter in the wizard's laboratory, he had only just noticed the strange metal frames on the table. Frowning, the Asura slipped into the chamber and went to the table, picking up one of the frames. It was the base of a ghostfire lamp.

The metal was cold to the touch. Far colder than it ought to have been, given the temperature in the chamber. Holding that metal lamp base in his hand, he glanced around once more. Another table, this one shoved into a shadowy corner, drew his attention.

The Asura sniffed the air, and a ripple of alarm went through him. *Death.* He had smelled it before, but now the scent was stronger. Ivar strode to the table in the corner and paused there, looking with horror upon the remains of an enormous lizard whose body had been dissected upon the wood. Other animals there were as well, dead and withered things. And against the wall, at the table's edge, a human head.

Ivar's nostrils flared. He glanced round once more, looking at the open door and at the spheres of ghostfire. Again he felt the sensation of being observed, of eyes upon him. The head was barely more than a skull, only dry skin pulled tight over bone, and a few wisps of hair. But he was sure that this man—if indeed it had been a man—had been experimented upon just as surely as the lizard and other dead animals upon the table.

Horrifying. And yet . . . and yet . . . the scent of death was not only here in this chamber, but elsewhere as well. Ivar frowned. Elsewhere. Farther below, to be precise.

Only then did he see the opening in the wall at the back of the chamber. It was to one side, cut into the stone so that with the brightness of the light, it would seem only a shadow. Instead, it was a passage.

Ivar paused only a moment. He ought to have gone back, he knew, and told Cassandra. But the scent of death and the presence of that decapitated head drew him on. He wanted to know the identity of the monster who had used this chamber as his magical laboratory. Careful to maintain the hue of his skin, to blend with his surroundings as best he could, Ivar moved to that passage and peered within.

Stairs.

He started downward, the wall curving once more, but after only two dozen steps, he came to a chamber so vast, it gave him pause. There was a strong draft within, cold air that slid over his skin as though it might seize him at any moment. This room must have taken up all of the available space in the base of the island, so that the outer, earthen wall of SkyHaven's undercarriage was little more than a hollow shell.

Ivar stepped inside.

There must have been a thousand ghostfire spheres, and hundreds of lamps as well, bolted to the walls all around that vast chamber. They flared to life, and Ivar brought up both hands to cover his eyes, so bright was their blaze. For a moment his control over his skin lapsed, his concentration slipping, and he felt the sensation of heat that always accompanied a shift in the hue of his flesh. The markings of his tribe appeared on his skin in dark black, controlled by his power over his flesh but on so deeply a subconscious level that no distraction could remove them.

Eyes narrowed, he peeked out from beneath his hands, blinking away the glare.

There were bodies strewn across the floor.

Ivar rushed to the nearest mage, a woman who wore the vestments of the Order of Molochai. Her skin was dry, almost scaly—as though all of the moisture had been drained from her. He felt for her pulse but knew what he would find. Her flesh was cold.

The mage was dead.

They were all dead.

How many mages had been reported missing in Arcanum in recent months? Ivar felt certain he had found them. The stench of so much death ought to have been overpowering, and yet instead there seemed to be only that unsettling odor he had caught before, an unsettling aroma like that of damp, moldy paper.

He withdrew slowly from the corpse, hot beneath the glare of so many ghostfire flames. Time to return to the halls of SkyHaven above, to find Cassandra and reveal to her the horrid secrets that lay below.

Ivar turned back the way he had come.

In the darkness of the stairwell, just outside the entrance to the vast chamber, someone waited, cloaked in shadows.

A man's voice echoed through the room. "Filthy savage."

The corridors of the Xerxis echoed with the thunderous footfalls of Lord Romulus. The Grandmaster had ridden with speed gifted by magic into the heart of the city of Arcanum, and dismounted his enormous horse in the shadow of the spire of the Xerxis, the headquarters of the Parliament of Mages. Breathing heavily, snorting much like his horse, he stormed the doors of the Xerxis. It was well that the sentries had swung the doors open before him, for the massive mage would have battered them down otherwise.

The gigantic Lord Romulus had to stoop slightly to walk through the arched doorways of the Xerxis, and even still the horns of his iron helmet scraped the frames as he passed through. The fur that was slung across his back flapped behind him as he hurried along a corridor toward the quarters of Alethea Borgia, the Voice of Parliament.

"Lord Romulus, please," called a sentry who had given chase from the moment he had entered the complex. He was a young mage with unpleasant features that made him seem rough, but a manner that belied the grimness of his face. He looked like a warrior, but whimpered like a coward.

"My Lord, Grandmaster or not, I cannot allow you to go any farther into the Xerxis without an appointment. You're entering the residential wing and—"

Romulus stopped so suddenly, the ugly man collided with his back. He rounded on the sentry, glowering down at him. He stood at least half again as high as the whining guard.

"My business is urgent enough, youngster, that I might break you with my bare hands if you delay me a moment longer."

The sentry's lip actually quivered. Lord Romulus almost shattered some of his bones for that alone.

"Yes, My Lord, it's only that no one is allowed—"

"There is too much at stake here for me to wait for an invitation."

Romulus's armor clanked and his horns scraped the ceiling loudly as he turned again. His footfalls shook the floor. The sentry continued to pursue him but no longer attempted to halt his progress. At the end of the corridor there was a grand staircase carved of wood. He pounded up those steps three at a time.

At the top he looked first left, and then right. There were doors in either direction, the quarters of some of the Parliamentary ministers. But only one of those doors was guarded by a quartet of combat mages from the Order of Tantrus, of which Alethea Borgia was Grandmaster. She was the wisest woman Romulus had ever met, and the highest authority in Parliament—the highest authority on all of Terra.

He turned right and started down the corridor toward the Tantric guards. The sentries began to shout at one another, all of them turning toward him with their hands up, magic sparking and spiraling around them. Their hands came up. Three of them formed weapons from pure magical energy, a sword and a spear. The fourth wore a black veil over her face, and now she tore it away. Where her eyes ought to have been, dark purple magic churned and danced like flames.

It was this woman, with the magic pouring from her eyes, who stepped past the others and held up a hand to stop him.

"Halt!" she snapped.

"I shall not," thundered Romulus, though he did pause ten feet away from them, glaring down upon them. "I am Grandmaster of the Legion Nocturne and I demand an audience with the Voice of Parliament. A crisis has arisen and she must learn of it immediately!"

The Tantric mages moved to form a half circle around him. The mage with the purple flames burning in her eyes remained in front of Alethea Borgia's door.

"You are known to us, Lord Romulus," the woman declared, her voice carrying along the corridor, fingers of purple fire emerging from her eyes like tentacles . . . or like serpents, swaying cautiously, waiting to attack. "But for the safety of the Voice, no one may enter her personal chambers without an appointment. You must follow the same rules as any other mage. Even a Grandmaster must do this. Others know this, and follow this protocol."

Fury raged in Romulus's heart, laced with suspicion. "Others? What others?"

The fire-eyed mage frowned. "It is hardly your place to—"

From within the chambers of the Voice there came a scream. The four Tantric mages spun and stared at the door.

"Blast you!" Lord Romulus roared. "Who is in there with her?"

The purple magic that snaked from her eyes receded to embers as she turned to him again. "Grandmaster Maddox of the Order of—"

"Out of my way!" Romulus bellowed.

As he shoved them aside, none of the sentries fought him. Magic roiled around his right hand as he clutched it into a fist, crimson light spilling out of his palm and enveloping his entire hand. The door would be sealed with magic. But Romulus had the strength in his muscle and bone of three men, and the magic of three mages, at least when it came to the sorcery of brute force. He brought his fist down like a hammer, streamers of red energy spilling off of it, and the door exploded inward, shattering into several pieces as it crashed to the floor.

Romulus had always thought Alethea Borgia was a beautiful woman, despite her advancing age. She was slender and silver-haired and had perfectly sculpted features.

Now, though, the Voice lay crumpled on the floor of her quarters, eyelids fluttering as she struggled to remain conscious. Her nose was broken, blood streaming from both nostrils, and she gagged loudly, and her hands batted the air as she tried to break the tendrils of night-black magic that encircled her throat, strangling her.

Silhouetted in the sunlight that spilled in through the tall, arched windows across the room, Leander Maddox stood grinning like a madman. When the door crashed inward and he saw Romulus and the Tantric combat mages rush in, he laughed. His face was utterly pale, and his eyes were as black as the ebony magic that he wielded in both hands.

And still, though they had caught him in the act of murder, he laughed.

Romulus roared. His hands swept up and, even as they did, a spell was upon his lips. Uttering words of a language spoken only in the deep forest by the Legion Nocturne, he crafted a battle-ax of pure magic, and minor spells dripped off of it like venom. The comparison was accurate. Its blade would poison anyone it cut.

Maddox looked sickly, even weak, but there was no weakness in that laugh, or in the magic that erupted from him like blood from a mortal wound.

"Leave her be!" Lord Romulus shouted.

With both hands above his head, he threw the ax. It turned end over end, spinning toward Maddox's face, toward those pitch-black eyes. At the last moment, Leander's head turned at an impossible angle and he grinned. Shimmering black light spread from his eyes and into a shield. The ax struck that magical defense, and was deflected.

"No!" Romulus barked, and he reached out a hand to summon the ax back to him.

"I think not," Maddox said.

But Lord Romulus knew Leander Maddox. The voice that issued from his mouth was not that of the man he knew, not that of the professor he had once respected. It was a voice that chilled him to the bone.

Maddox raised both hands. The tendrils that had been strangling Alethea dissipated into a dark mist, and then were gone altogether. The Tantric mage whose eyes were purple fire rushed past Romulus, shouting a spell that caused the air in the room to ripple with the power that was about to be unleashed.

The ax Lord Romulus had wrought rose into the air, controlled now by Leander Maddox, and flew at her. It struck her in the chest and she dropped, dead, to the floor.

Romulus screamed and ran at Maddox, forgetting about magic entirely now. The massive mage, whose size dwarfed even the burly Leander, curled his huge hands into devastating fists.

Maddox turned as night-black as the magic he had wielded, and then dissolved into mist. In a moment he was gone, as though he had never been there, and Lord Romulus was left with nothing to strike but the air.

Behind him he heard Alethea Borgia coughing, trying to speak. The Voice would live. He had arrived in time, or so it seemed. But the Grandmaster of the Legion Nocturne would not rest until Leander Maddox was dead.

Alastor hissed, baring its fangs as it leaped at Timothy. In that moment, the boy was more terrified and more confused than he had ever been in his life. Alastor had been Nicodemus's familiar, and when the Grandmaster had been destroyed, the cat had disappeared. Run off. But, somehow, Nicodemus—his soul, at least—was inside the cat, warping it, transforming it into a monster.

The creature slashed the air with its claws as it jumped up at Timothy, who was still seated atop his horse. The boy stopped breathing. Overwhelmed, he could not think to defend himself. He only stared, eyes wide, as those claws sliced down toward his face.

"*Cawwww! Cawwww!*"

Out of the corner of his eye, Timothy saw a swatch of darkness blotting out the sunlight. He heard the heavy flap of wings beating the air. The rook cawed loudly again, and long, almost like a war cry, and darted down from the trees above to come between the boy and the monstrous cat-creature.

The bird spread his wings wide, slowing as he struck the cat-creature. The rook raked his talons across Alastor's hideous face, dragging gory furrows into the cat-creature's flesh. The monster shrieked in pain and arched its back, twisting away from the attacking bird and dropping to all fours on the forest floor.

"Edgar!" Timothy cried happily. He did not know how his familiar had found him, but was thrilled to see the rook again.

"Back off from the kid, kitten, or I rip your eyeballs out!" Edgar said, and he circled around Timothy and then began to dive at the creature again.

The creature—half Alastor and half Nicodemus—hissed and sat up on its hind legs, claws up and ready to fight the bird.

"Oh no, you don't," Timothy said. He snapped the reins on his horse and the steed trotted forward. The fear that he had felt moments before drove the boy onward. His heart pounded and he knew he never wanted to be that afraid, never wanted to be that close to death again. He kicked the horse's flanks, intending to trample the cat creature beneath the animal's hooves. The thing was a freak of nature. An abomination . . .

Then he heard those words in his mind: *Freak. Abomination.* And he remembered them being used to describe him. Timothy pulled up on the reins as the cat creature's eyes widened and it realized it was about to be pummeled and broken beneath the horse's hooves. In that instant of hesitation, with those bloody scratches down its face, it took the opportunity to dart into the woods and disappear into the trees.

"Yeah!" Edgar cawed, flapping his wings, flying higher to peer into the woods in case it should double back. "You should run. And keep running, kitten, or I'll have your whiskers!"

But Timothy was no longer worried about Nicodemus. The cat-creature was gone. Edgar would guard against its return. The boy pulled up the reins again and turned the horse to see Caiaphas scrambling to his feet. Constable Grimshaw had attacked him, and the navigator's horse had bolted. Caiaphas had nowhere to run.

Grimshaw's clothes were torn and filthy and his hair was matted. His eyes were insane. But the Constable smoothed his mustache in that familiar way and grinned as he strode toward Caiaphas. Timothy could not see the navigation mage's features beneath his veil, but his eyes alone revealed his terror.

"Where will you go, fool?" Grimshaw snarled.

The last time they had clashed, Timothy had watched in horror as Verlis had bitten Grimshaw's arm off. But whatever black magic had wrought the Constable, a new arm was even more horrifying. The solid magic that had replaced his arm pulsed pink and white now, changing shape. What had been a tentacle now at least *looked* like an arm. Grimshaw thrust out a hand, and that magical arm erupted in pink-white lightning, a dozen bolts of sizzling power that spread out into a kind of cage that dropped down over Caiaphas. Where it struck the navigator's skin, it burned him, and Caiaphas shouted in pain and fell to his knees again.

"Caw! Leave him alone, you lunatic!" Edgar shouted as he darted through the air toward Grimshaw.

The Constable shot out his good hand, and a bright red light arced from his fingertips and struck Edgar. The rook cried out as the magic threw him back with such force that in an instant he had disappeared among the trees, several black feathers floating to the ground.

"No!" Timothy called.

Grimshaw laughed and started walking toward Caiaphas.

In his remaining hand, his good hand, the Constable summoned another spell. Dark magic churned there, black and red mixing together. Timothy had no idea what evil enchantment he was about to cast at Caiaphas, but did not want to find out.

Timothy shouted, imitating the riders he had heard among the Legion Nocturne. He kicked the horse's flanks again and held on to the reins, standing up in the stirrups as the steed thundered toward Grimshaw.

The Constable was so focused on murdering Caiaphas that it took him a moment too long to realize what was happening. He spun just as Timothy and his mount bore down on him.

But the boy had no intention of trampling Grimshaw.

Timothy drew one foot up onto the saddle, braced himself, and then sprang from the back of the horse. The animal's momentum propelled him at Grimshaw with incredible force. He collided with the Constable, wrapping his arms around the man and dragging him into a tumble of limbs on the ground. The instant they made contact, his arm and the cage around Caiaphas disappeared.

Grimshaw cried out in fury and then grunted in pain as they struck the ground. He flailed with his remaining hand, trying to pry Timothy loose, to get away from him, but the boy held on. He had wrestled and sparred with Ivar hundreds of times growing up. The Asura had taught him how to fight.

"Get off me, boy!" the Constable roared.

But his magic was gone.

Timothy's heart was racing with fear and anger, and it was all because of this man, this hateful, evil man who would not leave him alone. Still, he tried only to hold Grimshaw down, waiting for Caiaphas to come help him. But the Constable got one hand loose and reached up to grab Timothy's throat, choking him.

The boy hit him in the face, three times in quick succession. Grimshaw's grip faltered. His eyes rolled up. He was dazed.

Timothy jumped off of him and backed away. "Caiaphas!" he shouted.

And the navigation mage—his friend—was there.

His blue robes torn and dirty, Caiaphas still seemed majestic as he stepped up beside Timothy. The mage contorted his fingers and sketched them through the air. He muttered something in words Timothy could not understand. Grimshaw was shaking his head, had one hand propped beneath him, trying to rise.

Bolts of golden light burst from Caiaphas's hands, crackling as they arced out and struck Grimshaw. The Constable let out a single, short yelp of pain, shuddered, legs spasming, and then slumped back to the ground, unconscious, fallen leaves stuck in his hair.

"Wow," Timothy whispered.

"Caw, caw!" Edgar cried. The rook flew in a circle above them and then landed on the path not far from the fallen constable. "Well done, Caiaphas. I didn't know you packed that kind of wallop!"

Timothy was filled with relief at the sight of Edgar. He had feared the worst when the rook had been struck by Grimshaw's magic.

Beneath his veil, Timothy thought Caiaphas might be grinning. "Well," the navigation mage said, "I was angry, but I would never have the magical strength to defeat one as powerful as Constable Grimshaw. Timothy lowered his defenses, you see? It was easy, after that."

The boy was happy to see that the navigator seemed unharmed. He looked at the rook. "Edgar, where did the creature go? The cat-thing?"

"You saw it take off into the woods," the bird replied, pinning his wings behind his back and thrusting his chest out proudly. "That thing isn't coming back, kid. Trust me. Not when it knows I'll be with you. Guess I got here just in time."

"You certainly did," Timothy assured him, sitting comfortably on his horse, feeling now as though he had been riding the beasts all his life. "We'd best take Grimshaw and get back to SkyHaven. If Alhazred really is alive, Parliament must be warned."

CHAPTER ELEVEN

Cassandra Nicodemus stood atop the western wall of SkyHaven. The fortress was massive, with its many towers and courtyards, but the wall surrounded it all. The island floated far above the roiling ocean, and the view from the western wall was breathtaking. The sun shone brightly, the sky almost green today, and in the distance, across the waves below, she could see the shore of Arcanum. Beyond that, on a day as clear as this, the highest spires of the city were visible. If she squinted, she was certain she could see the Xerxis.

The girl loved to walk the walls and battlements, to stand atop the towers and search the horizon or simply gaze at the endless power of the ocean. Usually it brought her peace.

But not today. There was too much going on that frightened her, too much she didn't understand.

"Mistress Cassandra!" a voice shouted.

She spun, hands coming up defensively, fingers warm with the bright green magic that crackled in her grasp. The magic was almost the same shade as her robes. When she saw that it was merely an acolyte, running toward her along the battlement, she let out a breath and relaxed her stance. But the anxiety in her heart remained, for there was fear in the acolyte's eyes and a tremor in his voice.

"What is it?" she demanded.

The young mage, member of the Order of Alhazred, ran to her. He was not a sentry or a combat mage, only a household servant at SkyHaven, and he bowed to her with deep respect.

"Something terrible has happened," the acolyte said.

"What? Speak, man!"

He took a moment to catch his breath and then he steadied himself, gazing at her. "Grandmaster Maddox . . . he . . . we have just received word from the Xerxis. He made an appointment with the Voice yesterday—unbeknownst to any of his aides—and he went there . . . he tried to kill her, Mistress. Grandmaster Maddox attempted to murder the Voice of Parliament."

Cassandra stared at him. The wind blew her long, red hair across her face, and she pushed it away. She shook her head. It made no sense. "How can that be? He was here. I left him with Carlyle less than an hour ago, in his chambers!"

The acolyte nodded. "We went to his chambers immediately when we heard, Mistress. The Grandmaster is gone. Carlyle was unconscious, attacked by some sinister magic or other. He has come round now, but it is too late. He is frantic, Mistress. He sent me to fetch you."

A cold anger filled Cassandra, not directed at Carlyle or this acolyte, nor even at Leander. It was simply that she had had enough.

"Fetch me?" she snapped. "I am not one to be fetched. With Professor Maddox obviously no longer capable of serving as Acting Grandmaster, it falls to me to assert myself. From this moment on, I am Grandmaster of the Order of Alhazred. Let the word go out. All should be on guard for Professor Maddox's return. If he comes back to SkyHaven, he is to be captured—unhurt, if possible, but certainly alive."

The young mage hesitated, his mouth opening and closing. "But, Mistress . . . Grandmaster . . . there's more."

"More?" The idea stopped her cold. Cassandra swallowed hard, and a knot of ice formed in her stomach. "By the gods, what more can there be?"

The acolyte's nostrils flared in distaste. "That . . . thing . . . the metal man. The creation of the Un-Magician—"

"His name is Sheridan," Cassandra said angrily. "What of him?"

The young mage stood up taller, back straight, properly chastised for his demeaning attitude toward the mechanical man. He nodded. "Yes, Sheridan, that's it. I came upon him as I left the others with Carlyle, rushing to find you. It . . . Sheridan claims that the savage . . . Ivar . . . has disappeared. The Asura warrior is nowhere to be found."

The icy knot in Cassandra's stomach twisted even more

painfully. She took several long breaths, nodding. She was Grandmaster now. She had to act like it.

"All right," she said, pushing her hair once more away from her eyes. "Place on the walls every sentry to look out for Leander's return, and rouse every acolyte and servant. Search all of SkyHaven."

The acolyte looked horrified. "For a savage?"

Cassandra slapped him across the face, hard enough to raise red welts on his skin. The mage's eyes widened and then flashed with anger, but he only lowered his gaze and said nothing.

"Never mind," she snapped, pushing past him and rushing along the top of the wall. "I'll do it myself."

The air above Tora'nah was battered by the sounds of the miners at work, shattering rock and digging ore. On the first day, Verlis had watched the birds in the area take off in great flocks from trees and shrubbery, scattering across the sky for a time before attempting to return to their nests. But the noise was almost constant, thundering upon the ears, and the birds would quickly take flight once more.

It had been hours since Verlis had seen a single bird in the sky above Tora'nah. They had been driven off entirely, now, and he wondered if they would return.

The Wurm stood atop a rocky outcropping in the face of the hill that contained the graves of the Dragons of Old. The memorial fires burned again, and he could not avoid the somber feeling that came over him whenever he lingered here. Yet there was nowhere else at Tora'nah that he wanted to be. His quarters were too cramped for him to really spread his wings, and he tried not to spend too much time soaring the skies above the ancient home of his people. It made the miners nervous. Made the *mages* nervous.

And without Leander there to calm them, Verlis thought it might be unwise to do anything that would cause more trouble between him and the mages than already existed. If they came after him again he might be forced to use his heart's fire to burn them, or might be driven, perhaps, to eat one or two. Not that he had any interest in such conflict. But if attacked, Verlis would defend himself.

The ground rumbled beneath him. Verlis turned his gaze toward the mining operation. The sky was green, and the air crisp and cool. The wind carried a sharp odor, like live sparks, or one of Timothy's matches burning. It was, he had learned, the smell of rock being crushed and ground against still more rock. Even now he saw the Burrower digging a fresh tunnel into a hillside not far away. The enormous drill at the front of the thing was tilted somewhat downward, and dirt and ground stone collected beneath it before being swept back and out behind the vehicle by special scoops Timothy had built into the design. It was an extraordinary machine, and Verlis knew that, to the mages, it must seem its own form of magic. Yet it was precisely what they needed to mine the Malleum from Tora'nah.

Timothy was a good boy. A smart boy. Verlis was filled with bittersweet emotion thinking about Timothy, for he knew that the boy's father would have been so very proud to see how brave and clever his son had become. It made the Wurm long to return to Arcanum—to the Cade Estate—as soon as possible so that he could be with his own family.

Soon enough, he thought. *For now, you have a job to do.*

Someone had to watch over the dig at Tora'nah to be sure the ancient, sacred lands of the Dragons of Old were not disturbed any more than was absolutely necessary. And Verlis had more experience with mages than others of his kin. He was the only real choice. It would have been easier for him, however, if Timothy had not had to return to Arcanum. Verlis wondered about Leander's health. He hoped the Grandmaster would recover quickly from whatever illness was plaguing him.

I don't want to stay with these ignorant fools a moment longer than I must, the Wurm thought, snorting in derision. Tiny flames flickered from his snout, and plumes of smoke rose from his nostrils. Many of the mages were cruel and full of hate. Some were kind, but they were the minority.

Verlis spread his wings, leathery skin rasping as they unfolded. He dropped to his haunches and then lunged off of that outcropping, wings beating the air, soaring into the sky. The memorial fires burning far below made his heart leap with pride. This was the great history of his people, and he had been made its guardian. He would not falter in that task.

The wind slipped around him and he glided on the air. Verlis let out a long breath of determination and satisfaction, fire spilling over his fangs and lips and churning in a cloud around his snout as he flew. Then he inhaled again, and out of the corner of his eye he saw a single mage down below, on the open ground between the miners' camp, the little village where they were all staying, and the mine itself. The mage was waving to him, and it took Verlis a moment to recognize Walter Telford, the project manager.

Walter was a serious man, but courteous. Verlis respected him. He dipped his wings into the wind and darted toward the ground. For a moment he allowed himself to plummet toward the rocky terrain, feeling the pull of gravity and the rush of air past him. Then he pulled his head up and his wings back and he banked in a slow circle before coming to rest a dozen feet away from the gray-haired project manager.

"Amazing," Walter said, nodding to himself. "That really is a fairly amazing thing to watch. A Wurm in flight."

Verlis gave a short bow. "Gracious of you to say so, friend."

The man smiled at the word.

"How does your work proceed?" Verlis asked.

Walter scratched the back of his head. "Pretty well, actually. Better than we ever could have expected. The Cade boy's machine—the Burrower—well, it's saved us, really." The man grinned and shrugged sheepishly. "We rely so completely on magic—most of us, anyway—that the idea of taking on a job this big without using spells and enchantments is pretty daunting. But it's really working. We've already got enough Malleum that the blacksmiths have begun their work. The forges are burning."

Verlis widened his eyes. He glanced back toward the mine and then back to Walter. "That is excellent news." The Wurm nodded his heavy head, plumes of smoke snorting from his nostrils. "Truly excellent. Once heated and then cooled, Malleum is almost indestructible and cannot be melted again, even by the hottest fire. If Raptus manages to bring an invasion force through from Draconae, every piece of Malleum armor will be vital to your defense."

The project manager clasped his hands behind his back and smiled, pleased with himself for some reason. He rocked a bit on his feet. "Yes, sir. That is what we're hoping. Actually, though, we were all hoping you would come and have a look at what's already been forged. You know—to see if you have any suggestions, to let us know if we're doing it properly."

The Wurm gestured for the mage to lead the way. "I will look, but I am no blacksmith myself."

As they strode together across the hard ground, the two exchanged pleasantries and discussed other less than pleasant topics. No word had arrived on the condition of Grandmaster Maddox, and they were both concerned for him. Walter Telford hoped Timothy could return soon. The boy's inventiveness was indispensable to them.

Soon they came over a rise and in view of the Forge, a long, gray building made of stone and metal. Inside were four massive furnaces over which the Malleum could be heated so that the smiths could do their work shaping it into the armor and weapons they would need to combat a Wurm invasion. Once it had been properly shaped, magic could be used upon it to add symbols or clasps and buckles, but once magic had touched it, the Malleum would be impossible to alter. Its shape was set.

Verlis had yet to visit the Forge. Now, as he strode down the hill toward it, he felt the heat rising in his own furnace, the one inside his chest. It was a good feeling, and he exhaled little streamers of fire from his snout. Perhaps if there were any place in this encampment he might feel at home, it would be here at the Forge.

As they approached, a door opened and a bald mage poked out his head. "Ready, Walter?"

Verlis and the project manager were perhaps one hundred feet away. Walter smiled and threw up his hands in a gesture of opening.

The mage swung the large door wide with a creak of metal, giving them a view into the dark, fiery inner workings of the Forge. At first Verlis's attention was on the two enormous furnaces that he could see within, the flames leaping above them. There came the clanging noise of metal being worked and shaped inside.

A group of mages emerged from the fiery orange gloom within the building, first just a few and then many others. They called amiably to one another, these men and women in their heavy aprons and gloves, these metal workers, armorers, and weaponsmasters.

"What is this?" the Wurm asked, confused by the friendly, welcoming expressions on their faces.

"They wanted to meet you," Walter said as they continued walking nearer. They were fifty feet from the nearest of the mages now. "Well, some of them you've already met, but the smiths wanted to make sure you knew that not all of us think the worst of strangers."

A warmth spread within Verlis's chest that had nothing to do with the fires there. The very corners of his mouth turned upward in a sort of smile. His wings beat softly, and he held his talons at his side.

Then he saw what was coming from within. From the darkness within and to one side of the door, four more mages appeared. They carried a massive helmet, forged from Malleum so pure that it was a gleaming silver-white. It had been worked into a long shape, perfect to fit over the snout of a Wurm.

The smiths gathered around him. One of them, a stout woman with a rugged face and streaks of soot on her face, stood forward. "I'm Charna Tayvis, good sir. The supervisor here at the Forge." With bright blue eyes she glanced around at the others. "We're told that when the time comes, if the Wurms on the other side of that wall get through and want to do some killing, you're going to stand with us. It's appreciated. Nice to know we're not alone if bad times come."

Verlis was amazed. He stared at Charna, then at the helmet, then glanced at Walter, who only nodded, urging the stout woman on.

"This is . . . for me?" Verlis asked.

Charna crossed her arms and gave him a solemn look. "It's the very first thing we forged, from the first batch of Malleum the miners brought up. The very first thing. We wanted to make sure you knew that you're not alone either. We stand together."

Then the woman held out a hand. Verlis did not know, at first, what the purpose of this gesture was. It took him a moment to realize she meant to shake on it, the way the mages did. He reached out his massive hand and took her tiny one in it, talons curling around her wrist.

"You have my thanks," he said.

Then Verlis glanced around at all of those gathered there: friendly faces, grinning with pride in the work that they had done. He looked at Telford, who came over and clapped him on the back.

"Try it on!" called one of the smiths, a young man, powerfully built, with a long beard.

Verlis took the helmet from them, turned it over in his hands, taking a second merely to appreciate its beauty, and then he fit the metal helm over his head. The metal was still warm from having been inside the Forge building, so near the fires. The helmet sat up high enough from the top of his skull that his horns were not in the way. It was snug around his eyes and nostrils, so that he could see and breathe perfectly.

"It is wonderful," he said.

Some of the smiths actually cheered. Charna and Walter

congratulated them all on a job well done. They started talking excitedly among themselves, and then Charna began to herd them back into the Forge, getting them back to the important work they were doing. Some of them wished Verlis luck and waved. He raised a hand and waved back, the gesture unfamiliar and odd.

Walter strode over to the massive door of the Forge with Charna and they were talking together, leaving him for a moment to himself.

Verlis blinked in confusion.

There was a strange hum inside the helmet. The metal itself seemed to be vibrating slightly, setting up a kind of harmonic tone, a ringing in his head. He started toward the building and it diminished some.

Then he took several steps back, away from the Forge, and it increased.

Verlis frowned. He swung around, peering out from within the warm metal. He moved several steps in one direction, then another, and another, testing a theory. In moments he had found that if he moved toward the village, the hum would increase its intensity.

Leaving Walter behind, he unfolded his wings and sprang into the air, flying toward the village.

But it wasn't the village that was causing the hum.

It was Alhazred's Divide.

Verlis hung in the sky, hovering as best he could several hundred feet above the village, wings beating the air. He stared at the crackling barrier of magic that stretched up to the heavens and to either side as far as he could see. Milky colors swirled in the fabric of that magic.

The wall that separated two worlds.

The barricade that even now he knew Raptus's sorcerers were attempting to tear down from the other side.

The hum in his helmet increased again, now a kind of trilling noise added to it. Verlis snorted fire. He had not moved closer, but the hum had grown.

Verlis caught a scent on the breeze. A familiar smell. The scent of Draconae. He could almost feel that other world, and the presence of so many Wurm warriors, bent on the destruction of Terra and its mages. With that hum in his head and the way he sensed Draconae, so nearby, Verlis trembled with the sudden, alarming certainty that the barrier between worlds was growing thinner.

Walter Telford and his miners and smiths would need to hurry.

Even then, they might soon run out of time.

SkyHaven ought to have been in chaos. Cassandra knew that. With the Grandmaster having attacked his primary aide and then having rushed to the Xerxis to attempt to murder the Voice of Parliament . . . the floating fortress should have been just as frantic as the wild beating of her heart. And yet it was not.

She stood on a balcony at the front of the fortress, from which she could see the western wall and the spires of Arcanum beyond, as well as the courtyard below. Combat mages ran in quartets across the lawns toward stone stairs that would take them up the inner wall to the battlements, where they could watch for Leander Maddox's return. They were trained to fight in groups, to use coordinated magical attacks. The Order of Alhazred combat mages were simultaneously among the most peaceable and the most capable in all the world.

"Mistress Cassandra!"

With a final glance at the sky above the mainland, searching for the sign of anyone approaching, Cassandra turned and left the balcony, stepping through wide-open doors onto a mezzanine that ran along the inner wall of the main entry hall of SkyHaven, high above the stone floor.

A small group of acolytes stood awaiting instructions. One of Leander's aides, a handsome mage with skin the color of rust, seemed to be in charge of them. But both the aide and the mages had turned at the sound of that voice. It belonged to Carlyle, and all of those gathered in the main hall seemed surprised by his arrival. The man's face was flushed red and there was a quickly fading bruise on his forehead that seemed to change colors even as he strode across the hall to stand below the mezzanine, looking up at her.

"Carlyle!" Cassandra said happily. She did not like the man very much, but found that she was very pleased to see him up and around. "I'm glad to see you looking well, but shouldn't you be resting?"

The stout, oh-so-proper man crossed his arms and

arched an eyebrow. "After what happened earlier, do you honestly think I could rest?" he asked. Then, hearing the edge in his own voice, he stood a bit taller. "My apologies, Grandmaster. You'll understand if I feel somewhat under stress. Forgive my tone."

Cassandra pushed her hair away from her face and smiled. "There is nothing to forgive. I see word of my tyranny has already reached you, however."

What happened next was a first in her experience. Carlyle actually laughed. "Indeed. And I applaud you, Mistress. You never did suffer fools, and now you've even less reason to do so."

The man had once been indispensable to her grandfather, and later to Leander, but she had never had the feeling he felt any fondness for her at all. Apparently, though, upon regaining consciousness Carlyle had swiftly learned of her asserting herself as Grandmaster and of her treatment of the acolyte who had questioned her. Why else would he call her Grandmaster?

"Well, if you insist on being on your feet, sir, are you prepared to assume your duties as head of household once more?"

"I am at your service, Grandmaster," Carlyle replied, executing a short bow.

"Excellent."

Cassandra strode along the mezzanine and came to a curving staircase that led down to the floor of the vast chamber. She bunched her robe in her hands and raised the hem several inches to avoid tripping, then started quickly downward. All along, her ears were attuned to listen to any sound from outside the fortress, any signal that trouble was afoot. But all seemed quiet for the moment.

"You," she said, nodding to the bronze-skinned aide who had herded the acolytes into the room and who had stood in silence with them, awaiting instructions. "Uriah, is it not?"

"It is, Grandmaster," replied the mage, inclining his head.

Carlyle came to meet her at the bottom of the steps. The large bruise on his forehead had faded almost completely; only a small yellowed area remained to show where he had been struck. The Order's healers had done their work quite well, as always.

"Well, then, Uriah," Cassandra said, "take this group down to the aerie. Search for Ivar there. Most other areas of the fortress have already been assigned search parties, so presuming you find no sign of Ivar there, you'll have quite a task ahead of you. I'll want someone to examine the open window in the base of SkyHaven, in the center of the Aerie, and then the underside of the island, as well as the waters below, for any sign that he might have left the fortress through that passage, either of his own accord or through sinister means."

Uriah signaled to the acolytes to follow. As one, they touched their foreheads in a gesture of respect and hurried from the hall through an arched doorway in the northeastern corner.

"You seem to be taking to your new role with little difficulty," Carlyle said.

Cassandra sighed heavily and shook her head. "It's an illusion, I'm afraid. Now that we no longer have an audience, I can confess that much. I hope you're well enough for me to lean on you a bit."

"How may I help?"

"Supervise the search for Ivar, please. I want to go out to the wall to speak with the captain of the——"

They were interrupted by the most welcome sound Cassandra had ever heard, the heavy flapping of wings and the cawing of a rook. Her eyes went wide, and she spun to look up at the mezzanine where she had been standing only moments earlier. The black bird darted in through the open balcony doors and circled the entire chamber.

"Caw! Caw! Cassandra, there you are! We need a sky carriage!" Edgar called, his voice shrill. The rook's wings fluttered, and he came to rest atop a bust of Alhazred that sat upon a small table near the bottom of the stairs she had just descended.

Cassandra felt her heart skip a beat, her breath catching in her throat, and she could not suppress the grin that spread across her face. "You've found them, Edgar? Is Tim . . . are they all right?"

The bird shuddered, feathers ruffling, and flew from the small statue to the banister of the stairs. He cocked his head and looked at Carlyle, black eyes gleaming with distrust, then back at Cassandra.

"They're fine, babe. Trust me on that. But they've got dark tales to tell from this trip. Leander's gone crazy, but there's more than that. We've got a prisoner: Constable Grimshaw. He was hunting them out there, like he knew where they'd be, you understand? And he wasn't alone. He had . . ." Once again, his feathers ruffled. "Well, maybe I'd better let the kid tell you."

Cassandra hesitated. Certainly she knew that Leander was not in his right mind, but this news about Grimshaw was dire. And what else was Edgar not saying?

"Well, come on," the rook cried. "They're on horseback. Should be getting to the shore any minute now. Timothy sent me on ahead. They need transport—"

"Enough!" Carlyle shouted.

His voice echoed through the chamber.

The bird cocked his head. "What's your problem?"

"The next time you speak to the Grandmaster with such impertinence, I'll have you for blackbird pie," Carlyle snapped.

Edgar cawed and turned those gleaming eyes on Cassandra. "Grandmaster, huh? Well, looks like you've got a story of your own."

The horses should have been exhausted. Timothy himself was exhausted and his stallion had been doing all of the running. All he'd had to do was hang on, but even so, he was tired. He and Caiaphas rode side by side along an old trading road that hadn't seen much traffic in recent years. There were trees to the east and a slowly rising hill to the west. Due north was

Arcanum, and though the sky was fairly clear, they could not see even the tallest spires yet.

They rode on, the horses' hooves thundering on the hard-packed earth of the road.

"Nearly there!" Caiaphas called to him.

Timothy smiled, gritting his teeth against the wind that blew back his hair and caused his tunic to flutter at his back as he rose up off of the saddle. The Legion Nocturne were no ordinary mages. He had known this before, but riding one of their horses made him realize it all the more. Much as Lord Romulus would hate to admit it, Timothy probably had more in common with the Legion than any other mages on Terra. They lived in the wild and knew how to hunt. They relied on magic for a great deal, but not for everything, as so many mages did.

"How's our captive?" Caiaphas called, eyes sparking blue above his veil.

The boy reined in his horse just a little and dropped back a few feet. A rope of blue mist trailed behind Caiaphas, back to a floating sphere of energy—the same levitation magic he used as a navigation mage. Inside that sphere lay an unconscious Constable Grimshaw. Or, at least, he appeared to be unconscious. His eyes were closed. Even in sleep, though, his features were contorted with hate, his lip curled up in spite.

"Ha!" Timothy shouted, snapping the reins. The horse galloped faster, and soon he was beside Caiaphas again. "He's still out."

"Or he's pretending to be!" the navigation mage called, bouncing with the rhythm of the horse's momentum.

Timothy said nothing. Constable Grimshaw was too arrogant, too proud, to worry about being clever. If he had been conscious, Timothy was certain he would have been sneering at them and making pronouncements about their imminent doom at the hands of his master.

The boy smiled at the thought.

When he glanced ahead once more, he saw the tip of the Xerxis on the horizon like the brightest star in the sky. It was day, still, but the spire gleamed in the sun. With every step thereafter, more spires came into view. Arcanum had never really been home for Timothy, but he grinned with pleasure and relief, looking forward to visiting his ancestral home—his home—on August Hill again.

Soon. First, though, he had to find out what had become of Leander, and what secrets Grimshaw was hiding.

The road curved slightly eastward and, even as it did, the line of trees thinned out. Timothy caught the scent of the ocean on the breeze and then he could see glimpses of it through breaks in the trees. Another quarter mile and the trees stopped completely.

Timothy pulled on the reins and the horse stopped. Caiaphas saw him dropping behind and followed suit. He seemed about to ask what the delay was about when he noticed Timothy staring out at the water.

Caiaphas did the same.

Timothy cantered slowly up beside him on the horse and

together they gazed out across the water at SkyHaven, hanging proudly hundreds of feet above the whitecapped waves.

The boy took a deep breath. So many terrible and wonderful things had happened in his short life, all connected to that floating fortress. But this time, he was not sure what he would find when he returned.

"A carriage," Caiaphas said.

Timothy narrowed his gaze. It was so far away, he had not seen it at first. Now he spotted the sleek sky carriage gliding above the water toward the mainland.

"Edgar found her quickly," he said.

Then he spurred his horse on, and he and Caiaphas rode hard for the bluff overlooking the ocean. A long cliff stood above a short, rocky coast where the ocean crashed on the shore. His heart beat in time with the horse's hooves. As they rode, the sky carriage came nearer. Timothy glanced over his shoulder once more to make certain Grimshaw was still imprisoned, and when he looked back, the carriage was gently gliding toward the top of the bluff. The driver was clad in a veil and robes almost identical to those that Caiaphas wore.

There were curtains across the windows.

The carriage set down just a few moments before Timothy and Caiaphas rode onto the bluff. Twenty feet from the craft, the boy pulled the reins and drew the horse to a halt. He climbed down off of the saddle and tore his gaze from the carriage long enough to run a gentle hand along the snout of the beast.

"Thank you," he whispered to the horse. It nodded its heavy head as though it understood. "You'll find your way back to Romulus, I'm sure."

The horse snorted in agreement.

Timothy patted it on the side and shouted. "Ha!" The beast bolted, making a wide circle that took it daringly close to the edge of the cliff, and then it started back the way it had come. When the boy turned toward Caiaphas, he saw that the navigator had done the same. The horses trotted away together. The magical tether that sprang from Caiaphas's hand seemed to have lengthened, but that sphere still hovered over the ground, and within it, Grimshaw did not move.

"Welcome back."

His pulse quickened as he turned at the sound of that voice and saw Cassandra stepping out of the sky carriage. In the sun, her red hair was a halo of fire and he thought he had never seen anything so beautiful. Anyone so beautiful. The journey had been long and difficult and he was scraped and dirty, sore from the ride, and burdened with worry for Leander.

In that moment, none of it mattered. Once, he would have hesitated, not knowing what to say to her. Now Timothy dragged his fingers through his hair, straightening it, and strode over to her.

"Hello, Cassandra," he said. A little laugh bubbled out of him, surprising him, and he shook his head. "Gods, you have no idea how good it is to see you."

Her green eyes widened and her pale skin flushed scarlet. Cassandra glanced away a moment and Timothy realized that this time she was the one who did not know what to say. It also occurred to him, standing there beside her on the bluff, that he had become noticeably taller since they had first met, so that he was now only a few inches shorter than she was. When they gazed at each other they were nearly eye-to-eye.

"It's good to see you as well," she said. Her smile lingered for several moments, but then it disappeared, and her face was clouded with darker concerns. "I was . . . I was afraid I'd never see you again."

Cassandra reached out to take his hand. Timothy let his fingers touch hers. When Caiaphas approached, they broke that clasp, but he could still feel the warmth of her touch.

"Excuse me, Timothy," said the navigator. "Mistress Cassandra—"

"Grandmaster, now, I'm afraid," she said sadly.

Timothy felt his heart clench. "You're Grandmaster? Then, is Leander—?"

"Alive," she said quickly. "But . . ." Cassandra shook her head. "No, this is not the place. Let us return to SkyHaven, get Constable Grimshaw properly imprisoned, and then you shall hear it all."

CHAPTER TWELVE

Using a damp cloth and a pan of warm water, Timothy quickly washed the accumulated grime and dirt of his journey from his face and body. He wished he could have taken time to relax, to catch his breath, but that was a luxury that would be denied him until Leander was apprehended and Ivar's whereabouts were discovered.

He was drying his face and upper body with a towel when there came a gentle knock upon his door. Caught up in thoughts of what had transpired since he'd first left for Tora'nah, he absently walked over and opened the door to his chamber.

Cassandra stood on the threshold, red hair wild and unkempt. "Oh my," she said at the sight of him, averting her eyes.

It took him a moment, but then he looked down and

realized that he was still exposed from the waist up. "Sorry," he said, turning but leaving the door open so that she could enter. He retrieved a fresh tunic from his chest of drawers. "Guess I'm a little distracted. I was running through everything in my head and trying to put the pieces together, make some sense out of it all."

"That's all right," Cassandra replied. She had entered his room behind him but still appeared a bit flustered, a pink blush spreading across her normally pale cheeks. "Would you like me to have the kitchen prepare something for you to eat?" she asked. "You must be famished after your travels."

"No, thank you." He slipped the cream-colored tunic over his head. "With Ivar missing and Leander on the loose, I don't really have much of an appetite."

She nodded, and now that he was fully clothed, made eye contact with him. "Does it hurt?"

He had no idea what she was talking about. "Excuse me? Does what hurt?"

Cassandra again averted her eyes, the rosy heat returning to her cheeks. "When I first saw you . . . without your tunic . . . well, your side appeared badly bruised."

He'd been so caught up in the whirlwind of his adventure that he'd practically forgotten about his injuries. The scratches on his face no longer stung, though the skin on his cheek was strangely tight. Carefully, he pressed a hand to his side. It hurt like blazes.

"As a matter of fact, it does hurt. Thanks for reminding me."

They both chuckled softly, and their eyes met. He felt

the warmth begin to rise to his own face as an awkward silence crept into the room.

"So," Timothy said abruptly, "can you tell me where Ivar was last seen?"

"In his illness, Leander talked of stumbling upon something terrible here in SkyHaven while doing research on Tora'nah," Cassandra explained. "Ivar was going to try to retrace Leander's footsteps."

"Then we should do the same," Timothy said, feeling the pull of exhaustion but shrugging it off. There would be time to rest later. He made a move to leave.

"I have already dispatched acolytes to search SkyHaven. Edgar, Sheridan, and Caiaphas have also gone to search. I thought that perhaps as his friend, the rook might have an advantage on other searchers. We can only hope."

"Probably so. Edgar is cleverer than anyone gives him credit for," Timothy said, striding toward the door. "Well, let's go join them."

Cassandra looked at him gravely, brow furrowing. "As Grandmaster, I feel that it is in your best interest to rest."

"Rest? You're joking. I can't rest now."

"You've been through a harrowing ordeal," she continued firmly. "It would be wise for you to renew your strength before again throwing yourself into danger."

Timothy turned away from her to open his door. "I appreciate your concern, but I just can't do it. I'm sorry."

"Please, Tim," she pleaded. "I don't want you to get hurt."

Timothy looked back into the girl's stunning green eyes; eyes that now shimmered with emotion.

"I've thought once that something terrible had happened to you," she continued. "I don't want to feel that way again."

Timothy was stunned by her admission, not sure how to respond. Then the opportunity to speak had passed, for they were interrupted by another voice.

"That's simply precious. It appears that our little Grandmaster in training has been smitten by you, lad."

Timothy and Cassandra moved back to back, to fight together against any attack that might come. They stared around the room, but there was no sign of any intruder. Only that voice that seemed to come from all of the shadows at once. And he knew that voice. But there was something about it that made the hair at the back of his neck stand on end.

"Leander?" Timothy called, moving farther into the room.

Cassandra grabbed his arm, attempting to stop him. "Careful, Timothy," she cautioned. "Remember, he isn't in his right mind."

Gently, the boy removed her hand and inched closer to his sleeping area. Dusk was gradually approaching, and his room was now draped in growing shadows. The corners were pitch-black.

"I must say. You do make a handsome couple."

Timothy stared into the inky gloom, trying to find the

source of his friend's distorted voice. "Leander, we know there's something wrong. Let us help you."

And there came the laugh, low and rumbling, like the growl of some ferocious animal. "I don't need any more of your help, boy," said the voice scornfully. "You've done more than enough already."

Leander exploded from a pool of shadow, a glinting dagger clutched in one of his meaty hands.

"Timothy, watch out!" Cassandra cried.

"Silence, girl!" Leander roared, even as a blast of magic erupted from his free hand.

Cassandra was unable to conjure a defensive ward in time. The spell struck her, bruise-purple energy crackling in the air as it slammed into her and knocked her to the floor.

Timothy lunged at Leander and spun the burly mage around to face him. "What's wrong with you?"

"Nothing your death won't fix," Leander growled. He raised the dagger with a twisted smile and a demonic twinkle in his eye, and brought it down in a swift arc.

Timothy knocked the attack away with a blow of his forearm, one of the earliest moves that Ivar had taught him. He darted past Leander and out of his reach.

"Stand still, monster," Leander cried. "The blight of you must be removed from the world if it is ever to return to its former state of glory."

Again Timothy evaded the deadly blade, the archmage's disturbing words reverberating through his mind. This man had become his mentor, like a second father to him. But this was not the Leander he knew. It was as if someone else were speaking with Leander's voice, someone who did not appreciate *the unmagician's* introduction to the world.

He didn't want to hurt his friend, but at the same time he couldn't risk being stabbed, either. Once again relying upon his Asura training, Timothy moved in close enough for Leander to attack him again. This time, however, the boy grabbed the mage's wrist and pulled it toward him, forcing the hand with the dagger over his right shoulder and using Leander's own momentum to get in closer. He turned sideways at the same time, all of it one smooth motion, and hooked his left foot behind Leander's ankle. Timothy got a fistful of the mage's dark green robes and forced him backward, tripping him and driving him to the floor.

Leander struck the floor hard, knocking the wind out of him, and for a brief moment, Timothy could have sworn he saw a flicker of new awareness in his eyes. But then the hatred returned.

"Damn you!" the mage screamed, thrashing about.

"Please stay down, Leander," Timothy begged, prepared to keep the former Grandmaster incapacitated on the floor at any cost.

A moan from across the room distracted him. Cassandra had pushed herself up onto her knees and was slowly rising to her feet.

"Ah yes, the girl," Leander sneered.

"No!" Timothy shouted.

But he was too late. Tendrils of solid shadow erupted from the mage's hand, entangling the still recovering girl in wisps of inky black. Cassandra gasped helplessly as the tentacles squeezed her, stealing away her breath. Her eyes went wide with surprise and pain.

Timothy moved to touch the mage, to lay a hand upon him and disrupt the flow of magic.

"Come no closer, or she dies," Leander commanded. "Her delicate frame will be snapped in two before your wretched curse can stop me."

Timothy stood above the man, fists clenched in anger and helplessness. "You're not Leander," he said through gritted teeth.

The man on the floor looked up at him and smiled evilly. "Are you so certain?" he asked. "So positive that I could not have seen the error of my ways and finally realized what an abhorrence you are?"

The boy slowly shook his head, fighting to keep his anger in check. There was far too much at stake to let Leander—or whatever it was lying upon the floor—taunt him into doing something foolish.

"You're not he."

Leander flipped the knife blade in his free hand, offering the boy the pommel of his weapon. "Take it," he said.

Timothy hesitated momentarily, but did what was asked of him.

"Excellent," the archmage hissed, his other hand still crackling with the power of the black magic. "Now I want you to listen very carefully. I want you to take that blade and plunge it into your heart."

Timothy reacted as if struck. "I will not!"

Leander manipulated the magic holding Cassandra, and the girl began to scream. "You have no choice. Either do as I tell you, or the object of your affection perishes quite horribly."

He knew he could never live with himself if he was responsible for Cassandra's death. Hefting the blade, Timothy brought the tip to his chest.

"Very good," the archmage cooed. "Now, plunge the knife into your heart."

Timothy stood, knife poised to strike at his own chest. His mind raced, searching for options, but he could think of no course of action that could guarantee his own life and the safety of Cassandra Nicodemus. The blade shook as he hesitated, frantic to find any other way out of his predicament.

"Do as I say, boy, or the girl dies!" Leander spat, scrambling to his feet with anticipation.

Drawing back his hand, Timothy closed his eyes and prepared to drive the blade home.

"Yessssssssssssssssssssssssssssssssss," Leander hissed like some great reptilian beast, eyes glistening as he licked his lips expectantly.

The door to his room exploded inward with a thunderous crash and Carlyle stood on the threshold, magic crackling from his outstretched hands.

"Out of the way, boy!" Carlyle bellowed, a spell flying from his fingers in blades of golden light that severed the tentacles of shadow holding Cassandra. "There are creatures most foul to be dealt with this day!"

Leander screamed as though the magic that he wielded was somehow a part him, and the attack had wounded him. The archmage staggered back and then turned to escape as he had entered, through the shadows.

"You are going nowhere," Carlyle said. He raised his hands to reveal blazing spheres of magical illumination that spun on his upturned palms. He hurled them upon the floor and their brightness dispelled the shadows in the room, stealing away Leander's magical escape route.

Timothy ran to check on Cassandra, watching in awe as the fussy little man, the annoyingly proper assistant, cast a spell of enough force to shake the very walls of the bed chamber. A blue light sparked in the center of the room and then blossomed like a flower, growing in an eyeblink to extraordinary size and swallowing Leander Maddox in its petals.

"Are you all right?" Timothy asked, helping Cassandra to rise.

She nodded, giving him a brief smile, and he felt his heart skip a beat. It was almost as if *she* had worked some kind of magic upon him, but of course he knew that was impossible.

"I must look a fright," she said, attempting to fix her hair.

"You look perfect," he said, and smiled.

The two joined Carlyle, who was maintaining the integrity of the magical prison that now held their friend. The former Grandmaster bellowed like some wild beast, striking at the bubble, trying to break free.

"Not too close, now, Timothy Cade," Carlyle cautioned, not wanting the boy's negating power to interfere with his magic.

Timothy stepped back, stunned by the man's ability. "How did you . . . I never would have thought . . ."

"Have I surprised you, Timothy? I may be merely an assistant *now*," Carlyle said, manipulating the magical sphere around Leander so that it began to constrict, "but long ago I was something more."

Leander shrieked and cursed as his prison limited his movement.

"You were a combat mage?" Cassandra asked.

"They were difficult times that I would prefer to forget," Carlyle said gravely. "But when called upon, the memories return. And my training will be a part of me forever."

The magical entrapment around Leander continued to constrict until it clung to him, totally immobilizing him.

"What has happened to him?" Timothy asked, filled with fear as he looked upon his friend, growling on the floor, trying to free himself.

"This is merely the shell of Professor Maddox," Carlyle explained.

Cassandra left Timothy's side for a closer look. "He's been behaving so strangely, so erratic, that we were all afraid something was wrong with his mind. But Leander is possessed!"

"What do you mean?" Timothy demanded.

"Mistress Cassandra is correct. Something dark and terrible is inside his body even now, and his soul has been at war with it. Even as it has tried to control him, he has been fighting back. I was a blind fool not to see it sooner, but this kind of magic—only the darkest of wizards ever dared to summon creatures to possess their enemies."

"Who could do such a thing?" Timothy asked.

Carlyle balled one of his hands into a fist and slowly turned it in a circle. "That is something I intend to find out," he said, and he began to murmur a spell in a tongue that Timothy did not recognize.

The boy watched, horrified, as Leander began to thrash upon the ground, screaming as if in excruciating agony. "Stop!" Timothy cried, almost running forward but managing to stop himself.

"It is a spell of eviction," Carlyle stated. "It is not your friend that cries out, but the enemy that hides within."

With those words, the possessed screamed all the louder, his mouth opening wider and wider as he shrieked. Then the unthinkable happened. Something stirred in the darkness of Leander's throat, something that was now emerging into the light.

Cassandra gasped, returning to Timothy's side. "What is it?" she asked in a breathless whisper.

Timothy wasn't sure, at first. He could only watch in

disgust as the creature that had possessed Leander slowly drew itself up and out from the archmage's mouth, scrambling to crouch upon his chest.

"Grooak!" said the beast. Its dark brown skin was slimy and covered with warts, its sacklike throat expanding and contracting as it squatted there.

"This is the thing that possessed Leander? The evil that has been controlling him?" Cassandra asked.

"Yes," Carlyle replied. "Implanted there by its master. It may not speak, but its evil has been manipulating Leander's actions for some time."

"But this is no monster or demon. It's . . . it's just a mud-toad," Timothy said with confusion and revulsion.

"No. Not *just* anything, Timothy," Carlyle agreed. "If I'm not mistaken, there was once an extremely powerful mage who had a fondness for these grotesque creatures, used them as his familiars and harbingers, as his lackeys."

Timothy felt an icy chill run up and down his spine. "Let me guess," he said, fearing for a moment that the name would become stuck in his throat and choke him.

"Alhazred."

"It's useless!" Edgar squawked, fluttering his wings in frustration.

He was perched atop a wooden chest in the last of the document storage chambers that had yet to be searched. They had been at it for hours, and had come no closer to discovering Ivar's whereabouts.

"Now, now, Edgar," Sheridan consoled. "That's not the attitude of one who has recently brought our beloved master back from the wilderness, is it?"

The bird sighed, shaking his head from side to side. "When you put it like that, you'd think we'd have no problem finding Ivar," he croaked.

A group of acolytes stood in the doorway but made no effort to help them. Cassandra had given them all a task—to retrace Ivar's footsteps—but that was not as simple as it sounded. He was an Asura, and that meant he was very good at doing things without being seen.

"Are you sure none of you saw any trace of him?" Edgar asked.

The acolytes said nothing, some averting their eyes.

"Didn't think so," Edgar grumbled beneath his breath. No matter how hard they tried to fit in, they were still outsiders to the people of SkyHaven. He had to wonder if there would ever come a day when they would be accepted.

Sheridan clanked to the center of the room, segmented hands upon his hips. "If I were an Asura warrior, where would I be?" he asked aloud, a burst of steam hissing in release from the valve atop his metal head as his body slowly spun in a full 360-degree circle.

"You think the guy would have had the common decency to leave us a few clues," Edgar crowed in annoyance.

"Perhaps he did and we simply cannot see them," the mechanical man said, reaching up to his circular yellow eyes.

"I haven't used this function in quite some time—since leaving Patience, in fact—but it might prove useful."

Edgar watched as Sheridan massaged the sides of his head with his fingers. The mechanical man's eyes suddenly rotated backward to expose another set, this pair apparently made from thick pieces of glass.

"What's the story with the new peepers?" Edgar asked curiously.

The acolytes watched, fascinated, from the entryway.

"This is special glass that magnifies," the mechanical man explained. "Timothy thought they might help me to locate hidden veins of Vulcanite, or assist him with some of the more delicate aspects of his inventing."

There was a bit of a commotion near the door, and Edgar looked to see Caiaphas coming into the room. He was wearing new robes of sky blue, replacing the torn and dirty clothes he had worn upon his return from the wild.

"My apologies for the delay," he said with a slight bow. "After dining and cleaning up, I'm afraid I dozed off for a few minutes."

"No problem, Caiaphas," Edgar said. "You earned a little nap for helping to keep our Timothy safe."

The navigation mage bowed again. "It was my pleasure—though Timothy kept me safe, more often than not. We survived together."

"That certainly sounds like him," Sheridan said, bending forward slightly to survey the room with his new eyes. "But now our concern must be on locating our other wayward friend."

"You have had no luck, then?" Caiaphas asked, stepping into the room to assist them.

"Not yet," Edgar answered grimly. "I think Grimshaw's got to know something about it, though. If we don't find something soon, we may have to beat the truth out of him."

"That would make us as cruel as he is," Sheridan said.

Caiaphas grunted softly. "I could live with that."

Edgar would have replied, but then he noticed that the acolytes had stopped in the doorway and now simply stood there, not helping at all. The rook clacked his beak in annoyance and tilted his head to stare at them.

"Don't worry about a thing, guys," he squawked. "We got everything under control here."

He was not sure if Caiaphas's presence moved them, or if his jibes had finally hit home, but some of the Alhazred acolytes came into the room and began to help in the search for clues.

"There has to be something," Sheridan muttered, scrutinizing every inch of the storage room.

It wasn't long before everybody was searching—all the acolytes putting aside their prejudices and fears to help— but they still came up with no sign of Ivar's presence. Edgar was about to call a halt to the search and suggest that they move on to the storage chambers on the southern side of the floating estate, when the unexpected happened.

"Excuse me," said one of the acolytes, a short, chubby

man with a wild head of curly black hair. He was squatting down at the far end of the chamber before a large bookcase, and seemed to be looking at something on the floor.

Sheridan quickly clomped across the room, scattering acolytes as he moved with great haste. "Yes?" the mechanical man asked eagerly.

"Look," the acolyte said, moving some dust around on the floor with a fat finger.

"Yeah, it's a real mess in here," Edgar commented. "What this place needs is a good dusting."

"No," said the acolyte. "Here, the dust has been disturbed. And it looks like the stone has been scraped."

Sheridan bent at the waist for a closer look. The familiar, still atop his shoulder, listened to the whirring of the mechanics inside his head as he examined the spot of floor.

"I do believe he's right," Sheridan said, a hint of excitement in his voice. He turned his attention to the bookcase pushed up against the wall. "It appears this bookcase has been moved away from the wall and then pushed back again—and recently."

The chubby acolyte jumped to his feet, staring in amazement at the bookcase. He grabbed it and pulled . . . and it swung open.

"There was a lock here, but a spell has been used to force it open," he said.

"Great," Edgar croaked, eyeing the storage unit. "Maybe we're on the right track after all." The rook fluttered his wings. "Ready to go, Sheridan?"

"Quite ready," the mechanical man answered, flexing his arms.

There was a doorway behind the case, leading to a set of stone stairs descending into a sea of darkness.

Sheridan moved closer to the doorway, reaching up to click the buttons on the side of his head that would return his eyes to their normal setting. The glow from the twin orbs illuminated the descending staircase, but only a little way before the light was swallowed up by the darkness.

"Do you think Ivar is down there?" the mechanical man asked.

"I'd bet my tailfeathers on it."

"Then we go down."

"No," Edgar said. "Cassandra was very specific about what we are to do if we find anything of importance. You guys stay here," he said, lifting off from his perch and flying toward the exit. "She is going to want to see this for herself."

CHAPTER THIRTEEN

Timothy held the lantern high. It was one of his own special lamps, with oil inside that burned with hungry fire. Ghostfire was magical and would have gone dark the moment he touched one of those lights. Now he held his lantern out ahead of him and peered down the winding steps into the impenetrable darkness below.

"Are you sure about this?" Edgar asked. "Who knows what you're going to find down there."

The boy looked away from the stairs, back to his friends. "I'll feel much better knowing that all of you are safe, and that things are being properly looked after up here."

"And, besides, he won't be going alone," Cassandra said, sidling up alongside him.

Timothy felt himself begin to frown. As much as he was starting to enjoy the girl's company, or perhaps because of it, he wished that she would stay behind. Magic could not hurt him, but it could kill Cassandra. But he knew it would be useless to even suggest it. She was Grandmaster, after all. She was in charge here.

"I do wish you'd allow us to accompany you," Sheridan said fretfully.

"We'll be fine," Timothy said. "Are you ready?" he then asked Cassandra, lifting his lantern to light their way.

The girl nodded, a look of steely determination upon her delicate features. "Let's go find Ivar and bring him back."

Timothy turned to his gathered friends for one last time. "Look after Leander and keep him safe," he told them. "And keep your eyes open for anything unusual."

"Of course," Edgar squawked. "You just be careful."

Timothy smiled and waved good-bye. "That's my intention." He held his lantern of hungry fire out before him and carefully descended the steps, watching out for himself as well as for the girl who followed slightly behind him.

"I don't know why you insisted on bringing that clunky lantern along," she said. "I can easily cast a spell of illumination that will provide us with more than enough light."

"What if we're separated?"

Cassandra made a small noise of displeasure. "Let us hope that doesn't happen—though I see your point."

It seemed as if they were descending forever, down and down the staircase into eternal darkness, deeper into the floating island than seemed possible.

"How can something as extensive as this exist without

anyone knowing?" Cassandra asked, her hand reaching out to clutch his in the small pool of golden illumination that flickered from Timothy's lantern.

"It was likely done in secret," the boy replied.

At last the hint of a glow could be seen below, growing brighter with each new turn of the spiral stairs. They were getting closer, but to what, Timothy wasn't sure.

"Yet another bit of wickedness I'm sure that my grandfather can lay claim to," she said angrily.

Timothy said nothing, not wanting to upset her more by agreeing. The flickering of light grew more pronounced upon the walls, and Timothy found himself quickening his descent, eager to see what awaited them.

Nearing the bottom at last he came in sight of a ghostfire lamp that was set in a detailed sconce upon the wall. He found himself mesmerized by the magical flame, remembering his time with the Children of Karthagia and their feelings about ghostfire.

"Almost there," he said, pulling his eyes from the dancing soul fire and continuing with their descent. At last, upon the final step, they stood in front of a heavy wooden door set between two more sconces.

Timothy steeled himself and then reached out to push against the wood. The door swung slowly open to reveal the room beyond. Ghostfire lanterns came to life, revealing a kind of magician's workroom.

"I've read about places like this," Cassandra said, leaving his side and surveying the chamber.

Timothy placed his lantern upon a tabletop, its natural light no longer necessary with the multiple lamps of ghostfire burning. "What kind of place is it?" he asked, staring at myriad jars of unknown contents stacked upon multiple shelves. He could have sworn that something inside one of the jars was moving.

"If I'm not mistaken, this is a wizard's laboratory," she explained. "A secret place kept by the Wizards of Old so that they could practice their magical arts unhindered."

Timothy approached another table, drawn to the pieces of metal lying atop it. He reached down and picked up one of the pieces and studied it. At once he recognized it as one of the metal frames used as a base for a ghostfire lamp. Again, he recalled his discussion with the Karthagian called Finn.

He placed the metal upon the tabletop and looked about some more.

"Do you think it's possible, Tim?" Cassandra asked in a hushed whisper, hurrying to join him as if afraid to be alone.

"Do I think what's possible?"

"That a wizard from days gone by could still be alive today, and hiding inside of SkyHaven?"

Their eyes fell on another table, and what lay upon it, in unison. Cassandra gasped, averting her eyes from the sight of the dissected animals resting there. He wasn't sure if she had seen the desiccated human head, and made it a point to steer her away from the table before she could.

"I think we've seen enough of this room," he said, ushering her toward another doorway. Timothy wondered what new grotesqueries awaited them beyond it, and prepared himself.

There were more stairs to walk down, the passage lit by even more ghostfire lamps attached to the wall. Around a final corner, at the bottom of the stairs, he could see an entrance that would take them into yet another secret room below SkyHaven.

"Hopefully we'll find some answers at last," he said, leading Cassandra by the hand into the next chamber.

The two gasped in unison.

Everywhere they looked there were lamps of ghostfire—thousands of them, by Timothy's rough estimate—bolted to the walls and stacked on tables and shelves. Their brilliance seemed to grow more intense the further into the room the pair went.

"This isn't right," Timothy said, shielding his eyes as he attempted to look about the massive stone chamber. It seemed to go on forever, filled with stone columns and archways, but still just one enormous room. He could scarcely imagine the countless souls that were entrapped here.

"What isn't?" Cassandra asked.

"On my travels through the wilderness I learned some interesting views about ghostfire," he explained as he lowered his hands, his eyes better adjusted to the brightness. "Some cultures believe that it's wrong to use the soul energies of the mages who've passed."

"That is how it's always been," Cassandra said.

"Yes, but just because it's always been this way doesn't make it right." Timothy walked farther into the room. Everywhere he looked, there were vessels of ghostfire. "I can't help but wonder if all these souls aren't being kept from moving on to someplace better than this."

Cassandra stooped to peer at a row of the brightly burning lanterns resting upon a shelf. "I . . . I never thought about it like that," she said, looking with new eyes at objects she had seen her entire life.

Timothy was certain that most mages were kind and good, and that the use of ghostfire was simply a tradition that they had always followed. Most would be horrified to even consider that keeping portions of the spirits of their ancestors trapped in ghostfire lamps and torches might in truth be a torment for the dead, that their loved ones might be suffering because of that old tradition.

"Could . . . could it be so?" She looked at him, clearly hoping for an answer that he could not give.

"I don't know," he admitted. "But the question haunts me."

He watched as she moved around the chamber, reaching out to gently touch the spheres and lamps. "How cruel if it *is* true," she said.

Cassandra stopped suddenly and looked at him. "Why do you think they're all here? There are so many of them, they can't all be here for the purpose of lighting the room."

"No," Timothy said, tilting his head to one side. "I can't

imagine that they are." He had seen something through the nearly overpowering brilliance of the ghostfire lamps, up ahead in the chamber, lying upon the floor. Now, he started deeper into the room to investigate.

Cassandra followed closely behind. "What is it, Tim? It's so bright in here, I can barely make it out."

Timothy shielded his eyes from the light and tried to peer through slitted lids. It was so difficult to see that he nearly stumbled over the shape that lay on the floor. At first it appeared to be a sack of clothing, but on closer examination, Timothy realized it was something more. With a tentative hand he reached down and flipped back a piece of material to reveal the skeletal face of a mage.

Cassandra gasped, jumping back from the withered corpse hidden within the robes. "Oh no, the poor man."

Timothy nodded grimly, an idea beginning to formulate in his mind. "One of the missing mages, I'd wager."

They looked up and scanned the chamber that stretched before them. Among the columns were other figures on the ground, other bodies littering the floor. Something moaned in the distance, and Timothy felt his blood turn to ice. As if drawn by some invisible force, he began to inch his way toward the sound.

"Wait," Cassandra hissed, gripping his arm. "It could be a trap."

Timothy looked into her green eyes and removed her grip from his arm. "Then let's find out together. It's what we've come for. And I'm not leaving without Ivar."

They moved together toward the other bodies, searching for telltale signs of life, but there were none to be found. Timothy was disturbed by how many bodies there were. A far greater number of mages had apparently gone missing than had been originally thought.

Instinctively, he pulled Cassandra closer to him.

They heard the sound again, weaker than before but this time much closer. They moved cautiously toward the source of that sound and found themselves standing before a tangle of multicolored robes and withered skin. Whatever had been done to them, it had changed their flesh so much that they did not stink of death but of a kind of damp mold, as though there was nothing left of them but skin and bone and clothing. Someone had made a pile of corpses. How many mages had been thrown into this particular heap, Timothy could not begin to fathom.

And then the bodies began to move.

Timothy cried out, jumping away from the writhing pile of the dead, Cassandra in tow.

Yet it was not the bodies that moved, but something buried beneath. A pale hand and arm shot up from among them, and someone began to emerge.

"Ivar?" Timothy cried, rushing to assist his friend.

Cassandra helped him, each of them taking the struggling Asura by an arm and aiding him in crawling out from beneath the pile of dead mages.

"Are you all right, Ivar?" Timothy asked when his friend was finally free.

The Asura was weak, his legs unable to support his weight. Carefully they lowered him to the ground. His skin was strangely discolored and dry to the touch, as if he had been attacked by the same force that had caused the dead mages to wither, but had managed to survive.

Or maybe, Timothy thought, *whatever was doing this to him didn't get a chance to finish the job. Maybe it was interrupted.*

Cassandra gently laid the Asura's head in her lap.

"Ivar," Timothy said, kneeling at his friend's side. "Ivar, what's happened—who did this to you?"

Ivar's head thrashed from side to side as if in the grip of some terrible nightmare. He started to moan, and then his eyes snapped open and he stared at them, fear etched upon his face.

"It's me, Ivar, it's Tim and Cassandra. You're going to be all right," he assured his friend.

"No," the Asura rasped, his voice as dry as the desert. He reached a trembling hand up and grabbed hold of Timothy's arm in a powerful grip.

"Run," Ivar croaked, his dark eyes bulging. "Run for your lives."

CHAPTER FOURTEEN

In his dream, Leander Maddox could feel a breeze on his face that carried with it the scent of the ocean. It was only the deep ache in his gut and the ragged pain in his throat that forced him to realize that he was not dreaming after all. He moaned, softly, and knitted his heavy brows in consternation, all without opening his eyes.

The moment he did open them, narrowing them to slits to protect against the sudden bright light of day, memories swam through his mind. The pain in his belly tripled and he caught his breath, swallowing, shaking his head weakly upon his pillow.

"No," he said, sorrow welling up inside him.

"Professor?" asked a voice.

Through narrowed eyes, Leander saw the shadow of a figure loom over him. He blinked to clear his vision and saw that it was Carlyle.

"You're awake," Carlyle said, obviously pleased though there was also caution in his voice. "How do you feel?"

Leander ignored him. The mage had called him professor, which was in itself confirmation of his worst fears. "I remember . . . terrible things. They weren't nightmares, were they?"

Carlyle averted his eyes. "No, sir. No, I'm afraid they were not nightmares at all."

The former Grandmaster sat up. Nausea gripped him and he became dizzy, but he only paused to let it pass and then swung his legs off of the bed. "Is Timothy all right?" he asked. "And what of Caiaphas? Please, tell me that they're safe."

Carlyle nodded solemnly. "They are, indeed. Despite the evil that influenced you, Professor, you did them no permanent damage."

"And Alethea? The Voice?"

"She will recover."

Leander let out a long breath and sagged a moment at the edge of the bed. The memories of his actions were blurred, but he recalled much of what he had said and done. Even as the presence that had overtaken him had been beating Timothy and forcing him out the window of that sky carriage—speaking with Leander's voice and moving with his limbs—inside he had been screaming in fury, frustration, and fear.

"Thank the gods," he whispered.

Then he snapped his head up and stared at Carlyle. "But

the evil remains. Here in SkyHaven. The black-hearted wizard made me his puppet, but I won't let him harm anyone else. Where are they all now? Timothy and his friends, Cassandra, Caiaphas?"

A flicker of concern went across Carlyle's face, and then he frowned. "You need to rest. I shall have the kitchen prepare you some broth and perhaps a bit of poultry."

Worry creased Leander's face. His pulse quickened and he rose from the edge of the bed, towering over Carlyle. "Where are they?"

Carlyle glanced away from him. "You must understand, Professor. Mistress Cassandra—now Grandmaster Nicodemus—learned that before your behavior had turned so erratic, so cantankerous, you had been searching through the archives of SkyHaven. She sent the sav . . . the Asura, to search for you. Ivar never returned. Now that Timothy and Caiaphas have returned, the entire fortress is searching. Only a short time ago, that damnable rook appeared to tell the boy that a . . . a secret passage had been found. He and Cassandra both went immediately to investigate, in hopes of finding the Asura. They are in the lower levels of SkyHaven, even now, in the tunnels."

The news staggered Leander. He brought a hand up to cover his eyes, and his legs weakened beneath him. Shame and guilt burned within him. This had all happened because he had let down his guard, allowed himself to be taken by surprise. He had simply not had the strength to defend himself, to fight off the evil influence.

"Oh, Argus, my old friend. I am so sorry," he whispered. "You would have been stronger."

"Professor?" Carlyle said.

Leander stood up straighter. "Brace yourself, my friend, for a shock. The thing that possessed me was a servant of Alhazred. It would seem that, after all this time, the wizard is still alive. And the worst rumors we have heard of his nature have proven true."

"As we suspected," Carlyle said grimly. "When we evicted the presence that had been possessing you, it was in the form of a mudtoad. Alhazred's familiar was such a creature. I . . . I have difficulty accepting that the founder of this Order could be a creature of such darkness, but I turned a blind eye to the horrors perpetrated by Cassandra's grandfather. I will never make such a mistake again."

Leander had barely heard him. He stared at Carlyle. "They knew Alhazred's evil lingered, and still, they went into the secret passages?"

"The Asura is missing," Carlyle said gravely. "You know Timothy better than anyone. You don't honestly think that any danger could frighten him away if he believes one of his friends in peril?"

"Foolish boy!" Leander thundered.

Carlyle flinched, but he had the grace not to point out the obvious. It was not Timothy with whom Leander was so furious, but himself. Leander did not know if he would ever forgive himself, but such self-indulgence would have to wait. Alhazred had been hidden away in secret tunnels in

SkyHaven's belly for generations. From what Leander had been able to piece together, the ancient mage had been little more than a husk himself, his body for all purposes dead but his spirit lingering. It had taken great magic, enormous amounts of power, for Nicodemus to restore him.

Nicodemus had been stopped. The wraiths he had enslaved, the spirits of dead mages under his control, had been freed. But it was too late. He had gathered enough magic, enough of the life aura of other mages, to resurrect Alhazred. Enough so that when Nicodemus's own body had been destroyed, his spirit had been able to force itself into the body of his familiar, that hideous cat. Now Nicodemus and Alastor were one, a monstrous thing. Far worse, Alhazred was back, and whatever insidious horror he had planned, it would have been set in motion by now.

The question was whether he had left SkyHaven. Leander doubted that he had. The history of Arcanum, of all of Terra, was that of arrogant mages vying for control of the guilds, and later of Parliament. And none had ever been more arrogant than Alhazred.

"He is still here," Leander said, snatching up his cloak where it lay draped over a chair by the bed. "Timothy must not go near him. Alhazred is just as clever as he is cruel. He will find a way to destroy the boy. That must not happen."

Leander started for the door, but he was still weak and became disoriented. He paused a moment, swaying, breathing deeply to clear his head. Then he shook it off, anger building within him, and his fingers flexed at his side. Magic began to gather in his fist.

"Professor, you must not go. You are in no condition—"

"Then who will face him?" Leander barked, whirling on him, trembling. "Who? Yes, the Parliament will oppose him, but how long before word can reach them? How long before they believe it? You know as well as I that they will deny the truth until they are forced to accept it. By then, Timothy will be dead.

"By then, we may all be dead."

With those words he stormed from the room, still unsteady on his feet but without any hesitation at all. The time for hesitation had long since passed.

Ivar's words still echoed in that vast, stone chamber. Columns of masonry were all about the enormous room, as though they supported all of the fortress above. It was oppressive there, claustrophobic to think that the weight of SkyHaven pressed down upon them.

"Run for your lives," Ivar had said.

"I will not leave you," Timothy told him.

Together, he and Cassandra helped the warrior rise to his feet. He was weak and his skin drawn tight and dry. Even the black tribal markings that slid across Ivar's skin seemed to have paled, the pigment faded, but Timothy thought that might just have been the brightness of the room.

The ghostfire.

Hundreds, perhaps thousands of souls, trapped in spell-glass spheres and lanterns throughout this sprawling chamber. This dungeon.

"We must go," Ivar replied, wetting his lips. He shuddered as he took a breath, but then he separated himself from them, forcing himself not to be their burden. He blinked slowly and shook his head to clear it. "Now. We must go now."

Cassandra was barely paying attention. Timothy glanced over to see her staring at the corpses on the ground. Mages, most of them withered, their skin like parchment paper, some of them little more than skeletons with wisps of flesh and hair remaining.

He grabbed her hand and she flinched as she spun to stare at him.

"Let's go."

Her eyes were wide with sorrow and fear, but she nodded. The three of them started back the way they had come. Some of the strength had returned to Ivar, and he crouched slightly as he walked, on guard against an attack. Timothy wanted to ask him what had happened, who had done this to him, but if they had not yet drawn the attention of the evil in that chamber, he did not want to give their presence away now. And, in truth, he felt he already knew the answer.

A cold certainty settled upon Timothy's heart as he gripped Cassandra's hand more tightly and they moved beneath an arch propped up by two of those stone columns. They were being watched. There was no way they were leaving this chamber safely.

"Ivar," he whispered, glancing at the Asura.

The warrior only nodded in confirmation of Timothy's fears.

"Foolish boy."

The voice seemed to come from the ghostfire itself, from the souls of thousands of dead mages, from every lamp and lantern in that vast subterranean chamber.

Timothy and Cassandra spun around, searching for an enemy, for any sign that they were to be attacked. Ivar only froze, listening, all of his senses attuned, waiting for what would come.

"You see the dead arrayed around you. Some of them were the most powerful mages in their guilds. Yet you think that you can face me? You should never have come here. It will only mean suffering, now."

"What are you doing down here, Alhazred? What do you want with me?" Timothy called, his voice echoing back at him.

But the other voice did not echo. It came from everywhere at once.

"You were beneath my notice, but then you disrupted the work that Nicodemus conducted on my behalf. Grimshaw was supposed to remove you, yet you defeated him as well. I'm impressed. But now you must be removed from this game."

"Game?" Cassandra shouted, her cheeks flushing with anger and her eyes flaring. "This is a game to you? All of these mages dead?"

"Quiet, little girl. You'll be taken care of soon enough," the

insidious voice sneered. *"And these others . . . unfortunate, but sacrifices were necessary. I needed their power to restore myself, and to give me the strength I need for what's to come."*

Something moved in the chamber. There came the rasping noise of something being scraped across stone. Each and every one of those columns seemed to hide an enemy now. Each and every one held a threat, and Timothy shielded his eyes from the brightness, trying impossibly to see past them.

"Ivar," he whispered. "You've got to blend. Make yourself unseeable."

"I cannot. Not now. I have not the energy," the Asura replied, his voice so low that it seemed a hush just beside Timothy's ear, though Ivar was several feet away.

"For what?" Cassandra called into the chamber, and the echo came back to them. "What do you need all of that magic for?"

"This is only the beginning, don't you see?"

And with that, he emerged. A figure that was little more than a shadow carved from the brightness of the ghostfire stepped from behind a column up ahead, between them and the exit. Timothy blinked, and the image quickly resolved.

Alhazred floated above the stone floor. Blue fire danced in the palms of his hands, and even in that small flame, Timothy thought he saw faces. The souls of dead mages. He had thought he had imagined seeing them before, but now he knew that whatever Alhazred was doing to them must have roused them somehow, focused them. All ghostfire was comprised of such souls, but somehow in Alhazred's presence they were *aware*. Timothy wondered if what had focused them was fear.

The wizard's eyes burned blue as well. He was hairless, his flesh gray—at least what little of it was visible. For, other than his hands and his head, there seemed nothing of substance to him. Only shadow. His cloak was patterns of gray upon gray, dark upon dark, and where it hung open, there seemed only deeper shadows.

Timothy held his breath. Courageous as he had become, in that moment, the unmagician was terrified.

"I did not arrange all of this to leech borrowed magic from a handful of pitiful fools," Alhazred said, his voice still seeming to issue from every flicker of ghostfire in that chamber, from every corner, every sconce and sphere.

The wizard smiled, and Timothy clutched Cassandra's hand tightly and they took a step backward. Ivar did not move.

"I want all of the magic," Alhazred rasped. *"Every bit."*

Timothy had forgotten that other sound, the scrape upon stone that had come from behind them in the chamber, hidden behind one of those columns. Now there came a hiss like water seared by fire. Cassandra cried out and lifted her hand, summoning a spell. Timothy spun just in time to see the monstrous cat-man, that strange hybrid of feline and mage that her grandfather had become.

"No!" Timothy shouted as he lifted his hands to defend himself.

The creature had disappeared in the Yarrith Forest. He had

no idea how it had come to be here—through Nicodemus's magic or Alhazred's—but when he saw it, all the breath went out of him. He had not known how to tell Cassandra the terrible news of her grandfather's transformation, but he had thought he would have more time to find a way. Now he wished he had told her sooner, but it was too late.

The cat-man was easily taller than him now, and it hissed even louder as it brought its claws down, raking Timothy's arms and drawing blood that spattered the stones and the monster's fur.

Then it was on top of him, driving him down. Timothy's head struck the floor, and for a moment he was lost to darkness. When his eyelids fluttered and he regained awareness, Cassandra was pulling the cat-man away by the fur on its head with one hand, and in the other there shimmered a golden sphere of magic, a combat spell that would blast the creature across the room. The cat-man twisted around to hiss at her, threatening with those claws, and she got a close look at its face for the first time.

In those feline features, the cat-man's true identity was plain to see.

"Grandfather!" Cassandra gasped.

"Yes, a lovely reunion, is it not. The Nicodemus family, together again."

Timothy struggled and grunted, forcing the cat-man's arms away from him, but he managed to twist just enough beneath his attacker to see Alhazred, wondering when the mage would strike.

But Alhazred had moved only a bit closer and was making no move against Timothy and Cassandra. He did not have to. The wizard of shadows floated above the stones, blue fire still dancing in his eyes and his right hand . . . and in his left, he clutched Ivar by the throat. The Asura had dropped to his knees. Golden light seemed to flicker from his skin and run up Alhazred's fingers.

"Oooh, that's nice," the wizard said, and sighed. *"That's very nice."*

Edgar perched on top of Sheridan's head, talons barely able to cling to the metal without sliding. His black feathers ruffled, wings fluttering almost unconsciously. His patience had worn thin.

"All right, that's it!" the rook announced. He cocked his head and stared at Caiaphas. "We're going in. I don't have a clue what's going on down there, and I try to give the kid as much space to make his own mistakes as I can, but you two just got back from nearly getting killed. That's what happens when he goes off without Sheridan and me. So there's not going to be any more of this waiting-around crap."

A puff of steam hissed from the valve on the side of the Sheridan's head, ruffling Edgar's wings further. The rook cursed under his breath, but when Sheridan spoke, he listened.

"Something terrible is here in SkyHaven. This is not the first time this place has revealed its hidden secrets," the mechanical man said, his tone far colder and harder than Edgar had ever heard him. "After today, there will never be secrets in SkyHaven again."

Edgar cocked his head and gazed at Caiaphas. The navigation mage was not officially a member of SkyHaven's staff because he was personally employed by Leander. Still, the acolytes that surrounded him seemed to look to the mage for leadership. They had all given a wide berth to Sheridan, suspicious even now of Timothy's creation. And they were certainly not going to do anything at the command of a bird, no matter whose familiar he was.

"Mistress Cassandra instructed us to stay here," Caiaphas said. "But this one time, we cannot obey our Grandmaster. There has been far too much tumult in our Order of late. She and Timothy have been gone too long. We must go to their aid."

"That is precisely what you must *not* do," bellowed a voice that echoed along the stone walls of the corridor.

Edgar cawed and took flight, startled into the air by the voice. He glided in a quick circle, wings outspread, and came face-to-face with Leander Maddox, lumbering down the hall. The massive mage's face was pale and drawn, but there was a light of determination in his eyes and magic crackling at his fingertips. So intense was his expression that Edgar beat his wings, trying to get out of Leander's way.

"Grandmaster!" Caiaphas said.

"No longer, old friend. Merely 'Professor' once more," Leander said quickly.

Edgar landed on Sheridan's shoulder, wings still fluttering, and regarded him. "So you're not crazy anymore, I take it? Not going to try to kill anyone today?"

"None of my friends, at least," Leander replied darkly, gaze darting into the wizard's laboratory, where the bookcase had been torn away to reveal a hidden passage. Then he whipped his head around and stared at Sheridan and Edgar.

"Timothy is in terrible danger. He faces an evil unlike anything he has ever encountered. Cassandra is a powerful mage, and skilled for her age, but our enemy is too strong. The two of you will want to join me, I know, but you cannot help. Not here. Timothy will only be frightened for your safety, and that will make your presence more dangerous than your absence. Go with Caiaphas."

The former Grandmaster turned to his navigation mage now. Above his blue veil, Caiaphas's eyes sparkled with determination and strength.

"You must hurry back upstairs and find Carlyle," Leander told him, his gaze darting from Caiaphas to the nearest acolyte, and then taking all of them in. "Parliament is being notified, even now. After what I did to Lord Romulus under Alhazred's control, I am sure he will be among the first to respond to our summons. Parliament will send combat mages, and they must. But we at SkyHaven—the Order of Alhazred—we must take precautions. If the worst should happen, and Timothy, Cassandra, and I should all fall, the rest of you must keep the evil contained within the fortress until Lord Romulus and the Parliamentary forces arrive."

Edgar cawed softly, wings fluttering. He shook his entire body. Sheridan hissed steam.

"But—" the bird began.

"Go, now!" Leander snapped at them. "If you wish to serve your friend and master, this is the best you can do for him. And the rest of you, your Grandmaster's life is at stake, but so is everything you know. Not only the Order, but every guild, the entire Parliament of Mages. Go!"

With that, Leander stormed into the wizard's laboratory and through that hidden entrance, disappearing down the stairs on the other side.

"You heard Professor Maddox!" Caiaphas snapped, urging the acolytes on. "We must go!"

They started back the way Leander had come. Edgar expected Sheridan to follow, but the mechanical man did not move. The rook cawed softly.

"Do you not trust Leander?" Edgar asked. "The evil presence has been evicted from his—"

"No, that is not it," Sheridan replied, voice as soft as steam. "I suspect he is right. If this villain is so powerful, we would be of little help, and if we distract Timothy, that could be fatal. But if you don't mind, Edgar, I'd like to stay right here and wait. If the worst happens . . . well, I shouldn't like to be too far away from him."

Edgar felt a terrible dread settle on him, but he said nothing, only perched on Sheridan's shoulder and waited for the outcome, for better or worse.

* * *

In that moment, Timothy was torn. Cassandra was grappling with the cat-creature, which was hissing and yowling. She knew, now, that it had once been her grandfather. As he glanced at them, he saw it slash at her again, and its claws caught her forearm, drawing even more blood. Her sleeves were stained, and the crimson was dripping from the fabric to the floor.

But Alhazred had Ivar, who had nearly raised Timothy and had taught him so much about honor and nobility, and how to be a warrior. He whipped his head back and forth, heart breaking as he realized he could only help one of them.

Then Cassandra screamed in anguish, forced to attack her grandfather—or the thing he'd become. She raised both hands and sketched at the air. A burst of golden light erupted from her fingers, and the cat-creature was thunderstruck, the impact of the spell blowing the fiend back off of its feet and slamming it into a stone column.

"Go!" Cassandra cried. "Help Ivar!" She ran at the cat-creature, another spell already coalescing around her hands.

Timothy spun toward their real enemy, the evil behind all the horrors they had faced. "Put him down!" the boy shouted.

Alhazred clutched Ivar by the throat, the shadow wizard hanging there above the stone floor, darkness swirling around him. He was draining Ivar's life essence, and the tribal magic of the Asura. The markings on Ivar's skin seemed to fade even more, and his face seemed to wither.

His eyes opened and shifted toward Timothy, but instead of fear or sadness, the boy saw a warning in them. Ivar was more afraid for Timothy than he was for himself.

That, more than anything, was what spurred him to act.

He started toward Alhazred, gritting his teeth against the fear in him, and he flexed his fingers. The entire world ran on a matrix of magical power that flowed through everyone and everything . . . except him. Timothy was a black spot, a short circuit in the magical matrix. Any magic he came into physical contact with was disrupted, spells broken, charms shattered. If he could get his hands on Alhazred . . .

"Come another step, boy, and I will snap his neck," the wizard sneered. The blue light danced in his eyes, and shadows flickered across the gray flesh of his face.

Timothy hesitated.

And Leander Maddox stepped out from behind a stone column only a dozen feet from Alhazred. Leander said nothing as he raised his hands to attack, but Timothy smiled, and the shadow wizard must have seen it and understood what the boy's expression meant, for he began to turn, ready to defend himself.

Too late.

Leander shouted two words in some ancient language of wizards, and waves of red and orange light flowed from his outstretched hands. Bolts of power like lightning shot from his fingers, plunged into the shadows inside Alhazred's cloak, and threw him across the room with such force that he struck the far wall of the chamber, crushing ghostfire lamps and spheres, dousing some of the light, and collapsing as some of those lights tumbled down on top of him.

"Timothy, get the others out of here! Now!" Leander cried.

But already, Alhazred had begun to stir.

CHAPTER FIFTEEN

Grief welled up inside Cassandra with such power that she could barely stand. Nicodemus staggered a bit as he forced himself up onto all fours. All along there had been those who had called Timothy an abomination. But, this . . . this thing was truly abominable.

All her life her grandfather had been kind, but distant. And how often had she seen a hunger in his eyes, a cruel and cunning thirst? Yet he was her only family, and so she loved him, for she knew nothing else. His death had left her lost, alone, and somehow hollow inside. But it had also given her a freedom she had never imagined, and her experiences with Timothy and with Leander had offered a perspective on honor and nobility that had helped her to heal. She had learned the truth about Grandmaster Nicodemus, that he was a black-hearted, cruel mage who had committed heinous crimes and taken the lives, warped the spirits, of others for his own gain.

His death was terrible. Learning the truth—that he had taken those lives to resurrect his master—even worse.

But, this . . . seeing this creature that was so obviously her grandfather, twisted into some other form . . . this was worst of all.

Its yellow eyes locked on hers and it hissed again. But this time, the hiss was a word. This hiss was her *name*. "Cassssssssandra."

For a moment she was locked in place, frozen as though mesmerized. Then there came voices nearby, shouting, and she mustered all of her will to tear her gaze from the cat-creature's eyes. There was a sound like shattering glass nearby and she turned to see Alhazred crash into the wall, ghostfire lamps crashing to the ground. Her pulse raced and hope sparked in her as she saw Leander standing in the midst of that vast chamber, framed by arches and columns. His hands were outstretched, and magic danced all around him. Not far away, Ivar was sprawled motionless on the floor. Leander shouted something at Timothy, who turned to look at Cassandra.

Their eyes met. Her hope blossomed even further, and she managed a smile. He raised a hand to wave her toward him, called her name . . . and then Timothy's eyes went wide.

Cassandra twisted around too late to save her own life . . . if the cat-creature had been coming for her. But the hideous thing with her grandfather's face bounded away from her, loping across the chamber. She saw immediately what was about to happen.

"No!" she cried.

She shook her hair out of her face and raised her right hand. Rage and fear intermingled in her as she started to run after the creature. Magic simmered within her, drawn up from somewhere deep within, such power as she had never dared to wield. The air around her warped and wavered as she ran and golden light burst from her hands. Her fingertips began to burn. The magic was too much. But still she held on to the spell that she had summoned.

With a grunt of pain she came to a halt and thrust out her hand, eyes tracking the running creature, taking aim. Then the cat-man lunged behind a stone column. The ghostfire was so bright all around that she had to squint. Cassandra blinked and the beast was so swift that it had moved to the next column.

Again she ran, panic rising in her.

"Cassandra!" Timothy shouted.

"I know!" she snapped.

Then the two of them were running side by side, both of them shouting. Timothy was crying out for Leander to turn, to see what was coming, and Cassandra was screaming for her grandfather to stop—if he had ever loved her—to stop.

Leander was focusing on Alhazred, watching the ancient wizard carefully, ready to battle. Their warnings were drowned out by one another's voices. All he must have heard was their shouting, but none of the words. Still, the tone made him begin to turn . . .

Just then the monstrous cat-creature lunged out from behind a column and at Leander's back. Part Alastor, part Nicodemus . . . but both of them had always despised Leander Maddox. The thing struck him with its full weight in the very same moment that Leander saw it coming. He had no time to defend himself. Leander struck the ground with the twisted animal on top of him and it laughed with her grandfather's laugh. The burly mage tried to shrug the creature off, his hands beginning to glow with a defensive spell. Cassandra stopped again and raised her hand, fingers still burning, tips charred black and seared with pain.

Her entire body shook as the magic was channeled through her.

The cat-creature swept its long claws across Leander Maddox's throat. Blood flew, and all the magic that had been crackling around Leander winked out. The mage lay still.

"No!" Cassandra and Timothy screamed together.

Her face contorted with hatred, tears springing to her eyes, she let loose the spell that burned her hand, shaking with the power. Golden light streaked with scarlet leaped across the room and struck the cat-creature with such force that she heard its bones shatter as it was thrown across the room. It rolled onto the stone floor of the chamber, throwing strange shadows beneath the ghostlight, and then it, too, lay still.

Unable to breathe, Cassandra ran to Leander. His eyes stared into nothingness, gleaming in the flicker of ghostfire illumination, and she knew that he was dead.

She had never felt so cold, so numb.

Cassandra walked to the cat-creature. Its limbs were splayed around it at strange angles, and a trickle of blood ran from the corner of its mouth. Of her grandfather's mouth. His black heart had driven him to evil once more, and she had lost him a second time.

She wept for him, and for the loss of Leander Maddox, and, most of all, for herself, Timothy, and Ivar.

Alhazred would surely slaughter them all.

Leander is dead.

The thought was like a spear through Timothy's heart. It echoed across his mind, and for a moment he thought he might just collapse. All the strength was gone from his body. He saw Cassandra fall to her knees not far from the corpse of that strange hybrid of Alastor and Nicodemus, and he knew how much she grieved.

Timothy had not forgotten Alhazred's presence, but the shadow wizard was still struggling to rise from the debris of shattered ghostfire spheres and lamps he had crushed when he'd struck the wall. Black, oily mist rose from his eyes, twining with the blue flames that had already been there, but as he tried to get up, his body buckled and he went down again.

The boy forced himself to look at Leander again, stared

at the unmoving form on the stones at his feet. The open eyes, staring forever into nothing. Unblinking. Unseeing.

"No," he whispered.

When Argus Cade had died he had asked Leander to look after his son. Now, with Leander dead, who was there to watch over Timothy? No one. There was no one. That meant he was going to have to take care of himself.

"Timothy," a voice rasped.

"Ivar?" he said, spinning around.

The Asura had begun to rise to his feet. The tribal markings on his flesh were still faded and his voice was little more than a ragged whisper, but he was alive. Timothy's heart thundered in his chest, relief flooding him.

Then, beyond Ivar, he saw Alhazred begin to rise. Smiling.

"No!" Timothy shouted.

His voice drew Cassandra's attention and she jumped up and ran to his side, but Alhazred was also in motion. He shot out a hand, and those tendrils of oil and blue fire wrapped themselves around Ivar like tentacles and lifted him from the floor.

"Do not move!" Alhazred commanded.

Timothy and Cassandra barely dared to breathe. The shadow wizard—for surely Alhazred was no mere mage, but as powerful as one of the Wizards of Old—held Ivar up before him with those magical tendrils as though the warrior was a shield. The blue fire that flickered in Alhazred's eyes faltered slightly and he staggered, but he only pulled Ivar closer so that they could not attack.

"Stand your ground, children," he said, that thin smile stretching the gray flesh of his face. The shadows beneath his robe seemed to billow out below him into a cloud of darkness that rose up as though it might swallow both Alhazred and his living shield.

Then the wizard reached out a hand and grabbed the nearest floating sphere. His eyelids fluttered, and darkness seemed to spill out around the edges of his eyes like tears of black mist. Alhazred crushed the sphere in his hand and brought the open flame to his lips.

There were eyes in those flames. A face in the fire. And its mouth was open in a silent scream.

Alhazred sucked the ghostfire right out of the air and swallowed it. He shuddered with pleasure and reached for another.

"Gods, no," Timothy whispered, grief welling up within him. "It's true, all of it." He glanced at Cassandra and saw her face contorted with the same anguish that was in his heart. She knew, then, just as he did. "It's true."

"All my life," Cassandra said. "And I never knew."

Alhazred laughed. "Ah, so you understand at last?"

He took a lamp from the wall and shattered the top of it, then put his mouth over the broken spell-glass and almost seemed to *breathe* the ghostfire in. When he stared at them again, Timothy could have sworn he looked stronger, his eyes brighter, his flesh not so gray. The shadow tendrils that gripped Ivar tightened and the Asura groaned, twitching. The wizard only drew him closer.

"All of the mages Nicodemus enslaved—"

"Not only Nicodemus," Alhazred boasted, "but Grimshaw as well. They were my tools."

"They brought you . . . victims," Cassandra said, fresh tears streaking her face. She did not even try to wipe them away.

"At first they only siphoned the magic for me, keeping some for themselves and feeding the rest to me. I thrived. As you see," the shadow wizard said. He grasped another sphere in his hand, but only gazed at it a moment before turning back to them. His blue-black tentacles tightened on Ivar again. Something snapped in the Asura's body.

"Let him—"

Alhazred's expression kept Timothy from finishing the demand. The wizard scowled. "You still only know the beginning. The missing mages, yes, they fed me. I have kept myself strong with their souls, with their magic, and the spirits I have taken from ghostfire. But for every one I have consumed I have collected hundreds more, preparing for this very moment. And now every soul in this chamber, every ghostfire light in SkyHaven, will fill me. With that power I shall enter the very fabric of the magic that controls this world, and I shall be the most powerful mage in the history of Terra. First, though . . . I must be rid of a small nuisance."

He pointed a single finger at Timothy. "Come to me, boy. Or I snap the savage's neck. And then I come for the girl."

Timothy drew in a sharp breath. He had never imagined, after all he had experienced in this world, that he could feel the depth of horror that churned within him. After Nicodemus and Grimshaw, he had thought he knew evil, but what he'd seen before was only a taste. Now his mind spun. He glanced around the chamber, risked a quick look at Cassandra.

"Boy!" Alhazred screamed. "You have no choice."

He would not accept that. There was always a choice.

"Cass. Get Ivar," he whispered.

Then he screamed. The sound came almost unbidden, erupting from this throat as he threw back his head. It was fury and sorrow and a cry for justice, all merged into one terrible roar.

Timothy ran at Alhazred.

The wizard's eyes widened in astonishment for a moment, and then he grinned. Casually, he grasped another ghostfire lamp and raised it to his mouth. He forced his tongue through the spell-glass with a crackle and began to suck up the soul inside. The face in the flames pressed itself against the glass. And all the while, the oily tendrils of magic Alhazred used to hold Ivar were beginning to constrict further. The Asura grunted in pain. His skin had begun to change color to match the strange blue magic and that inky black mist that was crushing him.

"Now!" Timothy shouted.

Cassandra darted toward them as well, but out to one side. Her red hair flew behind her and her emerald gown flapped and for an instant Timothy thought again of the first time he had seen her, on a high tower above SkyHaven, and the way just the sight of her had stolen his breath away. Just having her beside him gave him hope.

"Monster!" she screamed, and she raised both hands up.

Out of the corner of his eye he saw golden light blossom from both of her hands, seeming to explode across the chamber. For the first time he saw that her fingers were burnt black, like those of Nimib assassins, channeling magic too powerful for her flesh to contain.

In his mind he had imagined her tearing Ivar away from Alhazred with some spell. But this was combat magic. The blast slammed into both the shadow wizard and the Asura warrior he held captive. The black tendrils dissipated and Ivar was thrown aside, striking the stones and not moving. Alhazred staggered backward, his head banging against the wall. Blood sprayed from his nose as though he'd been hit by a fist.

Timothy thought, afraid Cassandra had killed Ivar just as she had the cat-creature.

"Destroy him, Tim! Send him into the shadows forever!" she cried as she darted past him and raced to Ivar. Emerald energy shot from her fingers like lightning, picked the Asura warrior from the ground, and carried him forward as she fled deeper into the chamber for cover.

Praying Ivar would be all right, Timothy raced at Alhazred now, while the shadow wizard was staggered. Already the blue fire was burning in his eyes again.

Cassandra's attack had done him little harm. No matter how much raw power she wielded, he had more. The fiend had consumed dozens, perhaps hundreds, of souls. Ghostfire had been used for centuries, and the world of mages had never really understood the cruelty of the practice. Timothy's heart broke when he considered how long some of their souls had lingered in this world without being able to move on to whatever afterlife truly awaited.

But Alhazred had been the first to discover that the magic that lingered with their souls could be consumed.

As the boy ran at the wizard, he felt the eyes of every soul in that room, every flicker of ghostfire, upon him. He would set them free. Somehow, he would set them all free. Or he would die trying.

"No matter, boy," Alhazred sneered. "I will simply kill you first, and then your friends will die."

He rose up then, hovering once more in the air. The shadows that swirled beneath his cloak billowed and grew darker. His gray lips pulled back to reveal gleaming pearl teeth. A cruel smile.

Timothy ran at him and brought his fist up, putting his entire body into it, just as Ivar had taught him.

Alhazred slid aside and Timothy punched the stone wall, grunting with pain.

The wizard struck him with the back of his hand, breaking Timothy's nose and staggering him. The boy took two steps back, blinking the pain and shock away.

"I cannot kill you with magic, you fool, you insect, you

pitiful waste of flesh. But that does not mean I cannot kill you. It's fortunate your father is dead. How embarrassed he would be to see what a nothing his son had become."

Timothy felt cold inside, and strangely calm. Alhazred had caused so much death and sorrow, and it was time to bring an end to it, to generations of evil. His right hand throbbed with pain from striking the wall, but he shut off the pain from his mind, just as Ivar had taught him to do. Timothy was surprised by how swift and brutal the wizard was, but he was not afraid. He had spent his entire life learning from the last of the Asura, and without magic, Alhazred would be no match for him.

His nostrils flared and he flexed both fists, not feeling the bruised knuckles at all. Alhazred smirked at him, gray flesh wrinkling, shadows spilling from his eyes. The wizard reached for another ghostfire lamp, another soul to consume. . . .

Timothy stepped in close, swinging his right fist with all of his might. Alhazred sneered and twisted to move out of the way, but the boy pulled his punch at the last moment, shifted his weight and momentum, and rammed his left fist into the wizard's chest. At first all he felt was the resistance of that charcoal gray cloak, as though Alhazred were entirely substantial. Then his fist struck withered flesh and bone.

The shadows and blue fire leaking from Alhazred's eyes dispersed, and all the magic coalescing around his hands blinked out as though it had never been there.

"No," the wizard whispered, eyes widening, as the blow

forced him back a step. Alhazred shot out a hand, trying to claw at Timothy's face, but the boy had misjudged once and would not do so again. He swept his right arm up and knocked the wizard's hand away. Again, Alhazred attacked, and Timothy used his left to block a second time. He danced back a step, then put all his weight into another blow, this one with his bruised right hand. He struck Alhazred in the jaw.

Without magic, the wizard's eyes were blank white like those of a blind man. Timothy shuddered at the sight.

But Alhazred was not through. The wizard reached for him again. A spark of magic lit up his eyes, which shouldn't have been possible.

The null field that Timothy's body generated was not something he could feel. But when he focused, he could feel a tingle on his skin. It was not the null field, but the brushing against it of the magic that was outside of him. And if Timothy concentrated on that feeling, he had learned that he could extend the null field. Focusing his mind he could reach out and short-circuit magic *without* touching it, as easily as blowing out a candle.

Alhazred had been feeding off of the magic of other mages—their life essence, their souls—for ages. How much power had he stored up inside him?

It doesn't matter, Timothy thought as the shadow wizard's fingers clutched his throat. *Magic isn't real strength. That's in the heart.*

He shot his hand out, fingers straight, and jabbed at

Alhazred's throat. The blow cut off the wizard's air a moment, and he lost his grip. Timothy hopped backward, then spun his entire body, pivoting on one foot even as he brought his left leg up and kicked Alhazred in the face with such force that the gray skin of his face cracked. There was no blood inside, only a puff of dust.

The shadow wizard fell. He slumped to the ground, his back against the wall, flickering light upon him from the ghostfire flames burning in spheres and lamps all around. Some of them cascaded to the floor from the walls, rolling across stone. Faces gazed out at Timothy, and he thought he saw hope in the ghostly eyes of the dead mages whose souls were trapped inside.

"It cannot be," Alhazred rasped, his voice hollow now, no longer filled with that commanding tone that had seemed to spring from every flame of ghostfire in the vast, sprawling chamber.

In that moment, staring at the pitiful creature, Timothy was overcome with grief. He shuddered and felt his face flush with hatred. Leander was gone. Ivar was either dead, or nearly so. Cassandra had been forced to kill the twisted thing her grandfather had become at Alhazred's hands. And all the hatred, all the secrets that lingered in this world—the suspicions of the Parliament of Mages, the prejudice against Wurms, the betrayal and slaughter of the Asura—all of it was because of Alhazred.

"Why couldn't you just have died?" Timothy asked, his voice barely a whisper.

And blue flames flickered in the shadow wizard's eyes. Weak, but they were there. A grin spread across his face, splitting that dry, gray skin even further.

Alhazred thrust his hands out to either side of him. "You don't understand, boy. I am a part of the magical matrix now. There is so much of the magic in me that I cannot be separated from it. Not even by your freakish nature."

The wizard snatched up a ghostfire sphere in each hand, and as Timothy watched, his fingers slid through the spell-glass as though it weren't there at all. There was no mage on all of Terra as powerful as this ancient spellcaster.

"*Yessssssss!*" Alhazred screamed.

His voice came from every ghostfire flame in that chamber, every flicker from one end to the other, every lamp and sphere and lantern. Timothy shook his head.

"No. I don't—"

But he could not finish, for as he watched, the ghostfire inside the spheres Alhazred had plunged his finger into disappeared. It winked out, the light extinguished. The souls absorbed into the wizard's flesh.

"Stop," Timothy whispered, taking a step forward but not knowing what else he could do. "Leave them alone."

The blue flames danced in Alhazred's eyes again, and that split in his skin healed. He opened his mouth and let out a throaty laugh, and a billowing mist of oily black shadow unfurled from between his lips, gusting on his breath.

"Foolish boy," Alhazred said, but his eyes were rolled up in his head, the lids fluttering with pleasure, and he wasn't even looking at Timothy anymore. "You're too late, don't you understand?"

He had not moved his hands—he still clutched those two darkened spheres in his grasp—but now other lamps began to be snuffed out. Ghostfire faces screamed in silence and then seemed to be sucked backward into nothing, drawn out through their glass enclosures only to wink out as though they had never existed.

Alhazred began to laugh. The blue flames in his eyes danced higher and higher. Timothy thought he saw faces in it.

Then it grew worse. One by one the ghostfire lights began to dim. Spheres winked out. Lamps. Lanterns. With a strange rhythm, like the pulse of the dark wizard's heart, the lights in that vast chamber went dark. A dozen. Four dozen. One hundred, and it was spreading quickly.

"Stop it!" Timothy screamed, not knowing what to do. Alhazred was destroying them all, taking all of those souls, all of that magic, and if he really was linked with the magical matrix, Timothy didn't know if even his strange affliction would be enough to stop the horror unfolding before him.

At last, the laughter stopped. The lights continued to wink out, and the part of the chamber they were in was thrown into shadow, a gloomy near-darkness that grew deeper by the moment. Alhazred's eyes glowed, and when he stared at Timothy now, there was a calm in him that frightened the boy more than anything that had happened thus far.

"It is only a matter of time. I will consume them all, you see? All of the souls of the dead mages, all of their magic. I have gathered enough power now. Had you discovered me even days ago, you might have stopped me. But I have the magic now to jump from one flicker of ghostfire to the next. I begin here, with the spirits trapped in this room, and then I will spread through Arcanum, and then throughout the matrix, absorbing every one of the bound souls, the ghostfire, the captured magic of millions of dead mages . . . and then, boy, do you see?"

Timothy was horrified. He did see. Alhazred was mad, but the history of Terra was filled with stories of his scheming and manipulation. He wanted to rule, to control them all. And if he took that much magic into himself, if he could take control of the entire magical matrix, he would command every mage in the world. Timothy wanted to free the trapped souls, the suffering spirits of the dead, and Alhazred wanted to absorb their essence within himself, to *eat* them.

The darkness had continued to spread through the chamber. Timothy could almost feel the pleading eyes of hundreds of ghosts upon him. But by the light of that blue fire in Alhazred's eyes, he looked and saw that the wizard's fingers were still thrust into those hollow, spell-glass spheres.

Connected to the magical matrix.

Timothy glanced around. Several areas of the chamber had gone dark now, arches and columns almost black against the gloom. One by one, they continued to extinguish. Alhazred was absorbing them all, his power spreading. . . .

But what if I can disconnect him?

He took a step back and tried to steady his breathing. The pain in his right hand and his broken nose began to throb again, but he pushed it away. Eyes wide open, he *felt* in the darkness. All across his skin, on his face and his hands, even beneath his clothes, there was that tingling sensation that was the magic that slid over him but never touched him, just beyond his reach.

Taking long breaths, Timothy focused on the entire surface of his body, on that tingling . . . on the magic . . . and he *pushed*.

He felt it give way. The null field grew, ballooning around him. A smile touched his lips, and he glared down at Alhazred. The shadow wizard was still laughing, that blue fire burning in his eyes, darkness pouring from his mouth . . . but when he saw the smile on Timothy's face, Alhazred's laughter faltered.

Timothy took a deep breath, held it a moment, and then with every ounce of his self-control, every bit of his will and inner strength, he pushed as hard as he could, forcing the null field to burst away from him, spreading and stretching out to encompass that entire massive chamber. . . .

Alhazred's eyes went dark.

Every piece of glass in that vast chamber disappeared in an instant, the spells that had created the spheres and lamps and lanterns shattered. A massive flare of ghostfire lit the room as those flames were free. And in that flash of brilliant soul-illumination . . .

SkyHaven began to fall.

Timothy heard Cassandra scream somewhere nearby. Alhazred shouted in fury and fear. The boy's own heart seized as he felt the stone floor drop below him and felt that they were falling. The entire floating fortress gave way to freefall, and in that moment, when he felt he might throw up, his mind cried out in panic as he pictured SkyHaven tumbling down into the ocean, sinking, drowning everyone who wouldn't be killed by the impact alone.

One. Two. Three seconds. Through fear and instinct, he drew the null field back to him, and the freefall of SkyHaven stopped.

The sudden halt of their descent slammed Timothy to the floor, and he cracked his skull against stone. He blinked, forcing himself to stand, dizzy because all of his balance was shot by the fall. Three seconds, only. They had not hit the ocean, they were not going to drown.

You disrupted the whole matrix, he said. Everything must have winked out for a second, all of the magical power in the area . . . possibly the whole city . . . and maybe farther.

Suddenly he was very afraid.

The ghostfire was no longer captured by magic and it flashed brighter, and brighter still, and Timothy spun and saw the faces in them, all of them gazing at him, smiling, able at last to go to their rest.

Then they began to fade.

As they did, Alhazred began to howl. Timothy spun to look at him in that dimming light as the entire room faded to blackness, and he saw Alhazred's gray flesh begin to split all over, withering and crinkling like burning paper. Darkness puffed out of him, and in moments, as the last of the light faded, he saw the wizard crumble into nothing but ash on the floor.

Then all was darkness.

And in that utter blackness, he heard Cassandra call his name.

"Are you all right?" he asked.

"Yes. And . . . Ivar's going to be okay, too, I think." Her voice came through the darkness, bouncing off the walls of that chamber. He wanted to crawl to her, to hold her hands in his, and know that she was safe. "What about you?" she asked. "Are you okay?"

Timothy thought about that question, but he said nothing for a very long time.

He was not at all sure how to answer.

In Tora'nah, Verlis spread his wings and flew high above the ground. He had been watching the miners more closely, enjoying the feeling of progress as they dug more and more Malleum out of the hillside. He had made his peace with the mages—at least some of them. The helmet the smiths had made him at the Forge had been a kind gesture, one he had not expected.

Still, he felt a certain unease with them working so close to the burial grounds of the Dragons of Old. But he would work with them. He would give them the benefit of the doubt.

The sky was cloudy, and the afternoon wearing on. The air was chilly, but the fire in his own belly and gullet warmed him. Smoke plumed from his nostrils as he dipped one wing and banked to the left, circling around again.

When he heard that buzzing hum in his skull, he nearly dropped out of the sky. He faltered and began to drop, but quickly caught himself, flapping his wings harder, soaring upward. His heart thundered in his chest, and alarms of danger raced through him. Before, he had heard that hum because he had been wearing the helmet—the metal it was forged from was tied intrinsically to the Wurm, and he could feel them on the other side of the barrier.

But in that moment, something had happened. He didn't need the helmet to feel the connection now.

Beating his wings, Verlis flew straight toward Alhazred's Divide.

Fire streamed away from his snout as he rode the air currents.

The barrier lit up, from ground to sky, from horizon to horizon. Verlis spread his wings, stopping himself, eyes wide as he was filled with terrible dread.

The light dimmed. All of the magic in Tora'nah winked out for just a moment.

Before Verlis's eyes, the barrier fell.

And the murderous, barbaric Wurms that had been trying to break it down from the other side began to come through.

Catch a sneak peek of the next
Magic Zero adventure,

BATTLE FOR ARCANUM

The intensity of the buzzing hum inside his thick, thorned skull nearly forced Verlis from the sky above Tora'nah. He faltered and began to drop, but quickly regained his senses, flapping his leathery wings all the harder, and soaring upward again. His heart hammered in his broad chest, and alarms of danger raced through him. The last time he had experienced this hum, he had been wearing a helmet forged of Malleum—the metal tied intrinsically to his kind, the descendants of dragons known as the Wurm.

But now it appeared that he didn't need the helmet to feel this connection.

Verlis sped through the air toward the magical barrier between dimensions that separated Terra from Draconae, the world to which the Wurm had been banished many decades past. It was called Alhazred's Divide. On the other side was a Wurm civilization of savagery and tyranny, lorded over by a general called Raptus, who wanted nothing more than for his sorcerers to tear down the Veil so that he and his army could invade Terra and destroy the world of mages.

Filled with a terrible dread, Verlis spread his wings and hovered before the barrier. The light of Alhazred's Divide shone from ground to sky, from horizon to horizon, as it had for centuries, but now its ethereal light had dimmed. The hum in Verlis's skull increased and he hissed in pain, flinching away from the magical barrier.

As it winked out, all the magic in Tora'nah cut off for just a moment.

A moment was long enough. The barrier fell with a sound like breaking glass, the spell at last destroyed, and with a murderous roar of triumph, the barbaric Wurm that had been trying to break it down from the other side began to come through. The sky beyond—the sky of Draconae— was filled with dark, winged figures, the Wurm gathering like storm clouds as they realized what had happened.

The first wave emerged on foot, cautiously, from the large rip that had been torn in the fabric of reality. The edges of the dimensional tear hissed and sputtered. Verlis watched them come, for a moment unable to believe that the barrier had been broken, and then he remembered the mages at the mining operation nearby, digging for the precious metal Malleum, and realized their safety was now in jeopardy.

Spurred to action, Verlis swooped down out of the sky toward the invaders. He opened his massive jaws and a stream of liquid fire erupted from his gullet, bathing them in flames as he flew past and away. They were his kinsmen, these Wurm, but not like him at all. They had waged a civil war upon his clan, who wanted only peace. To him they were the enemy.

Two of the Wurm soldiers roared in pain as Verlis's fire engulfed them, and the others were distracted by his attack, some even hesitating on the threshold of this world. But Verlis knew that this was at best a temporary distraction. He only hoped that it would provide him enough time to warn the workers at the mining operation that what they had feared most had happened.

Wings pounding the air, Verlis soared over the ancient home of the Dragons of Old, desperate to reach his human comrades in time. He flew low above the mages' encampment, finding it deserted as expected. Most of the workers would still be toiling at the mines, and he redoubled his speed, hurrying toward them. The mages were excavating dangerously close to the burial grounds of his ancestors, but he had kept them away from the actual graves of the ancient dragons.

The air was filled with the droning, grinding noise of the digging machine Timothy Cade had designed, and as Verlis swooped down toward the mining operation, he saw the metal thing burrowing into the hillside, boring a hole from which the mages would excavate tons of Malleum for weapons and armor to fight against the Wurm.

Or, at least, that had been the plan.

Time had suddenly run out.

Verlis caught sight of Walter Telford, the project coordinator, who stood talking animatedly with a pair of miners. They all wore troubled expressions, and Verlis understood. They wouldn't know yet that an attack was under way, but they were suffused with magic—they would have felt the magical matrix flicker.

"Walter!" the Wurm roared, smoke furling from his nostrils, the wind whipping past him.

Telford glanced up and lifted a hand. "Greetings, Verlis," he cried over the sounds of the digging machine. "I see you felt it as well. Do you have any idea—"

"The Divide has fallen!" the Wurm bellowed over the noise of the excavation, streams of fire leaking from his jaws.

Telford stepped back, the look upon his face showing that he wasn't sure he had heard correctly. The coordinator's eyes bulged as he turned to another worker, saying something into his ear. The worker ran to stand beneath the Burrower, waving his arms to shut the noisy machine down.

"Are you sure, Verlis?" Telford called. As the site fell silent, all mining operations ceasing, the men and women gathered around. "Absolutely certain?"

"I saw the barrier fall with my own eyes," the Wurm growled. "Whatever interrupted the flow of magic gave

Raptus and his sorcerers the opening they needed. Alhazred's Divide has been torn down. The Wurm of Draconae are invading!"

The coordinator's body seemed to diminish in size; his head slowly hanging low. "We're not ready. There are no weapons, no armor, except what's at the Forge right now."

From the distance came a sound that could have been the rumbling of a distant storm, but Verlis knew otherwise.

Telford heard it as well, craning his head to listen. The others began to mutter worriedly, some already starting to move away from the machine and the mine, searching for some kind of cover. In the distance Verlis saw the workers from the Forge, wearing their heavy gloves and thick aprons, begin to emerge from the building where the Malleum was being processed.

"That's not a storm, is it?" Telford asked, looking up and out of the valley at the slate gray sky.

"No, it is not," Verlis replied, his inner fire roiling within his chest, causing steam to rise from the sides of his mouth. The sound was moving closer.

"Come on, all of you!" Telford shouted, and he started at a run toward the Forge.

Many of the miners followed, but others took that as their signal to flee in earnest. Instead of hurrying away, they were sprinting, perhaps thinking to take shelter in some cave or other. None of them ran toward the village. It would be in flames soon enough.

Verlis took flight, keeping pace with Telford and the

miners courageous enough not to run for their lives. The Wurm glanced back repeatedly, and he saw dark figures against the sky, Raptus's soldiers at last taking flight. Black smoke rose on the horizon, the first of the huts now burning in the small village encampment the mages had built.

Telford led them to the Forge. The workers there were all moving outside, curiosity and fear etched in their faces. Verlis saw Charna Tayvis, the Forge supervisor, but her focus was on Telford.

"What's going on, Walter?" Charna demanded. She was a large, powerful-looking woman, her face covered in the dirt and grime of her labors. The blacksmiths grumbled behind her, eager for an answer as well.

"We're under attack. Raptus has broken through."

The blacksmiths looked horrified, as well they should have. Raptus was a brutal savage and a cunning general, utterly without mercy. Verlis knew this from experience. But Telford did not allow fear to fester.

"Gather up whatever you've already forged, Malleum weapons, helmets, whatever there is," he instructed the smiths. "Not a piece is to be wasted."

Charna stepped forward, removing the heavy gloves from her hands. "A good many pieces were shipped out to Arcanum two days past," she said. "Enough to fortify a battalion. All that's left here is what we've worked on since then."

One of the miners, the man who had been operating Timothy's digging machine, came forward. Fear shone in his eyes, and Verlis could smell the stink of panic seeping from his pores.

"And what then?" he asked, gazing up toward the rim of the small valley in which they toiled. The rumbling was louder now—closer. "Once we gather the weapons—what then?"

One of the blacksmiths had left the Forge carrying a weapon he had obviously been working on. It was a Malleum spear, its head tapering to a nasty point. Forged from this metal, it would pierce even the toughest of Wurm hides, and their armor as well.

Telford took the weapon from him and hefted it in his hands. "We use them for what they were intended," he said in a forceful voice, eyes searching out every face in the crowd. "We use them to fight for our lives."

Miners and smiths alike dispersed quickly, rushing into the Forge to arm themselves.

"How long before they are upon us?" Telford asked, coming to stand at Verlis's side, spear still in hand.

"Not long," Verlis growled, watching the sky begin to darken with black smoke as the entire village was set aflame. Ominous winged figures cruised amid the smoke, the flapping of hundreds of pairs of wings sounding like the roll of thunder. "Not long at all."

Timothy knelt by the body of Leander Maddox, his friend and mentor, who had looked out for him since the death of his father. The mage had been a huge man both in stature and in heart, but he seemed so small now, there on the ground, no life left within him, no spirit, no magic. Cassandra had gone quickly back up to the room from which they had descended into this secret chamber and brought back the lantern of hungry fire that Timothy used. This, to him, was pure fire. Not magical. Not ghostfire, made from the souls of dead mages. This world had always perceived it as the rechanneling of magical energy to useful purpose, but Timothy had discovered that the ghosts of mages were trapped in the fire, unable to go on to their final reward, and he thought it criminally tragic.

Now Cassandra knelt by his side, hungry fire lantern in her hand, and shared in his sorrow over the death of the man who had been their teacher and protector. Not far away stood Ivar, last surviving warrior of the Asura tribe. He had suffered injuries in the battle with Alhazred, but he stood with his hands together as though saying a prayer over Leander's remains, and he muttered a kind of incantation under his breath, a chant to some higher power.

Cassandra placed the lantern on the floor beside him. "I'm so sorry," she said, bowing her head. "I knew him only a short time, but long enough to know he was a great man. Arcanum has lost a treasure today."

"He will be missed," Ivar said, his voice raspy and weak. "More than ever, the Parliament of Mages needs leaders like Leander Maddox."

Timothy heard their words of solace, but could not find his own voice. His mind was filled with memories of the man, of the kindness in his eyes, of the quiet strength that he had and that he inspired in others. Timothy recalled the first time he had seen Leander as he came through the magical doorway from Terra and into the world where the boy had been hidden away at birth due to his *affliction*. Even then, at that first look, he had known that the burly, bearded mage with the wild mane of red hair was a friend. Leander had been manipulated by evil, but in his heart, he had always remained loyal to the memory of Timothy's father, Argus Cade, who had been Leander's own teacher.

With a long, mournful breath, Timothy finally summoned the words in his heart. He held Leander's cold, stiff fingers in his own. "He always felt responsible, somehow, for the way the mages treated me. He blamed himself for their fear, their ignorance. I was born on Terra, but I think he wished that he had left me where he'd found me—to spare me from all that I've been exposed to since stepping through that doorway into this world."

Timothy studied Leander's pale face. If not for the spatters of blood that dappled the man's cheek, it would have appeared that the great mage was merely sleeping.

Cassandra put a comforting hand on his shoulder.

"He couldn't have been more wrong," Timothy said. "Sure, there are times when I wish I could run back to Patience and hide, but then I think about all I'd be giving up. My island home seems so . . . insignificant after seeing what exists beyond it."

He felt a wave of emotion threaten to reduce him to tears, but held it temporarily at bay. "You opened my eyes to wonders that existed beyond the doorway, Leander, and for that I will always love and miss you terribly."

Leaning forward, he placed a kiss on the man's brow and climbed to his feet, still fighting to not be overpowered by grief. He felt Cassandra and Ivar's concerned eyes on him, but only nodded to confirm that he would be all right.

Across the vast chamber, a tapestry adorned with the crest of the Order of Alhazred hung on the wall. Timothy went over and tore it down from the place where it had likely hung for centuries. As he crossed the room with the tapestry, he made a promise to himself that he would not suppress his grief forever, that he would give himself time to truly mourn the passing of his friend, but for the moment there were things to be dealt with that had to take priority over his anguish.

"Tim?" Cassandra asked. "Are you all right?"

"Not even close," he said, draping the tapestry over Leander's still form. "But now that the horror of Alhazred's schemes is done with, I will be. Everything will be better now. It has to be. Leander died to make it so."

He said a silent good-bye to Leander, then went to Ivar, whose face masked the pain he must have been in after the conflict with Alhazred. The dark wizard had drained some of Ivar's spirit, and it would take time for him to recover. As a child on the Island of Patience, Ivar had been his friend, and as great a teacher to him then as Leander would later become. All his life his friends had looked out for him. Now it was time for Timothy to return the favor.

"Let's get you to a healer," Timothy said. "And then we need to let the others know what happened here today."

Cassandra nodded in agreement, picking up the lantern from the floor to light their way up the stairs that led to a storage room where the secret passage to Alhazred's hidden lair was first discovered.

It seemed as though it took three times as long to climb the stairs as it had to descend them, and Timothy spent this time pondering the future of the Parliament of Mages and the world of Terra. Yes, Alhazred had been destroyed, but that did little to squelch the fear that he harbored over the potential threat of invasion from Draconae. Timothy shivered as he recalled his time in the Wurm world as Raptus's prisoner.

"We're almost there, Ivar," Timothy said, helping support his friend as they made their ascent of the winding stone staircase.

As they rounded a corner, a large shape was silhouetted in the doorway above them, and a bird fluttered over it. In the midst of his pain, Timothy found a spark of comfort at the sight, for the silhouette was that of Sheridan, the mechanical man he had built, with Edgar, the black-feathered rook who had been his father's familiar. Timothy was no mage, but Edgar was his familiar now.

"Caw! Caw!" Edgar cried. "It's them! By the tail feathers of my ancestors, it's them!"

"Timothy! You're alive!" Sheridan said, extending his segmented metal arms down the staircase to assist them in their climb. He clanked as he moved, and steam hissed from the release valve on the side of his head.

Another day, Timothy might have made a joke of Sheridan's pointing out the obvious, but there was nothing amusing in the mechanical man's concern for him. Not all those who had descended into the belly of SkyHaven to combat Alhazred were coming back alive.

Cassandra went first, with the lantern, and then Timothy helped Ivar through the door into the storage chamber, barraged by questions from their anxious friends. There were half a dozen mages in the room, acolytes of the Order of Alhazred, but though Cassandra was their grandmaster, as a sign of respect they would stay away from Timothy unless they were forced to confront him.

"Thank Zephyrus you're safe," said Caiaphas, the navigation mage who had served Leander long and well. Those who had studied that specialty all wore a distinctive veil that covered most of their faces, leaving only their eyes visible, but Timothy could see the relief in him. He could almost not bear to meet that gaze.

Caiaphas frowned and peered back down into the darkness of the stairwell. "But where is Master Leander?"

"Yeah," Edgar croaked, tucking his wings back and tilting his head, looking down from his perch on Sheridan's shoulder. "Where is he? Guarding Alhazred or—"

They all then saw the look on Timothy's face, and their expressions tore at his heart. *Just let me be strong now,* he thought. *Just let me be strong for my friends.*

"Alhazred is truly dead now," he said. "But Leander . . . if not for him arriving when he did, none of us would have made it out of there alive. But the cost . . . ," Timothy said, prying the terrible words from his mouth. "Leander was killed."

They were all thunderstruck, each of them falling silent. Caiaphas closed his eyes and turned away, hanging his head. Edgar fluttered his wings, beak opening as though trying to find something to say. Sheridan's glowing red eyes dimmed and his arms hung at his sides as though he had shut himself down. The other Alhazred mages muttered among themselves, some of them gazing at Timothy with open suspicion.

"What went on down there, kid?" Edgar asked at last, flapping his wings as he flew up to a new perch atop Sheridan's head. "It must've been awful. The whole place started falling. We thought it was the end for all of us."

"It was terrifying," the mechanical man agreed. "How can such a thing happen, that spells so powerful and intricate could falter?"

The acolytes watched Timothy with fear in their eyes, as if they knew that he was somehow responsible. The un-magician was to blame.

And they were right.

"It was Alhazred," Timothy began. "By absorbing the soul energies in the ghostfire, he managed to connect himself to the magical matrix. He was draining it, making himself stronger and stronger. He was going to try to take control of the whole thing, to command all the magic in the world. Leander tried to stop him, but Alhazred was too strong. If I hadn't done what I did . . ."

"What did you do, Timothy?" the black bird asked in a troubled whisper.

"Do I have family in the Imagine Nation?" Jack asked. "Are they superheroes?"

"You're a mystery, Jack. But that's all about to change."

Don't miss the thrilling adventures of Jack Blank, who could be either the savior of the Imagine Nation and the world beyond, or the biggest threat they've ever faced. And even Jack himself doesn't know which it will be. . . .

EBOOK EDITIONS ALSO AVAILABLE

From Aladdin
KIDS.SimonandSchuster.com

BE SURE TO CATCH ALL THE LEVEN THUMPS BOOKS!